Slocum emp[...]ng killers charging him [...] heads and dropped two, causing the others to stumble and fall. He pulled another stick of dynamite out of his belt and struck a lucifer. From the corner of his eye he saw two Sum Yop assassins. Flashing silver cartwheeled past his head. The two men grunted and fell, hatchets in their chests. Slocum turned to Ah Ming's father and knew that the old man had been a killer in his day.

"Thanks," Slocum said, then spun and tossed the dynamite before the short fuse burned down to the blasting cap. He had guessed right where the Sum Yop would attack next. He blew up three of them and caused an avalanche of crates, blocking that route.

While he had cut off one avenue of attack, he had also cut off a way of escape.

"Keep 'em busy for a few seconds," Slocum said. He reloaded his six-shooter, then heard what sounded like a vast army assembling out of sight. Six rounds would not put a dent in it.

Ah Ming's father stood with a hatchet in each hand.

"You got any ideas how to get out of here?" Slocum asked. He sighted and fired, winging a tong man trying to sneak across the tops of the crates. Slocum cursed under his breath. He had hoped to escape. It had not taken the tong killers long to figure out not only how he had gotten through the building so fast but also how to attack him . . .

DON'T MISS THESE
ALL-ACTION WESTERN SERIES
FROM THE BERKLEY PUBLISHING GROUP

THE GUNSMITH by J. R. Roberts
Clint Adams was a legend among lawmen, outlaws, and ladies. They called him . . . the Gunsmith.

LONGARM by Tabor Evans
The popular long-running series about Deputy U.S. Marshal Long—his life, his loves, his fight for justice.

SLOCUM by Jake Logan
Today's longest-running action Western. John Slocum rides a deadly trail of hot blood and cold steel.

BUSHWHACKERS by B. J. Lanagan
An action-packed series by the creators of Longarm! The rousing adventures of the most brutal gang of cutthroats ever assembled—Quantrill's Raiders.

DIAMONDBACK by Guy Brewer
Dex Yancey is Diamondback, a Southern gentleman turned con man when his brother cheats him out of the family fortune. Ladies love him. Gamblers hate him. But nobody pulls one over on Dex . . .

WILDGUN by Jack Hanson
The blazing adventures of mountain man Will Barlow—from the creators of Longarm!

TEXAS TRACKER by Tom Calhoun
Meet J.T. Law: the most relentless—and dangerous—manhunter in all Texas. Where sheriffs and posses fail, he's the best man to bring in the most vicious outlaws—for a price.

JAKE LOGAN

SLOCUM
AND THE
CELESTIAL BONES

JOVE BOOKS, NEW YORK

THE BERKLEY PUBLISHING GROUP
Published by the Penguin Group
Penguin Group (USA) Inc.
375 Hudson Street, New York, New York 10014, USA
Penguin Group (Canada), 90 Eglinton Avenue East, Suite 700, Toronto, Ontario M4P 2Y3, Canada
(a division of Pearson Penguin Canada Inc.)
Penguin Books Ltd., 80 Strand, London WC2R 0RL, England
Penguin Group Ireland, 25 St. Stephen's Green, Dublin 2, Ireland (a division of Penguin Books Ltd.)
Penguin Group (Australia), 250 Camberwell Road, Camberwell, Victoria 3124, Australia
(a division of Pearson Australia Group Pty. Ltd.)
Penguin Books India Pvt. Ltd., 11 Community Centre, Panchsheel Park, New Delhi—110 017, India
Penguin Group (NZ), 67 Apollo Drive, Rosedale, North Shore 0632, New Zealand
(a division of Pearson New Zealand Ltd.)
Penguin Books (South Africa) (Pty.) Ltd., 24 Sturdee Avenue, Rosebank, Johannesburg 2196,
South Africa

Penguin Books Ltd., Registered Offices: 80 Strand, London WC2R 0RL, England

SLOCUM AND THE CELESTIAL BONES

A Jove Book / published by arrangement with the author

PRINTING HISTORY
Jove edition / December 2007

Copyright © 2007 by The Berkley Publishing Group.
Cover illustration by Sergio Giovine.

ISBN: 978-0-515-14384-3

JOVE®
Jove Books are published by The Berkley Publishing Group,
a division of Penguin Group (USA) Inc.,
375 Hudson Street, New York, New York 10014.
JOVE is a registered trademark of Penguin Group (USA) Inc.
The "J" design is a trademark belonging to Penguin Group (USA) Inc.

PRINTED IN THE UNITED STATES OF AMERICA

10   9   8   7   6   5   4   3   2   1

1

John Slocum knew better but did it anyway. He gripped the dirty shot glass, stared at the amber liquid in it and then knocked it back fast. It hit him like a mule's kick. He was already close to being knee-walking drunk, and some dim, dark part of his almost-sober brain told him drinking in a saloon perched at the edge of San Francisco's Embarcadero with a crowd of rowdy sailors was worse than stupid.

It could be deadly.

He slammed the glass down onto the bar and tried to focus. His vision blurred. As if from a hundred miles away, he heard, "He's stronger 'n a damned bull. Tell the barkeep to put a stronger Mickey Finn in the next round."

"You want another, mister?" The barkeep thrust his ugly face into Slocum's.

Slocum blinked and fought hard to chase away the double vision. The man had muttonchop whiskers and was bald on top. His eyes were as bloodshot as Slocum's probably were, but his came from being in the dense smoke of the First Port Saloon all night long. Slocum had come by his from too much rye whiskey.

"Another?" the barkeep shouted at him and reached out to shake him.

Slocum reacted, knocking the man's hand away and moving to the side quickly enough to avoid the club descending toward his head. The heavy belaying pin crashed into the bar, broke glass and sobered Slocum enough to realize he was in a world of trouble. Shanghaiers. Two men had followed him from the last saloon where he had been drinking. In his alcohol fog he realized what was happening, but the liquor had also dulled his common sense.

His elbow collided with the shanghaier's nose and broke it. Blood spurted and caused the bartender to cry out, "Don't get no blood on my bar! I jist wiped it down!"

Slocum ducked a clumsy swing from the other sailor who had dogged him. He drove his fist into the man's belly, but he was weak from too much liquor, and the sailor's midriff was harder than an oak plank. The sailor grunted, and Slocum felt the pain from the impact all the way up into his shoulder.

"No shootin'! Don't go throwin' lead in my place!" The barkeep dived under the bar, and Slocum heard him scurrying about like a cockroach as he hunted for his weapon. It might have been a club weighted with lead or anything else deadly. From the corner of his eye, Slocum saw the man's bald head rise up. Those bloodshot eyes peered down the short length of a sawed-off shotgun.

Slocum tried to run. His legs betrayed him—and saved him. He fell facedown onto the sawdust-covered floor as both barrels of shot ripped past him. He curled up and thrust his back against the bar until he could sit up. The place had descended almost instantly into one big free-for-all.

Head spinning from the knockout drops and too much whiskey, Slocum crawled along the bar, avoiding kicking feet and flailing arms until he reached the end. Using the bar to pull himself up, he took two staggering steps outside into the foggy night. The cold breeze blowing off San Francisco Bay did not quite sober him up, but it helped him think more clearly.

It had been a damn fool thing to do, to go on a drunk

like this, but he had needed the release too much pop-skull gave him to help him forget. Getting into San Francisco had been easy enough. Getting over the Sierra Madres had been hell. The sudden autumn storm had taken them by surprise, and he had lost a good friend and a woman he had probably loved. Ulysses Larson had frozen to death on the second night they had been trapped in a cave, and his sister Anne, Slocum's lover—his love—had died the next morning. Slocum had awakened with his arms around her trim body, which had been wrapped in their horse blankets to keep her warm against the frigid temperatures. She had been cold and unmoving. It had taken Slocum a half hour before he could release her and accept that she, too, had been a victim of the storm.

Slocum had considered simply dying then and there, but something kept him moving. The blizzard had blown over and left the mountains sharp, crisp and white. The air had cut at his face and lungs, but somehow he had refused to die. One foot had gone in front of the other, their horses having perished, and finally he had been rescued by a Wells Fargo station agent.

For four days Slocum had been laid up with fever-induced delirium. And then he had taken the stagecoach into San Francisco. That trip had been another five days, giving him plenty of time to regret his decision to press over the mountains. He had been the experienced frontiersman, not Ulysses or Anne. He had convinced them getting to the coast would be easy.

"The storm," he muttered, staring into the gray fog. "The damned storm."

His hand went to the ebony handle of his Colt Navy. He almost drew it to put to his temple. He had killed a friend and the woman he had loved as surely as if he had shot them with this deadly weapon.

"Whoa, mister, we don't mean nuthin'," came a hoarse voice in the fog.

Instinctively, Slocum turned toward the speaker. He lifted his six-shooter and aimed it.

"You want to shanghai me?" Slocum asked. His voice came out in a whiskey-rough whisper.

"You got the wrong fellas," the man said.

Slocum fired. A foot-long tongue of orange flame momentarily illuminated the area around him. Slocum missed the man who was doing all the talking, but he caught sight of two others silently creeping up on him from either side. He might seriously consider killing himself, but he would not be shanghaied. There were things worse than death. Being consigned to a China-bound schooner for long, harsh years was one of them. As Slocum fired again, this time winging one of the men, he reflected that living with the guilt of Anne's death was no fit way to spend the rest of his days, either.

But it was better than hauling canvas sail and being the peg boy for a crew of hardened sailors.

He fired a third time, but the shanghaiers had already faded away, hunting easier game.

Slocum stood with his six-gun in his hand, staring at the formless fog. He wanted to fade into it and disappear, but that did not seem likely to happen. His head throbbed like hell, and his belly tried to turn itself inside out. He shoved his six-shooter back into the cross-draw holster and spun around to leave. He had to find a place to sleep off the whiskey.

He turned too fast and stumbled. Strong arms caught him and held him upright.

"Whoa there, cowboy," came a drawl. "You look to be three sheets to the wind."

Slocum forced himself back and reached for his pistol again. He did not draw.

"Who're you?"

"Looks likely I'm the salt who kept you from falling on your face."

Slocum squinted and got a better look at the man. He was smallish but with immense shoulders and forearms that looked more like a man's thighs. He had caught Slocum and supported his entire weight and had not strained himself at all.

"Thanks," Slocum said.

"You can buy me a drink. I just blowed into port, and I built up a mighty thirst out at sea."

Slocum knew the captains rationed their rum to keep the men in line. Too little, though, and the crew was likely to mutiny. Too much and drunken sailors fell overboard and drowned. From the captain's viewpoint, that was not the real loss. Not having an able-bodied seaman who could climb into the rigging was.

"I'm about done in," Slocum said. He still wobbled a mite, and he needed to find himself a place where he was safe enough to sleep for a few hours. He doubted that in San Francisco, along the waterfront, such a place existed.

"You owe me," the sailor said. A steely edge came to his voice. "You the kind what welshes on a debt?"

"I don't know it's much of a debt, but I'll buy you that drink. Just not back there."

"But First Port's supposed to be the best. Other than the Cobweb Palace, of course. Or Meigg's Wharf. Then there's—"

"Come on. I want to find a watering hole away from the bay."

"Landlubber," the sailor said, but there was a joking quality in the seafarer's insult. He slapped Slocum on the back, then grabbed a handful of cloth and pulled upward to keep him on his feet. "You need to get your sea legs, and you aren't even on a ship."

They wandered through the fog, homing in on another saloon more by sound than sight. The gray shroud surrounding them was damp and chill, and Slocum felt isolated, even with the sailor beside him occasionally breaking out into a sea chanty. Slocum decided he needed a new drinking partner to get away from the guilt and memory of Anne and her brother.

"There's a place," the sailor said. "You got anything against that one?"

To Slocum it was like all the others, except it was some distance from the waterfront.

"Looks good to me."

"Then buy me a drink or two. I'm so dry I'll match you two for one. Three!" The sailor laughed and put his arm around Slocum. Slocum did not like the familiarity, especially since the sailor was a good six inches shorter than Slocum's six-foot height. The muscular arm weighed Slocum down and almost caused his knees to buckle.

"Charlie, there you are," called someone at the far side of the large room. "We was wonderin' when you'd find us the entertainment."

Slocum stopped dead in his tracks. The hole in the floor afforded only a small path around it. He looked straight down almost eight feet and wondered why any saloon keeper would allow even the worst drunk to dig such a pit. Then he was no longer wondering anything. The sailor's strong arm moved behind him and a meaty hand shoved hard. Slocum went flying into space and crashed hard on the dirt at the bottom of the large pit.

"Way to go, Charlie. Damage him 'fore he kin give us a chuckle or two."

Slocum shook his head to clear it. Things, important things, rattled around loose inside. He forced himself to his hands and knees and then managed to get to his feet. He drew his six-shooter and looked around.

The dirt walls sloped slightly, making scaling them almost impossible. Even sober and with a running start, he would be hard-pressed to get to the lip of the pit. He pointed his six-gun up at the jeering crowd circling above. Slocum twisted about and aimed at the sailor who had pushed him into the hole.

"You gonna waste a bullet on poor li'l ole me, or you gonna use it on something worthwhile?"

"You tell 'im, Charlie."

"You're a dead man, Charlie," Slocum said, drawing a bead. He froze, his finger halfway toward triggering the round.

"Aren't we all, aren't we all?" Charlie laughed uproariously. "But you're gonna be in hell a damn sight 'fore me. Save a good spot for me and my mates, will you, cowboy?"

Slocum saw a small gate lift at the side of the pit directly under the treacherous sailor. Fiery red eyes peered at him and then the huge black body emerged. Long whiskers twitched, and yellowed fangs showed in a grin eerily human in its viciousness. The wharf rat took a few tentative steps, then launched itself at Slocum.

He fired. His .36-caliber slug hit the rat in midleap. It twisted and fell, half its body blown away.

"Told you you'd need your ammo, cowboy," taunted Charlie.

Slocum turned his pistol back upward. He heard a squeaking sound behind him. A quick glance over his shoulder confirmed his worst fear. Another gate had been pulled up, releasing a pair of the hungry wharf rats. These were the size of large cats. He shot twice more, each bullet killing a rat.

"Better reload fast, partner," shouted another sailor from the safety of the pit's rim.

"Fifty dollars," shouted another. "Fifty says he won't last ten minutes."

The betting began in earnest now. Slocum knocked open his Colt Navy and began reloading. He was sorry now that he had wasted three shots earlier in the fog. He had fired at phantasms. Now he had to shoot to save his own life.

He emptied the six rounds into four more rats. But six more were released. He could never reload fast enough to kill all the rats being turned free from their cages around the pit. If he went one way, the sailors on the far side of the pit loosed the chittering, snarling rats there. Slocum winced as he felt sharp teeth grab on to his tough boot top.

Those boots had protected him against mesquite thorns and even rattlesnake fangs, and they did not fail him now. He kicked out hard and sent the rat flying. But that rodent was replaced by two more. Four. Ten. Slocum spun around and around, the rats clinging to him with their teeth driving for his flesh. Some, the ones with weaker jaws, lost their grip and smashed into the dirt walls. Most were stronger—or hungrier.

He began clubbing the snapping rats with the barrel of his six-gun. This worked for a few seconds. The sailors let more rats free from their cages.

"We got a million of 'em," Charlie yelled down.

Slocum had no time to wonder how the sailor knew what he was thinking. It would not have been too hard, in any case. Slocum fought fiercely, swinging his pistol and then enduring the sharp, stinging rat bites in an attempt to reload. He could never hope to kill more than a half dozen of the rats with his bullets, but he wanted to take a few of the sailors with him if he was going to die.

"Get back, mates," Charlie called. "He's up to the point of wanting to kill us 'fore they gnaw his bones clean and white."

Slocum realized then that the sailors had done this before. Many times before, and had learned all the tricks. He was distantly aware of new bets being made—most of them at high odds against him. Some part of his alcohol-fogged, fear-shrouded brain wondered who was stupid enough to believe he would ever escape alive. Then he realized they all knew he would die. That was the point. They were betting on how long he would survive.

Slocum saw that he was not going to be successful reloading before the weight of the rats bore him down. He kept moving, swinging the barrel and knocking huge brown and gray clumps of the ferocious rats off him. He bled from a dozen bites. He pressed himself against the side of the pit, then put his chin down and ran as hard as he could for the far side. The toes of his boots dug into the hard dirt. He kicked and clawed and tried to get free. The lip of the pit was not that far above him. But his fingers caught at the loose dirt, and he slid back down into the undulating carpet of snarling rodents.

"I win!" cried a sailor. "Four minutes and he didn't make it out."

Slocum realized that if he had somehow succeeded in getting free of the pit, the sailors would have grabbed him and tossed him back to his death. Slocum had seen terriers thrown into a pit like this. A good dog could kill a hundred or more rats and, now and again, even exhaust the supply and survive to kill for the amusement of the saloon patrons another day.

Even if he had the advantage of a well-trained rat-killing dog, he had started more than half drunk. Slocum felt his strength ebbing quickly, and it would not be much longer before a rat got to his throat and ripped out his jugular. Or he lost enough blood from myriad other bites to weaken enough for the horde of rats to finally overpower him.

He clutched the butt of his pistol and considered shooting himself until he heard Charlie yell, "A hunnerd that he kills himself."

The bet was quickly covered, and Slocum's will hardened. He would never give the son of a bitch who had lured him into the pit the satisfaction now. He tried to run across the pit and climb the far side again. This time the sailors kicked and struck at him to be certain he did not escape.

He slid down the steeply sloping side, pulling in his arms to protect his face and throat from the snapping rats.

Fury burned away what whiskey remained in his brain. He fought with renewed strength, prompting another round of spirited betting on him.

But as Slocum fought, he felt the rage-inspired strength fading. The rats were winning. He smashed himself against a dirt wall and spun against it to get some of the clinging rats off. They were hungrier than he was strong. As he pressed his head against the dirt wall, though, he heard something peculiar. It was a rushing sound as if water raced along only inches away. He saw no way to use this— until he looked up and saw a Chinese woman just behind the ring of sailors light a stick of dynamite.

Slocum dived and slid along the dirt floor of the pit when the dynamite with its sizzling fuse arched up and

came down just behind him. The explosion was muffled.
He had worked in mines enough to know a dud, but this
was something else. The tiny *pop!* of detonation was about
what he would expect from a half stick of dynamite but a
curious crackling sound accompanied it. The only thing he
could equate it with was a breaking pot.

Then came an immense rush of water into the pit. He
had been right. A water main passed close by. The dynamite must have cracked the pipe enough to cause the water
to flow into the pit. Rats chittered all around as they swam
for their lives in the rapidly rising water. Slocum thrashed
about and let the gushing waters toss him about until he
flopped onto the floor of the saloon.

He got to his feet. The explosion and water filling the pit
had caused the sailors to hightail it out of the bar. All but
Charlie. The man stood stock-still, eyes wide in horror.

"You son of a bitch," Slocum said. He reared back to
swing a haymaker at the sailor, but Charlie simply sank to
the floor. He landed on his knees, then tumbled forward
onto his face. Standing behind him was the Chinese woman.
Slocum got a better look at her. She was dressed in a
somber gray padded coat that came to her knees. Under the
coat she wore what might have been a pale yellow silk
blouse and dark linen trousers. Slippers more appropriate
for the boudoir encased her tiny feet.

Slocum took all this in with a single glance. His green
eyes fixed on the slender needle in her hand. A drop of
blood dripped from the tip. Charlie's blood.

"Thanks," Slocum said. "You saved me the trouble of
killing him."

She knelt and wiped the bloody weapon off on the
sailor's shirt, then tucked it away in a knot of dark hair at
the back of her head.

"Come," she said. "They will return and be angry."

"I can see why. You made a shambles of the place."
Slocum saw that the water level continued to rise. The pit
had been filled to overflowing and now sloshed about at an-
kle level. Anyone not knowing the pit had been in the mid-

dle of the saloon might blunder in and find himself thrashing about in eight feet of churning, muddy, rat-filled water.

"The police will not like having water service stopped."

Slocum shook his head. San Francisco had underground water mains and sewers for its citizens. This was the mark of real civilization. Most places he frequented used outhouses, and young children or women fetched water from streams or lakes.

They stepped into the night-cloaked street, and Slocum saw the woman was right. The sailors had not gone far. They argued among themselves until they spotted Slocum.

He started to tell the Chinese woman to run for it, but she had vanished. Once more he was on his own and facing two dozen sailors intent on seeing him die in the messiest fashion possible. They advanced on him with clubs and wickedly sharp knives. He touched the six-shooter in its holster. He had been unable to reload. Fighting so many men would be like going against the horde of rats: impossible.

Slocum ran. His boots clattered against the cobblestone street, but the sound did not echo and rang out curiously flat. The fog! The fog muffled his steps. When a swirling gray cloud enveloped him, he darted for a building, found a doorway and crowded into it. The angry sailors rushed past, waving their knives and clubs and vowing to slit his throat and beat him to a bloody pulp.

Slocum waited for them to pass, then headed back in the direction of the saloon only to find he had not waited long enough. He ran into three lagging sailors. They spotted him instantly.

One advanced while the other two moved to flank him.

"Here. This way," came a soft, sibilant voice. He jerked his head around and saw the Chinese woman again. She held open a door. He never hesitated and darted through it. She slammed it behind him and dropped a locking bar into place.

From the way the door sagged under the repeated kicks from the sailors, the entire wall might come tumbling down in an instant. Slocum started reloading.

"No time," she said, tugging at his arm. "This way."

"That's twice you saved me," Slocum said. "I'm doubly in your debt."

She stood a good foot shorter than Slocum and appeared frail. Small and petite she might be, but Slocum quickly saw *frail* was not the right word. A stuck door at the rear of the room yielded to her powerful kick. She was through the door and hurrying along in a split second. Somehow she did not appear to touch the ground. Rather, she drifted inches above it like some kind of Celestial ghost.

But Slocum had felt her touch and inhaled her jasmine perfume. The occasional glint of light off the deadly steel needle she had tucked into her hair showed that nothing about her was incorporeal. Slocum found himself hard-pressed to keep up when they left the building and entered an alley. The woman was already a dozen yards away and being swallowed up by the fog.

Slocum ran flat-out now and caught up with her. They moved through the foggy San Francisco streets, down alleys, through spaces between buildings where Slocum had to suck in his breath and lose skin to get through. The entire while, the woman never appeared to rush or be upset.

"There he is! Get him, mateys!"

Slocum swung about as a burly sailor burst from the fog. Before he could fight the man, he found himself clutching the man's dead body. An ax protruded from the sailor's back. Two other seamen advanced on Slocum. As he watched, another sailor stiffened and corkscrewed down to the ground. A knife had almost severed his head from his body. The other sailor almost reached Slocum before two Chinamen silently appeared. One grabbed the sailor by the throat. The other split open his head with a small ax like the one in the first sailor's back.

"Come, hurry," the woman said, tugging again at his arm.

"Wait a minute," Slocum said. "Who are you? Who are these men?" He faced the three silent Chinamen. From some hidden arsenal concealed under their padded jackets they had retrieved other hatchets and knives and held them ready.

"They are On Leong," the woman said.

"On Leong? What's that?"

"They are *boo how doy*, tong assassins. Now come. Hurry. There is no time."

Slocum looked at the trio of hatchet men and repressed a shudder. The reputation of the Chinese tongs was one of sheer barbarism and brutality. Somehow, he had come under their protection. He had no idea how long that would last. He followed the woman deeper into Chinatown, the foggy streets making it impossible for him to figure out the route. For now, that was all right. For now.

"There is no doubt?" the woman asked from the safety of her hiding spot just inside the mouth of an alley.

"None, milady," said a huge Chinaman. He held knives in both hands.

"On Leong. Very interesting. Why do *boo how doy* protect an American?"

She stepped out into the street. Light from a distant gas lamp down the street fell on her. She wore a form-fitting white satin dress embroidered with writhing green-thread dragons and other mythical creatures fashioned in vibrant colors. Jade ornaments gleamed in her jet-black hair and at the belt around her trim waist. She thrust her hands into voluminous, dangling sleeves, turned and walked away unconcerned about the murder and mayhem all around her in the foggy San Francisco night.

None would dare interfere with her. They would pay with their lives if they so much as spoke to her. In minutes she left Slocum, the other Chinese woman and the On Leong killers far behind as she moved on to her rendezvous.

2

"Down," the woman said urgently. "You must go down. The street is not safe."

Slocum looked around. Through the billowing fog he saw nothing, heard nothing. As far as his every sense could tell, they were alone. Then he jumped as a Celestial came up and stood a yard away from him. Slocum had not heard the man moving.

"You're as good as any Apache brave I ever saw," Slocum said. Then he grinned ruefully and added, "Or as good as any brave I didn't see."

The Chinaman stood silently. Not a muscle twitched. As far as the man was concerned, Slocum did not exist. Slocum would have pressed the point except the man held a wickedly sharp hatchet in his hand. Blood dripped from the silver blade onto the cold ground.

"You sure it's safer down there?" Slocum looked past the woman into the darkness of the stairway leading down into the bowels of the earth. Slocum had heard all the stories about tunnels under Chinatown. Opium dens abounded, and those were some of the milder pastimes that could be found.

"The Sum Yop are on the prowl this night."

"Sum Yop? Another tong?" Slocum saw the smile curl the woman's lovely lips. For a moment.

"You learn fast. In Chinatown all is controlled by the tongs."

"That must come as a real surprise to the San Francisco police."

"No," she said. "It does not. They do not come down anywhere but Dupont Gai unless invited."

Slocum blinked at this. Dupont Gai was the main street through the heart of Chinatown, but the area spread out for dozens of blocks in all directions. No one knew how many Celestials lived in the area, but it was a considerable number. Every sailing ship from the Orient carried more coolies to work on the railroads, but not every Chinaman ended up carrying steel rail or driving spikes. Those who did not work for the railroad barons found it difficult to get any work other than in this patch of China transplanted just behind the twin peaks of the Golden Gate that protected San Francisco Bay.

"If not the Sum Yop, then the Suey Sing. We must get off the street. Now."

She turned and hurried down the steps, as if going first would relieve Slocum's anxiety about the underground danger. It did not. The back of his neck prickled as he followed. The hatchet men who had protected them on their way through the maze of streets pressed close behind. Slocum fancied he could hear the blood still dripping from the one killer's weapon.

The descent was done in complete darkness. Slocum braced himself on either wall and got splinters in his hands from the rough wood. He ignored the minor pain. There was not much else in the rest of his body that felt better. The rat bites burned like fire, and his head felt as if it might split open at any instant. Worst of all, he noticed how hungry he was. Too much tarantula juice had burned up what food he had eaten earlier before starting on his wild bender.

Hearing the soft padding of the woman ahead gave Slocum a way to guide himself through the passage. While hardly wider than his shoulders, he got the knack of walking along at a brisk pace without bumping into either side. When he saw a faint yellow outline of a door ahead, he slowed and let the woman go to it. The tong killer behind him shoved him forward roughly.

"Watch it," Slocum growled. He started to turn but felt the butt end of the hatchet pressed into his back. He kept walking. The Chinaman could easily have killed him if he had wanted.

"Enter, please," the woman said, bowing to him and pushing open the door. Although the light came from a single coal oil lamp, Slocum had to squint. His eyes had adjusted to the utter darkness, and even this small trickle of light burned.

"Please, sit. I must announce your arrival."

"Wait," Slocum said, reaching out to take her arm. She looked down at his hand on her delicate arm. This was enough for Slocum to draw back. "Sorry. I want to thank you, but I don't even know your name."

"Ah Ming," she said, bowing lower. For a moment Slocum wondered if this was some sort of answer in Chinese or if it were her name.

"I'm John Slocum."

"I am pleased to meet you, John Slocum." She bowed deeper.

"And I'm right pleased to meet you, Ah Ming, since you pulled my bacon out of the fire."

"What fire?"

"Just a way of saying you saved me."

"Yes," Ah Ming said, bowing again and backing off. "Please sit. Wait until I return."

She backed off another two paces, bowed a final time, turned and left. Although she never seemed to hurry, she vanished in an amazingly short time. Slocum looked around the small room. There was a chair and a blanket laid out on a hard plank of wood. That was all the furniture in the room. The solitary coal oil lamp sat on the floor near the chair. Slocum sank into the chair and leaned back, warily watching as the two hatchet men who had trailed him in the tunnel stood by the door. His eyelids drooped for a moment and when he snapped alert, they were gone.

Uneasy about his surroundings, Slocum took the time to reload his Colt Navy. The pistol had gotten drenched in the flood that had saved his life. He used an edge of the blanket to dry and clean his six-shooter. Then he carefully reloaded, making sure the action worked smoothly. He rested the six-gun in his lap and closed his eyes again. His wounds throbbed, but his weariness overtook him once more.

He dreamed his boots were being stolen. He protested a little, but soothing words calmed him. Soft touches on his arms and legs made him smile and then he rolled over and woke up.

For an instant he was disoriented. The room was darker than he remembered. The lamp had been turned down, and he was lying in the bed. He sat up, dislodged his six-shooter and made a grab for it to keep it from hitting the floor. Swinging his legs around and putting his bare feet down made him dizzy for a moment. Then he noticed the rat bites on his arms and legs had all been swabbed with a pinkish lotion and the worst of the wounds bandaged.

"It wasn't a dream," he murmured.

"No, John Slocum, it was not."

"Ah Ming?" He looked around for her and almost missed her sitting in the chair. She was hidden in shadow. Her pale gray jacket provided perfect camouflage.

"I saw that your wounds were tended by a healer. He said you were not seriously injured."

"How long have I slept?" Underground, in the darkness, he had no idea. He fumbled in his pocket and dragged out his watch. He peered at it, but it might be ten in the morning or ten at night.

"A few hours. No more."

"I am in your debt. You saved me from my own stupidity." The words burned on his tongue. How foolish to go on a binge and get knee-walking drunk the way he had. Losing Anne had been a shock, but she was not the first one he had loved and lost. He clutched the pocket watch a little tighter. It was his brother Robert's only legacy. Robert had been killed during Pickett's Charge. Slocum was lucky any of his older brother's personal belongings had reached him because he had been in Kansas at the time, riding with Quantrill and his butchers.

"You are," Ah Ming said. "It is good you recognize this. Many Americans do not have your sense of honor."

This put Slocum on guard again. He slid his six-shooter into his holster and stood on shaky legs. A few steps convinced him he was going to be all right. The alcohol had burned itself out of his belly and brain, and his wounds were all covered by the cooling pink poultice.

"Sounds like you want something from me," he said.

There was no answer. He felt the woman's dark eyes fixed on him, waiting. For what?

"Why did you save me? Just so I'd be in your debt?"

"Yes. I watched you from late this afternoon. In spite of your drunken nature, you acquitted yourself well. Such skill is needed to rescue my father."

"Rescue him?"

"He has been kidnapped."

Slocum heaved a sigh and sat. He had heard stories like this a thousand times. A man took off and the family wanted him back, sure he had been kidnapped. More often than not, the man wanted a new start. From what he had seen of the dark tunnels in Chinatown he would not blame any man for simply heading for the high country. Life in the Sierras would be miles better than eking out an existence in the middle of a knot of Chinamen intent on throwing axes at each other.

"You do not believe me."

"I do," he said. Slocum hoped he sounded convincing. "It's just that men get itchy feet sometimes."

"Not my father."

"I'm sure he didn't just light out and hunt for a better place to live." Slocum studied the woman carefully. The light caught her in profile. She was quite pretty. Fragile.

Exquisite like a fine porcelain doll, only her pale yellow skin made her seem even more exotic.

"The Sum Yop tong has kidnapped him."

"You know this for a fact?"

Ah Ming nodded once.

"They sent a note? They want ransom and you want me to conduct the exchange, swap your pa for however much they ask in ransom?"

"It is not so simple, John Slocum."

He heaved another deep sigh. It was never simple. He cursed Ah Ming for seeing his one flaw. He *was* an honorable man and owed her a debt. She had saved his life back in the saloon and quite possibly her henchmen had saved him again in the streets as they fled from the sailors.

"You have nothing to lose," Ah Ming said softly. "You are honorable and your life means nothing."

This caused Slocum to pay more attention to the woman.

"What do you mean?"

"You are, as the saying goes, 'drowning your sorrow.' A woman? You said more than once you have nothing to live for."

"You're giving me a reason to go on?" Slocum laughed harshly. Ah Ming did not seem the type to go in for the rehabilitation of men she did not know. From the way she had effortlessly used the needle to kill Charlie in the saloon, she had no qualms about any man.

Other than her father.

"I am not careless," Ah Ming said quietly. "You are a dangerous man. You have become a dangerous man who does not care if he lives or dies. I need such a one."

"You have an army of killers around you," Slocum said, gesturing toward the door where a Celestial stood, arms crossed on his broad chest, a hatchet ready in his right hand.

"They would never get close to the Sum Yop lair," she said. "The Sum Yop would not expect a cowboy to be of any danger to them."

"So you figure if I get my head chopped off, so what?"

She said nothing. That was good enough an answer for

Slocum. That was precisely what she meant. Risking her own people in a frontal assault would give less chance of recovering her father than having a white man try.

"How long did you follow me around?"

The question surprised Ah Ming. She hesitated longer than Slocum thought she would.

"For two days. Since you arrived on the stagecoach."

It was Slocum's turn to be surprised. He had thought she picked him out simply because the gang of shanghaiers had gone after him, marking him as someone who would never be missed.

"When do you want me to rescue your pa?"

"Now. Quickly. The Sum Yop will not allow him to live for much longer, and he is an old man."

"They're torturing him?"

Again the woman remained silent, giving Slocum his answer.

"How do I find him?"

Ah Ming rose and gestured for him to follow.

Anyone passing by might think it was an abandoned building, but Slocum had watched long enough to know the truth. At least four Celestials stood guard on the roof. Four more walked the streets along carefully laid out paths to always protect the single door off the alley. Windows were boarded up and the front door to the building had been sealed shut with brick and mortar. Rather than a dilapidated building, it was closer to a fortress.

The headquarters of the Sum Yop tong.

Slocum realized getting into the building was only part of his problem. Finding Ah Ming's father was another because all the Chinese looked alike to him. A slow smile came to his lips. Not all. The tong killers were burly brutes. And Ah Ming was distinctive in any crowd. She was like a hothouse flower—a deadly one. If the daughter was so gorgeous and murderous, her father might be easier to recognize than Slocum feared.

Slocum checked his pocket watch. It was only midnight.

How much had happened to him since he had begun his binge around sundown! He had been drugged and avoided shanghaiers and sailors intent on feeding him to rats. Shaking his legs reminded him of the rat bites. The poultice Ah Ming had applied had worked miracles. His muscles were sore, but he moved easily. He would have to move fast if he wanted to get in and out of that building alive with the Sum Yop's captive.

From the patterns the hatchet men walked, Slocum knew luring them away would not be easy. Seldom had he seen army posts with such dedicated sentries, even in Indian country.

He took out a quirley and lit it with a lucifer from a watertight tin in his pocket, which had preserved his matches. He sucked in the smoke from the quirley and blew a single smoke ring before sauntering across the street toward the front of the building. He stopped at the bricked-in front door and stared at it a moment. Small crevices showed where the tong watchmen peered out. Some of the holes were large enough for rifles and pistols to be thrust through to defend the building. Slocum puffed away contentedly and got only a hate-filled look from the nearest sentry.

The man turned at the end of his guard route and started away. Slocum moved like lightning. The guard was most of thirty feet away, but he was not Slocum's target. Reaching into his pocket, he pulled out a full stick of dynamite. He had personally crimped the fuse to the blasting cap to be sure it would detonate. One chance was all he was likely to get to rescue Ah Ming's father.

Slocum had cut the short black fuse so it would burn only ten seconds. He applied the tip of his cigar to the fuse, saw it begin to sputter, then turned and shoved the stick through a hole in the masonry.

The patrolling guard realized something was wrong and turned back to Slocum. The flash of a hatchet was all the warning Slocum needed. He drew and fired. The Celestial dropped on the spot an instant before the explosion blew out the front of the building. Bits of brick and mortar cascaded down on Slocum. He bent double to avoid any more falling, flaming splinters from the wood frame as he raced around the corner to the single way into the building.

Let the tong rush its men to the front of the building to see who was attacking. Slocum would go in and find the kidnapped man and be on his way before they knew what was going on.

That had been the plan. It began falling apart almost immediately after Slocum kicked in the door.

Just inside stood two men with drawn six-shooters. Slocum shot the one on the left, but the other returned fire and ducked into the maze of crates piled within.

Cursing, Slocum scooped up the pistol from the fallen tong killer and lit out after the fleeing guard he had failed to shoot. He twisted through the narrow paths made from the tall boxes, then stopped and listened. He heard the Chinaman yammering, someone barking out orders, others protesting.

Slocum looked up and knew he had to take the high ground fast. They had laid out this labyrinth to trap anyone clever enough to get inside. There would be decoys that would lead to ambuscades, dangers devised by cunning Oriental minds he could not guess at. He scrambled up the crates and flopped belly-down atop the pile. From the sounds rising from floor level he knew where the bulk of the hatchet men were. He stood and surveyed the interior of the building. Walls had been pulled down, making a large warehouse. The spot where a prisoner might be kept most safely would be in the rear of the building. Jumping from crate to crate, Slocum made his way past, taking time to empty the captured six-gun at two tong members who happened to spot him on his aerial route.

He dropped the empty pistol and drew his own trusty Colt. He had left most of the Celestials lost in their own maze by the time he jumped down next to an old man chained to an iron ring set in the brick wall.

Dull eyes turned toward him. The man might have been a hundred years old, but from the amount of blood on the floor all around, his aged look might have come from dedicated and profound torture.

"Ah Ming sent me," Slocum said. He saw a spark of recognition in the old man's eyes. He nodded once, as if he had expected this rescue.

Slocum had no time to talk. He spun and fired when a huge hatchet man burst into sight, a deadly ax in each hand. His first shot hit the Chinaman in the chest. It hardly slowed him. The tong killer had the stamina and size of a mountain man. Slocum knew what to do. His second round blasted out a nickle-sized hunk of forehead, snapping the hatchet man's head back. This killed the assassin instantly.

Slocum grabbed one fallen hatchet and used it on the old man's chains. The sound of steel on steel worried Slocum, but he finally cut through a link and freed the captive.

"Sorry, but you'll have to keep those shackles on a while longer," Slocum said. "I'll need more time and a hammer and chisel to get them off. When we get out of here, there'll be time to worry about such things."

The old man painfully lifted his hands. Both thin wrists were circled by iron bands, but the chain holding him to the ring was severed. He smiled and nodded.

"You know how to get out of here?" Slocum asked.

The old man pointed.

Slocum was not certain if Ah Ming's father only pointed to what he thought was a way through the maze of boxes or if he was warning of danger. Getting away suddenly seemed less likely than fighting to stay alive.

A half dozen Sum Yop tong killers swarmed from their rabbit warren of crates and rushed Slocum. All he could see rushing toward him were the uplifted, glitteringly sharp blades of their hatchets.

3

"Whoa there, little lady."

Lai Choi San looked out the window of the coach driving her through the San Francisco streets. At first she saw only the phantasms moving in the fog, then she saw the arm of a man thrust out on the street. Her driver. He must have died quickly and silently for her not to have noticed, although she felt she could be excused from such inattention due to the weighty matters on her mind.

"You killed him," she said in a sibilant voice.

"Why don't you get on out so we can get a good look at you?" The door opened and a grimy hand reached for her. She lithely avoided the grasping hand and stepped to the wet cobblestones. A single gas lamp burned down the street. Otherwise, all was cloaked in intense night. There were no policemen in view. Through this part of San Francisco they traveled in packs of five or more. Even the more brutal private police force known as Specials were loath to venture out alone.

She stood with her emerald green silk shawl wrapped about her.

"We got ourselves a chink whore," cried the one who had tried to grab her. From around the coach came three

24

more men. Each was uglier than the one preceding him. Lai Choi San stared at them with cold, dark eyes. After only a glance, she dismissed them as fools.

"You are delaying my journey. I must not be late to the museum."

"Museum, is it? Them folks at this here museum, they like their whores to be yellow?"

Lai Choi San remained impassive. She pulled her silk wrap a little tighter around her shoulders. The night was cold, and she was not accustomed to wearing clothing like this.

"What's a chink whore charge? Must be something to afford a coach like this one."

"It is rented," she said.

"Didn't think a whore'd own it," the first man said, moving closer. Lai Choi San's nose wrinkled at the odor. Westerners needed to bathe more often. In this lout's case, bathe more than once a year.

"Reckon whoever hired her for the night's fun is the one with all the money."

"Won't hurt to search her and see what she's got."

Lai Choi San did not move when he ran his fingers through her carefully coiffured hair and found one of the carved jade ornaments there.

"This must be worth a few dollars."

"It is priceless," Lai Choi San said.

"Well, everybody's got their price. What's yours for spreading them fine legs?" Another man lifted her skirt and leered at her well-muscled legs.

"Do not get any blood on my clothing," she said quietly.

"Blood? We ain't gonna get blood on you, 'less you're a virgin. But you're too old for that. I heard them Celestials don't value virgins, so you don't have a cherry to bust no more."

"I was not speaking to you," Lai Choi San said coldly.

"She wasn't—" The first road agent died in midsentence. The others whirled about, reaching for knives and slungshot. As one, they also died.

"You, Sung," she said, pointing to the dark-clad man who had silently approached and killed the robbers' leader. "Drive me the rest of the way to the museum. And be quick. I do not want to miss the exhibit."

The huge Chinaman bowed deeply and dropped to hands and knees so his mistress could return to the coach. She stepped onto the middle of his back offered as her footstool and closed the door behind her. He hastily motioned to the other Celestials who had killed the road agents for them to remove the bodies, including that of the driver. Only when he was sure they obeyed his silent commands did he agilely climb into the driver's box. For a moment, the reins and team confounded him, but he quickly figured out the arrangement and got the coach clacking along the cobblestone street.

Lai Choi San leaned back inside the coach and fumed. Such delays should never happen. She was on a mission of the utmost urgency. Why did she have to come to such a lawless city as San Francisco to complete her quest? She needed to burn more joss sticks to appease the gods. Later. After she had recovered what had been stolen.

Tess Lawrence wanted to scream. There were too many people crowded into the museum and not one in a hundred had the slightest idea what they were looking at. How much easier it was working in an office, dealing with Sir William's papers, even setting up such showcases as this than it was actually coping with them.

Tess bit her lower lip as she heard one matronly woman say "Why, they look so . . . tawdry. And old. They are so very old-looking. Not new at all." The matron thrust out her diamond-encrusted bracelet for all those nearby to admire. "Michael bought this for our anniversary. He had it made specially for me, of course, by the finest jeweler in all of Europe. It's from Italy. Or was it France? I simply cannot recall." She turned back to the case holding the jade ornaments and wrinkled her overpowdered nose. She sniffed and said, "Cheap-looking. Don't you agree?"

Of course the small knot of sycophants with her all agreed as they moved on, trailing the doyenne like a cloud of perfume, cloying and obvious. Tess closed her eyes and leaned against the cool plastered museum wall, wishing this ordeal were at an end.

"There you are, my dear. Have you seen to the lackeys at the door? I have heard they are being rude to some of our guests." Sir William Macadams never met her sapphire-colored eyes or appreciated her beauty. Tess wondered if he even knew her name, and she had worked for him almost six months.

Sir William cut quite a dashing figure, though, in spite of his lack of social graces. A preeminent archaeologist, he had little trouble raising money for his expeditions. He was middle-aged and balding, but his quick wit and manner always gulled the rich out of a few dollars to finance his often odd travels. He was muscular and brave and daring and, Tess had to admit, quite handsome.

Why wouldn't he at least call her by name?

"I'll see to it, Sir William," Tess said. "Uh, Sir William?"

"Yes?" The sandy-haired man looked not at her but at the matron who had found it so difficult to believe anything old could be valuable. Tess saw the dollar signs in his eyes—or pound signs since he was British—as he estimated how much he could get from her husband for his next expedition.

"Never mind," she said.

"Nonsense, my dear. Is it important?"

"I wondered what you were doing after the exhibition. I thought we could—"

"Always business, aren't we, my dear?" He laughed. It was rich and endearing, except Tess did not find it so at the moment. She had hoped they could celebrate the success of the jade exhibition in a somewhat more private setting. Sir William's hotel room would do nicely. All night long. With champagne and . . . Sir William beside her in the luxurious bed.

"Oh, Mrs. Clarke, wherever has your dashing husband

gone?" Sir William called. "I can't imagine why he would allow such a lissome demoiselle as yourself to be alone for even an instant." With that Sir William went to kiss the matron's hand. She giggled like a debutante.

Tess fought to keep from calling out, "Demoiselle means she's not married." She held her tongue, as she had on so many occasions. She was never certain how far Sir William went in his romancing of rich society matrons, but she had the gut-wrenching feeling he would go as far as necessary to enlist the women's aid in obtaining financing from their husbands.

She turned and almost fell. She was not used to wearing the formal high-heeled sandals and such a long, flowing skirt. Every step caused her to wobble a mite. Breathing also proved difficult due to the tightly cinched corset she did not need. Fashion. It would be the death of her yet. Tess patted her strawberry blonde hair back into place and settled herself. Dealing with the small museum staff had proven to be a chore almost as vexing as getting into the corset. They were as irritated over Sir William's blowing in with his fine collection of jade artifacts and assuming he was in complete charge as she was of dealing with the archaeologist's foibles. Sharing a mutual annoyance did nothing to calm the choppy waters since Tess could not openly say anything about her employer, and they could— and did.

"Raymond," she said when she approached the liveried doorman.

"You don't have to say anything more, Miss Lawrence," he said. The glum expression told it all. "I've already ordered the footmen and the rest of the staff to be more civil."

"There is one bright spot in the evening," Tess said.

"What's that?"

"It'll be over soon." She reached out and touched his arm, smiled as cheerfully as she could and then returned to the large exhibition hall where Sir William had pushed the existing cases to one side and installed his own in the center. They had leased the entire museum for a full week, allowing the curator to take a much needed vacation. Tess wished she could be with him, although he had been as surly as any man she had ever met. The vast money Sir William had offered for the lease had decided the matter, she felt. The museum was out of the way for the rich and curious, nearly outside town to the south of the Mission District, and merely survived. Sir William's exhibit had brought in more people in one night than the museum had seen in a month.

That was the way he went through life, in command and oblivious to anything that did not concern him personally. Tess made a mental note that she ought to offer the custom-made cases Sir William had ordered to the museum for their own displays after he left on his next expedition, wherever that might take him.

"This is a fine example of Tang Dynasty jade," Sir William said loudly to attract attention. It worked. Tess was pushed out of the way so several of the society women could move closer to hang on his every word. "I recovered it in a dig just outside Shanghai a few months ago."

"Oh, it looks so marvelous," cooed Mrs. Clarke.

Tess wondered if lightning might strike her. This was the woman who, only minutes earlier, had thought the imperial jade looked tawdry. Mrs. Clarke showed no sign that this hypocrisy troubled her as she batted long eyelashes at Sir William. He graced her with a dazzling smile, took her flabby arm and steered her closer to the case.

"This piece, I believe after long examination, is the crown of the Jade Emperor himself."

"The emperor is made of jade?"

Sir William laughed easily. "A common misconception. The Chinese believe he is of divine origin and jade is a divine stone. This crown once rested on the emperor's brow."

"How'd it come to be buried?" asked an ill-dressed man who stood with pencil poised over a folded sheet of foolscap.

Tess sighed. She had not wanted to allow reporters into the exhibit. A private showing for them would have been more beneficial for both the museum and for focusing the attention on the jade display. As it was, the reporters would concentrate more on who was here this evening rather than why. Although Sir William had not said so, Tess thought this was why he had invited the reporters. Showing off society friends and having their names listed in a front page story might be beneficial to his fund-raising. Tess had seen notes about excavations in South America that had turned up Chinese artifacts. It was like him to go exploring in Peru and Chile for what must be a will-'o-the-wisp—one that would require a considerable bankroll.

"You will have to wait for my soon to be published book describing my journeys throughout the Orient for that to be revealed," Sir William said haughtily. "Let me say at this time, it was a perilous trip and one fraught with danger at every step. Finding the jade crown was less of a chore than escaping with it. I was bedeviled by Chinese brigands at every step, yes, every step."

"I thought you were on a boat," the reporter said, looking confused.

"I was. That is a manner of speaking. A metaphor, as it were. Now, ladies and gentleman, in this case are a variety of jade combs and buttons." Sir William took Mrs. Clarke's arm to keep her from getting away and led the crowd to the next case.

Tess trailed, mentally keeping track of all the exaggerations and outright lies Sir William told that she might be required to back up with documentation. It was difficult being with him, but Tess could not imagine being without him. He was larger than life and had a flair that she had never encountered before. He was the brightest star in the firmament, the—

"Pardon me," Tess said. "I was not paying attention to where I was going." She looked at the short Chinese woman impeccably dressed in a white satin dress embroidered with writhing dragons and other creatures less recognizable. The green silk shawl had slipped down the woman's broad shoulders and draped over her elbows as she reached out to press her hands against the case.

"Exquisite," the woman said, not noticing Tess. Her attention was fixed on the jade crown inside the case.

"Yes, it is. You have a few nice carved jade items of your own," Tess said, seeing the glint of light off the carved green stone ornaments adorning the woman's jet-black hair.

The woman looked up, her ebony eyes boring into Tess's blue ones.

"These belong to the Jade Emperor."

Tess started to speak, then stopped and collected her thoughts. The woman's recognition of the contents in the case told of some education.

"They were recovered by Sir William recently. The term 'Jade Emperor' applies to any of the dynasty rulers. He has not yet determined which emperor wore this crown."

"All the emperors wore this crown," the Chinese woman said.

"Are you an authority? I'm sure Sir William would like to speak with you and profit from your knowledge and insight. He—"

"I am nothing, a ship's captain, no more."

"I beg your pardon? A ship's captain? That's—"

A loud shout from the foyer caused Tess to look away. Her eyes went wide at the sight of a dozen Chinamen rushing into the museum. They brandished long, curved knives. More than one waved a pistol. Once they forced their way through the door leading into the main room, they formed a V and advanced, coming straight for her.

"Sir William!" Tess cried. The explorer was already in action. He pushed Mrs. Clarke and several of the other women behind him and thrust his hands under his flaring dress coat. "Sir William, no!"

Tess was horrified at the sight of the pistols Sir William drew and pointed at the Celestials making their way through the exhibit, smashing glass cases and stealing the jade as they advanced.

She threw her arms around the Chinese woman and knocked her to the floor as Sir William fired a volley. The bullets tore through the space directly above, and one errant slug broke the glass. The cascade of shards caused Tess to flinch. The elegantly clad woman struggled to get free.

"Let me up, you fool."

"He's shooting, there's danger," Tess said. "Stay down or you'll be injured."

"Fool!" The Chinese woman pushed herself free from Tess's grip and got to her knees.

"At them, men! Attack! Give them what for!" cried Sir William.

Pouring from three smaller doors leading into the exhibit came armed Specials. They sprayed bullets everywhere. Some of them hit the Celestials who were still working on stealing the jade ornaments. Tess saw that the Chinamen were not cowed by the gunfire. It was as if they were used to such things, but they were outnumbered. If more of them had been armed with pistols, they might have made a better showing. As it was, the withering fire from the uniformed Specials dropped one robber after another.

Tess followed the Chinese woman to her feet. The side of the case holding the jade emperor's crown had been shattered by Sir William's stray round, but reaching the jade within the case was difficult.

"Don't," Tess said, grabbing the woman's wrist as she tried to reach inside. "You'll cut yourself. And there's no need to worry. The jade crown is safe."

"Aye, that it is, my dear," called Sir William. He opened the action on his Webley pistols and reloaded. He stopped beside Tess. "I'll fight to the death to defend my prize."

Tess felt as if she would wilt. He had called her his prize!

"Yes, the jade crown is the prize of this collection. No band of brigands will steal away my glory!"

Tess stood dumbstruck at the man's revelation over what he considered most valuable. He fired a few more times, but the Specials had surrounded the few remaining robbers—the ones they had not gunned down. Tess saw the expression on the Chinese woman's face. For a moment anger had flared but what replaced it was less understandable. She looked frightened. During the gunfire, she had been fearless while Tess had been scared. Now that the danger had passed, Tess felt relieved and the woman was in shock.

Tess shook her head. How people reacted under stress always amazed her.

"Bring that one to me," called Sir William. "The leader."

"Howja know which that is?" demanded a Special wearing sergeant's stripes. "Don't see no insignia." He guffawed at this.

"He's a sailor," Sir William said. "A mate, unless I miss my guess, and I seldom do. Bring him here."

The Special dragged a burly Celestial over and held him in a hammerlock.

"Answer the gent's questions, scum." The Special jerked hard and almost pulled the man's arm from its socket.

"No speak Ingrish," he said.

"And I speak no Mandarin. Or is it Cantonese?" Sir William wondered. "They are quite distinct languages, although the written language is similar. I doubt this one can read."

Tess glanced from the captive to the Chinese woman. Her expression had changed again to one of utter disdain. She started to speak, thought better of it and stepped away from Sir William. Tess saw the woman mouth a word that might have been "sung" and then turn and walk off.

"You'll tend to it, won't you, my dear?"

"What? What's that, Sir William?" Tess lost sight of the Chinese woman in the crush of people leaving the museum.

"See to cleaning up the broken glass, get the cases back into order, that sort of thing. I must go smooth some ruffled feathers. As invigorating as this evening has been for me, others have found it disquieting." He thrust his twin pistols back under his coat and called out, "Mrs. Clarke, here! All is well. There is no more danger. Allow me to see you home safely."

Tess turned in a full circle. The exhibit was a mess. The jade was safe, except possibly for a few pieces the Specials would steal. The emperor's crown was secure, though, and

this was the centerpiece of the exhibit. The brigands—
sailors, Sir William had said, and Tess had no reason not
to believe him—were all being taken out by the Specials.
Some bodies were dragged but a few went under their own
power.

In a surprisingly short time, she was alone in the vast
room. Tess stared down at the jade crown and then looked
up. Somehow she had expected to see the woman dressed
in the white satin gown. She shivered, put her arms around
herself, wishing Sir William had done that earlier, then
went to find the museum employees to begin the cleaning.

All that and she had to wear the uncomfortable corset.
It had been quite a night.

4

Slocum emptied his Colt Navy into the pack of tong killers charging him. He aimed for their heads and dropped two, causing the others to stumble and fall. This gave him a brief instant to act. He grabbed around his waist and found another stick of dynamite tucked into his gun belt. He pulled it out, got a lucifer from its tin and worked to light it. From the corner of his eye he saw two Sum Yop assassins rushing him. He got the fuse lit, but it would be too late—or so he thought.

Flashing silver cartwheeled past his head. The two men grunted and fell, hatchets in their chests. Slocum looked at Ah Ming's father just as he reached for another of the fallen weapons. Slocum knew then that the old man had been a killer in his day. He still was.

"Thanks," Slocum said, then spun and tossed the dynamite an instant before the short fuse burned down to the blasting cap. The explosion knocked him backward into the old man, and they went down in a pile. Slocum got to his feet, found another stick and lit the fuse on it, tossing it underhanded between the crates. He had guessed right where the Sum Yop would attack next. He blew up three of them and caused an avalanche of crates to come crashing down, blocking that route.

While he had cut off one avenue of attack, he had also cut off a way of escaping the building.

"Keep 'em busy for a few seconds," Slocum said. He reloaded his six-shooter, knowing there might not be a chance to reload again. He heard what sounded like a vast army assembling out of sight. Six rounds would not put a dent into the number of men that would be storming this position.

Ah Ming's father stood with a hatchet in each hand. His dark eyes darted about. Any hint of infirmity had disappeared when he had regained use of his favorite weapons.

"You got any ideas how to get out of here?" Slocum asked. He sighted and fired, winging a tong man trying to sneak across the tops of the crates. Slocum cursed under his breath. He had hoped to get back to this aerial highway and escape. It had not taken the tong killers long to figure out not only how he had gotten through the building so fast but also how to attack him.

The old man shook his head.

"What's wrong, cat got your tongue?" Slocum asked. He went cold inside when the man opened his mouth and pointed. His tongue had been cut out. "They do that?"

The old man nodded.

"We'll get you back to your daughter and then figure how to even the score," Slocum said. He had seen torture in his day. The Apaches were about the worst. Slocum had come across a man staked out naked in the desert sun with his eyelids cut off so he would go blind. The only mercy in the situation was that the man had been dead when Slocum had found him. Otherwise, Slocum would have been faced with the decision of getting him back to the nearest cavalry outpost or just putting him out of his misery. That was what he would have done for a wounded animal but doing it for a mutilated human being was different.

Sometimes, Slocum could not quite figure why, but it was.

What an old man so decrepit that he could hardly stand did to merit such torture was beyond Slocum. He fired twice more and drove back a renewed attack, but there was nothing he could do to escape through the building.

"Get down behind this crate," Slocum said, kicking the box in the man's direction. "There's going to be one hell of an explosion real soon."

He fumbled in his pockets where he had stuffed a couple other sticks of dynamite and came out with a bundle of five. Slocum chose one short fuse, lit it and then placed it against the wall. He hoped he had not gotten too confused making his way through the building to this spot and that he had figured out which was an exterior wall. Then all thought vanished as the explosion clutched at him like a powerful fist. Stunned, deaf, blinking dust from his eyes, he sat on the floor and stared stupidly at the gaping hole. Fresh air from outside blew in, carrying the fish scent of the Bay.

"Come on," he yelled, getting Ah Ming's father to his feet. The old man had endured the blast better than Slocum. He still walked with a limp when flat-out running was needed to get away from the Sum Yop.

Slocum pressed through the hole in the wall and then helped the man. He took a quick shot at a Sum Yop hatchet man running toward them. The slug only hit the man in the leg. He tumbled forward, then started crawling. Slocum was not certain he admired or detested the determination the tong members showed in doing their duty. He put a second bullet into the man's back. This stopped him.

"Go straight to your daughter," Slocum shouted at the old man. His ears rang, and he was not sure if the man understood. Slocum gently pushed him out in the direction of the street, then found himself in a gunfight with two men on the roof who opened fire on him. The bullets kicked up dirt all around his feet. He was in shadow while the two tong killers on the roof failed to realize they had silhouetted themselves against the night sky. The moon had not risen, but the starlight was enough for Slocum to draw a bead. He fired three times and then his hammer fell on an empty chamber.

He knew he had no time to reload. He ran after Ah Ming's pa and tripped over something by the curb that threw him to the ground with enough force to knock the wind out of his lungs. He lay gasping, sure that the Sum Yop hatchet men would be on him in a flash. He saw tiny dust clouds rising around him. He was still deaf, but he recognized bullets hitting stone. He tried to stand, but one foot tangled in whatever he had tripped over. Rolling, he came to a sitting position.

His heart almost exploded when he saw what had caused him to stumble. Ah Ming's father lay still.

"Come on, get up," Slocum cried, swiveling around to kneel by the man. He pressed his fingers into the man's throat. No pulse. He turned him over and saw a bullet smack in the middle of his back. If the slug had not killed him outright, the broken spine would have left him paralyzed for whatever remained of his short life.

Slocum yelped in pain when a bullet grazed his left arm. He looked to the roof of the building and saw a dozen Sum Yop lined up with rifles. They were getting serious about killing now. He dodged, ducked and stumbled across the street to the safety of the alley. Only then did he stop, bend over with hands on his knees and gasp for breath. He was lucky to be alive.

When he got his breath back, he slowly retraced his path through Chinatown until he found himself shadowed by a pair of burly men. He caught sight of one and recognized him as being Ah Ming's personal guard. Motioning, Slocum got the man to come closer.

"I got him out, but he was killed. Tell Ah Ming." Slocum was not sure if anything got through other than the name of the man's mistress. Within minutes, Slocum found himself shoved down a narrow stairway and once more in the intricate underground maze of passages below Chinatown.

Slocum made no effort to remember where he went this time. He was shoved along by the hatchet man following him, and eventually they came to the same room where Ah Ming had patched up his wounds and given him the chore of fetching her pa.

He sat on the bed, his head aching and his body ready to die around him.

Slocum looked up when Ah Ming came into the room. She now wore a midnight black silk jacket and pants that matched her hair and eyes. Tiny silver threads subtly highlighted her hips and breasts in ways no Western woman would consider. If anything, the silver chasing diminished her charm rather than accentuated it. It was as if Ah Ming wanted to disappear rather than stand out.

"He is dead," she said without preamble.

"I'm sorry. I got him out of the building. They had tortured him."

She stared without blinking at Slocum. He felt like a truant schoolchild.

"They'd tortured him. Cut out his tongue." He had no reason to bedevil her with such details. Her pa was dead from a bullet in the back. That ought to be enough.

"You freed him? Before he died?"

Slocum nodded. "I reached him inside the Sum Yop headquarters. They attacked, I killed a few. After I freed him, your pa used those axes like he was born with them in his hands to kill a couple more."

"The dynamite blew a hole in the wall."

Slocum looked more closely at her. She must have watched or at least had spies report back everything that was visible from the street. He nodded.

"You did not protect him as you escaped."

"I was taking fire. I told him to run for it, to get back to you. He understood that I was going to cover for him. I ran out of ammo, then I . . ."

"You stumbled over his body."

"That's right," Slocum said, feeling guilty. At the time he had thought he was the toughest hombre in San Francisco, going into that den of killers and rescuing the old man. Now he felt as if he had failed in every respect.

"You must retrieve his body."

"That's not going to be too hard," Slocum said. "The Sum Yop will leave it out in the street."

"They have taken it. They are hiding it."

"Why?"

"They want to dishonor him."

Slocum knew how that worked. Indians were always doing foolhardy things for honor. The Celestials had something similar in their devotion to "face." Honor meant everything. Slocum could understand that. Without honor, what was a man?

"You will get him?" Ah Ming came and sat beside him. Her fathomless eyes stared into his, and he felt suddenly dizzy, as if she had given him some knockout drops. Slocum tried to explain it away because of the heavy perfumed odor in the air. The Chinese burned incense everywhere. He took a deep sniff and caught some of the joss sticks but more of Ah Ming. Her hair was like a mountain meadow and that girlish figure looked less and less like a child's and more like a woman's with every passing second.

A million thoughts shattered in Slocum's head. He had loved Anne. There was no telling if he would have married her, but that was possible. And she had died in his arms. He still felt the cold chill along his body and arms as he had clutched her lifeless body, even knowing she had frozen to death.

Then the coldness went away and he found something warmer and more pliant in his arms. Ah Ming. She moved still closer until her body pressed against his. Her arms circled his neck and pulled his face to hers. The kiss was warm. Then it became molten. Slocum had tried to drown his sorrow at losing Anne, but he had sought refuge in the wrong places.

Ah Ming moved even closer and began moving slowly against him, rubbing herself like a cat, making small purring sounds as her tongue invaded his mouth. She pressed past his lips so her tongue could duel with his. They began to frolic, move back and forth in a slow, sensual oral dance that deepened. Slocum felt himself responding when he had thought he would never again feel anything for a woman.

"You are tense," Ah Ming said. "Let me make you hard, too."

She slithered down his body, moving as gracefully as a

snake. She dropped to her knees in front of him. Her clever fingers worked at his gun belt and then the buttoned fly of his jeans. Before Slocum realized it, she had released him. He sprang upright, fully erect and aching. The cool air in the underground room quickly became a distant memory as warm, soft lips closed on the purpled head of his erection. Slowly moving, Ah Ming took more and more of him into her mouth until he was squirming on the hard bed.

He felt the end of his manhood bounce off the roof of her mouth and go deeper. He groaned as she pulled back. Every inch of the way her tongue stroked along the sensitive underside of his fleshy shaft. She quickly took him fully into her mouth again, this time using her teeth to lightly score the top and bottom of his length.

Slocum reached down and ran his hands into the woman's silky black hair. He guided her in and out, demanding more speed from her as he felt the volcanic pressures mounting within him.

When he was sure he would erupt, he was suddenly left out in the cold. He opened his eyes and stared at Ah Ming. She got to her feet and took a step backward. With agonizing slowness, she unfastened her padded jacket and slipped out of it.

"You like this?"

"Yes," was all he could say. Slocum hardly trusted himself to speak. His throat was tensed and a knot built in the pit of his stomach as more and more pale skin appeared to torment him. A shoulder, then the other. The jacket slid to the floor, but he watched Ah Ming carefully unfastening the frogs on her blouse. The deep divide between her breasts appeared.

And then her breasts! What he had been missing! He had thought she was like a young girl, but those firm breasts were definitely a woman's. Capping each was a dark circle of aureola with a hard button popping up in the middle.

"You like?" Ah Ming stepped closer, cupping one breast.

Slocum showed how much he liked the offer. His tongue flicked out, snake-quick, and lightly touched the tip of one nipple. A shudder passed through her body. He carefully circled the nipple and then worked into the valley between her breasts. He put his arms around her waist and drew her closer. She came willingly. Moans escaped her lips as he continued to torment her with his oral assault.

One breast, then the other and he hardly noticed how she shucked off her blouse so she was naked to the waist. His hands worked over her bare back and then downward to the firm, small mounds of her ass. She moaned even louder as Slocum pulled her close. He ran his lips across her bare belly and then worked lower, getting his tongue under the waistband of her linen trousers. She reached down and slipped them off her hips.

The pants fell around her graceful legs. Slocum was delighted to see that she wore nothing under them. He moved lower. His mouth brushed her nether lips and then his tongue slipped into her. The dampness seeping out became a torrent as he flicked his tongue over the pink nub growing at the V of her sex lips.

She moved forward and pushed him flat onto the bed to crouch over his face as he continued to run his oral organ in and out of her. Then Ah Ming moved lithely down him, stripping his pants as she went. He lay flat on his back, jutting upright. For a moment. She rose, then dropped, taking him fully into her tightness.

They both gasped at the sudden intrusion. Slocum was surrounded by soft heat that clutched at him with increasing power. She rose, squeezed down and tried to hold him within her. She was too wet for that. He slid free like a watermelon seed. She lowered herself slowly, taking him all the way in.

"You're wearing me out," Slocum said. He had not thought he would ever be aroused by a woman again. Now he was acting like a young buck on his first exploration into the wonders of a woman. He twitched and jerked about within Ah Ming, then arched his back and drove himself upward as hard as he could when she began massaging him with her knowing inner muscles.

She rose and fell faster now. The friction along his length burned like a forest fire. It spread throughout his loins and then exploded like a stick of the dynamite he had used on the Sum Yops.

She pumped fiercely for a moment, let out a tiny cry of pleasure and then sank down, her cheek resting on his chest.

"You are not like other men," she said.

"Is that a good thing?" Slocum did not know how to take her comment.

"It is very good."

"You're more than good," he said.

Ah Ming did not answer. She lay on him. He felt her hot breath and the pressure of her body and the way her legs clamped down around one of his. She moved the slightest bit, stimulating herself against his thigh.

He was surprised to find that she got him hard again so quickly. And after they had finished a second lovemaking, she whispered in his ear, "You will bring back my father?"

"His body?"

"Yes, his body. He must be returned to the Celestial Kingdom for burial."

With his arms around such a lissome, willing woman, who had brought him back from black despair, Slocum could only nod. He knew how difficult that would be, but somehow for Ah Ming he would do it.

5

Tess Lawrence looked at Sir William. Seldom had she seen him more cheerful. The cold wind off the bay blew her strawberry blonde hair about, forcing her to constantly touch it. She worried he might think this was a bit too forward, but the explorer took little notice. He stared not across the carriage at her but out into the city. He sucked in a deep breath and let it out in a big gust.

"This is a fine day to be alive," Sir William said. "Yes, I say it is."

"I suppose," Tess said uncertainly. "Why do we have to go to the police station? The officers are quite capable of interrogating the robbers and finding who sent them, aren't they?"

"I doubt it. Did you see their heavy brows and undershot jaws? Definitely brutes of low caste and even lower intelligence."

Tess wondered if he meant the police or the robbers. Asking would have made her sound either ignorant or cheeky. Neither of those would increase her stature in Sir William's eyes.

"What do you hope to find out?"

"I will personally conduct the interrogation. Those

sailors, and sailors they were from their clothing and the curious way they walked—did you notice that, my dear?"

"They acted as if the floor was rolling about under them," she said.

"Exactly! Sailors used to the bounding main. They have only recently come ashore. How is it that a crew of Chinese sailors takes it into their heads to rob me of my fine exhibits? That is a poser. It is also a question I will answer by careful deduction. I doubt if any of the police in this city even speak Chinese."

"Mandarin or Cantonese," she murmured.

"Exactly right. You catch on quickly. By learning what dialect of Chinese they speak, we will learn much. Are they from the north? Or the south? If the latter, they are likely to be South China Sea pirates."

"Why would they want the jade?"

"Anything of value is their goal to steal," Sir William said haughtily. "What finer collection in all of California can there be but mine? It is destined to be shipped to Boston soon. You have made those arrangements, haven't you?"

"I am finishing them now. I think by rail would be safer and quicker," Tess said. Her head spun. She had juggled so many items for Sir William that they all blurred together, and she struggled to keep this and her own affairs in proper order. Setting up the exhibition at the museum had been time consuming, but nothing like determining the best way of shipment for possibly fragile jade ornaments. The vibration from the steel wheels for weeks on end had to be considered against the somewhat smoother trip in a sailing ship around the Cape. Vibration was more destructive than even the most severe battering of a storm, but Tess had decided the chance of a ship sinking was greater than the jade being stolen by train robbers. There would be armed guards accompanying the shipment, in any case, but even if the train derailed, its cargo would not be consigned to the depths of the ocean.

Even if train robbers stole the jade, there was a chance of ransoming it back. This was what she had told Sir William.

So many details made her head ache. And now Sir William wanted to confront the thieves personally.

"What is it you expect from me when we arrive at the police headquarters?"

"My dear, you will take notes. Every utterance I make must be recorded. This will make a splendid chapter in my autobiography, don't you think? Yes, yes, it will. I also want you to study those ruffians for any sign of lying. They will be expert at it, mind you, being both sailors and Chinamen, but I am sure you will be able to detect it."

"How?"

"There will be a furtiveness. Their eyes will dart about. They are not clever enough to conceal such mannerisms inherent in lying."

"What if they play poker?"

Sir William looked at her, startled. Then he laughed. "You do have a quaint wit, my dear. Imagine that. Poker faces!" He laughed loudly, causing the driver to turn and look at him curiously to see what the joke was.

"There it is, driver," Sir William called. "The police precinct where the surviving robbers were taken for incarceration. Pull over here and wait for us, that's a good chap."

Sir William hopped down and took a step toward the front door before he remembered his manners, swung back and took Tess's extended hand to help her from the carriage.

"Thank you, Sir William," she said. The brief touch had been electric for her. How brave and daring he was!

Then Tess had to hurry to catch up with him. He took the steps three at a time in his hurry to begin the questioning.

"You, my good man," Sir William barked, pointing to a sergeant behind a large desk. "Where have you put my prisoners?"

"Yer prisoners, now, sir? Who might you be and who might they be?"

Sir William puffed himself up, thrust his thumbs into the armholes of his waistcoat and struck a pose with one foot slightly before the other. Tess thought he must have looked the same when he climbed the highest peak in Africa or discovered the trove of jade in Shanghai.

"The brigands who attempted to steal the priceless jade artifacts from the museum last night. I captured them; I demand to question them."

"What's that?" The sergeant scratched his head as he studied Sir William. "I don't unnerstan' a word of what yer sayin'."

"Allow me, Sir William," Tess said.

"Yes, of course, my dear. You do have the common touch." Sir William stepped back and allowed her to go to the policeman's desk.

"Last night there was a robbery attempt. A gang of Chinese hooligans—"

"They were sailors fresh from the sea," Sir William cut in.

"Yes, of course," Tess said, irritated at the interruption. She had the police officer's attention. She knew he was more interested in staring at her bustle and undoubtedly fantasizing about what lay under the undulating wire structure, but she had his attention.

"You was sayin', miss?" The sergeant ignored Sir William.

"The Chinese sailors who tried to rob the museum last night. There were many influential people there who are very disturbed. People from society. Rich men and their wives," she pressed. This caused a spark of understanding to flare in the policeman's eyes.

"Four of the bastards," the cop said. "No offense, miss. We got 'em in cells down there. Captain Reilly's in charge."

"Sir William," Tess said, inclining her head slightly in her employer's direction, "would like to be present at the questioning. He might speed up the gathering of information."

"You mean he wants to take a turn with the brass knucks? Why didn't you say so?" The sergeant got to his feet and went to a corridor. He bellowed down it, "A gent's here to help Captain Reilly!" The echo made Tess cringe.

"That's not what you wanted to do," Tess protested to

Sir William. "Is it?" She clutched at her throat when she thought it might be. Sir William had a wild, untamed streak that might cross over into barbarism.

"Nothing of the sort, my dear, nothing of the sort. But you did well. Broke the ice, got us through, all of that."

"Jist head on down. Last cell on the right."

When Tess started to go with Sir William, the sergeant reached out and took her arm to stop her.

"Wait a second, miss. What goes on there ain't fer delicate sensibilities."

"She has no 'delicate sensibilities,' my good man," Sir William said. "She's my assistant. Come along now. We must not keep the captain waiting."

Tess went with Sir William, doing her best to keep up as he hurried along. She glanced in some of the cells and winced at the sight. The prisoners were kept like animals.

"They act like animals, they should be caged like animals," Sir William said, as if he had read her mind. Tess decided her expression had conveyed her shock at seeing men in shackles in barred cages.

"Yes, of course."

"You must be Captain Reilly," Sir William greeted. He thrust out his hand. The police officer glared at him and did not shake his hand.

"You one of them lawyers who think the Cubic Air Ordinance is a crock of shit?"

"I have no idea what you mean. I am not a lawyer."

"Then why are you here?" The captain was a bulldog of a man, with fierce eyes and a beetle brow. He had ample red hair that he had worked into long sideburns and a bushy mustache to go with the curly mop top.

"I have some knowledge of the Orient and might help find what transpired last night." Sir William stepped to one side to get a better look at the prisoner. "I say, this one seems to have expired."

"He croaked," the captain said. "We got three more."

"What have you discovered?"

"Can't make head nor tail out of what they're yammerin'," the captain said. "They're speakin' Chinee, though it ain't what most of the others here in San Francisco talk."

"Cantonese rather than Mandarin," Sir William said thoughtfully. "It is as I suspected. Most Chinese sailors are from the southern provinces."

"We want to find who paid them to bust in like that and try to steal your jade. Already we got four complaints going all the way up to the mayor's office about this. They scared some mighty powerful gents in the city."

"I am sure," Sir William said dryly.

Tess felt faint from the smell and the sight of the body. The sailor was slumped down in a chair where he had been tied. The steady drip of blood from his face into his lap and onto his legs showed he had not been dead long. Otherwise, the blood would have coagulated.

"Get your notebook, my dear," Sir William said airily. "It is time to ask questions."

"You want her to see?" The captain was as skeptical as the desk sergeant had been about Tess's witnessing how they questioned their prisoners. And with good reason, if death was a common part of the interrogation.

"Why not? They're only Celestials, after all," Sir William said.

The captain shrugged and wiped his bloody hands on his uniform.

"This way, then," he said.

Tess followed reluctantly. She was both repulsed and drawn by the squalor in the cell block. It was the only time she had witnessed such debasement and made her wonder about the sights Sir William had endured on his travels throughout the world.

"This one looks to be the ringleader," Captain Reilly said. "Wake up there, boyo." He rattled the cell door hard enough to get the attention of the Chinaman inside. Tess saw bruises and more than one cut on his face.

"Has he been questioned already?" she asked.

"Naw, that was what he got for resistin' arrest last night. I wanted to get something on him from the others 'fore gettin' down to serious questionin'."

"I see," she said. She stared at the man and details from the prior night worked their way back into her memory. This was the man the elegantly dressed Chinese lady had glared at and mouthed a word to.

Captain Reilly opened the cell and stepped inside.

"He's harmless. He was cowed last night. Once their spirits are broke, the Chinee are as docile as—"

"Sung," Tess said. "Sung."

The prisoner reacted as if he had stepped on a rattlesnake. He shot from the chair, lowered his shoulder and caught the captain in the midriff. Tess heard the air gust from the policeman's lungs. Even Sir William was taken by the surprise attack. The Celestial shoved the explorer out of the way, stared hard and hot at Tess, then swung around and slammed the cell door. She heard it click. Both Sir William and Captain Reilly were locked inside while she stood with the escaping prisoner outside the cage.

"Wh-what are you going to do, Sung?" she added what must be the man's name in an attempt to slow him. The police station was filled with armed officers. They could stop Sung if she could slow his escape.

"Guards!" bellowed Reilly. "Prisoner on the loose!"

Sung reached through the bars, grabbed the captain's jacket and pulled hard enough to smash his head into the iron door. Reilly sank to the floor, unconscious.

"Run, my dear. Don't let him take you alive!" Sir William stepped away as Sung grabbed for him. The sailor backed off, glared at Tess again, then squared his shoulders and strutted down the corridor as if he owned the place. He turned a corner and vanished from sight. Tess heard a struggle and then nothing.

"Get the keys. Free us!" Sir William was agitated now.

Tess cautiously went down the corridor and peeked around. A policeman lay flat on his back, knocked out. The rear door to the jailhouse swung open and a key in the lock showed how the Celestial had escaped. Tess looked over her shoulder and saw a thick knot of police crowded in front of the cell. The turnkey was working to open the cell door and let out his furious captain. Blood trickled down the police officer's scowling face. Sir William strolled out as if he were on an afternoon jaunt.

"Aren't you frightened, Sir William?" she asked when he came up. "That man is dangerous."

"No more dangerous than others I have confronted in my years of roaming the entire world," he said. His eyes darted about as he took in the scene. "This looks to be jolly good sport."

"What?" Tess could hardly believe her ears.

"We can track the brigand through the streets, just as if he were a wild animal in the densest jungles of Borneo. When I bag him, it will be a great victory."

"You're going to shoot him?" Tess had a wild image of Sir William gunning down the Chinese sailor and then mounting his head on a wall somewhere.

"If circumstances so dictate. Come along, my dear. We have much to do."

"We didn't learn anything from him, and the police beat that one poor man to death."

"Poor man? Ha! Hardly. He would have snuffed out your life like a flickering candle flame if the opportunity had arisen. Society is better off without such ferocious, immoral animals."

Tess trailed her employer, uneasy at the continuing allusions to hunting and game in the wild.

"Back to my hotel, driver," he snapped. He hopped into the carriage and let Tess fend for herself getting in. Barely had she settled down when the carriage lurched forward. The driver whipped the horse to move at close to a gallop. He had worked for Sir William long enough to know the explorer's quicksilver moods and profit by them.

"What shall we do?" Tess looked at Sir William. He was lost in thought.

"Track him. We don't have beaters, and there are no native gun bearers available. Curse civilization!"

"The police are hunting for him," Tess pointed out. All around galloped officers on horseback, spreading the word about an escapee from the jail. The policemen had to know by now that Sung had disgraced their captain by locking him up in his own cell. Some would secretly rejoice at this, but no one would openly mention it.

"What do they know? They let him escape, didn't they?"

"If he goes to Chinatown, he will disappear."

"Ah, is that what the police think? They will cordon off the yellow section of town to prevent our escapee from reaching what looks to be safety?"

"I would suspect so," Tess said.

"But he is not of this town. He is a sailor. He will return to the sea. We begin our hunt along the Embarcadero."

Tess said nothing more. She had seen how many Chinamen worked as cargo handlers. If Sung—and she was sure that was his name—did not go to Chinatown, then he could as easily blend in among the dockworkers.

They returned to the hotel where Sir William changed into clothes better suited for the jungles of India. Reluctantly, Tess went along, staying close to the carriage as he drove this way and that for more than an hour before finally admitting he could not track his quarry.

Tess avoided him the rest of the day because of his foul mood.

Sung stepped out into the bright California sunlight and turned his sallow face to the sky. It felt good to be out of the foul-smelling jail cell. He rubbed his knuckles. He might have cracked one when he struck the policeman guarding the rear door to the jailhouse. A powerful blow had been necessary to keep him from crying out and alerting the others. As it was, Sung heard the clamor inside as the police captain raised the alarm.

Sung wished he had killed the man for what he had done to Ju Ling. Sung had listened to the blows and Ju

Ling's outcries turn from defiance to begging for mercy. Not once did the beating let up. Sung knew the precise moment when his friend had died. There were not even tiny moans of pain, but the meaty thunks of a club hitting flesh had continued.

He walked down the block until he was out of sight of the police station, then broke into a trot. As it was, the sight of a running Chinaman drew attention. He slowed and kept to the alleys and smaller streets that were not as well patrolled by the police. Always he kept his goal in front of him: the harbor.

When Sung reached the Embarcadero he walked slowly, hunting for a dinghy or rowboat carelessly left untended. More than once he looked up at the junk bobbing serenely on the waves in the bay. Returning to his ship was as sure a death as remaining in the police cell, but duty forced him to such a fate. He had sailed as a pirate most of his life and had fought fierce battles. Twice he had almost died, but always his opponent went down with his sword through his gut.

Sung resigned himself to dying now because he had failed his captain.

Not seeing a boat suitable for stealing, Sung went down to the shoreline and estimated the distance he would have to swim. Two miles. Not so much, although the water was freezing. He shivered, took a deep breath, then made a clean dive into the choppy waves. He went down low, the cold sucking away his energy and then surfaced. With a slow, steady stroke, he began swimming.

By the time he reached the junk he was almost blue from cold.

"Captain," he cried as he crawled over the railing and flopped on the deck. He rolled onto his belly and banged his forehead against the deck he had never expected to see again.

"Sung," Lai Choi San replied. She wore her ship's gear now, having carefully packed the white satin dress and the emerald green shawl in her cabin. She looked more regal in the padded jacket, cotton pants and knee-high black leather boots. She wore a broad belt woven from hemp with a dagger and a thick-bladed Chinese sword dangling at either hip. "Why have you returned?"

"To report, mistress," he said. He did not look up. The deck was no fit study, but he dared not look upon her wrath.

"Then do so. Why did you fail?"

Sung babbled out his tale of not expecting so many guards at the museum and then continued with how Ju Ling had been killed by the police just before his own escape.

"I do not care about Ju Ling or you," Lai Choi San said angrily. "The jade crown is all I want. You failed."

"I did, Captain. I failed. The entire crew failed."

"Do not blame them," Lai Choi San snapped. "You are first mate. It was your responsibility to recover the jade crown."

"I failed." He banged his head three times on the deck, kowtowing to her.

"I should carve out your foul, cowardly heart and toss it to the sharks."

"Give me your dagger, Captain, and I will do it."

He reached out without looking up.

"I do not want your vile blood befouling my blade," she said.

Sung remained silent. Sweat puddled on the deck under his face although the day was cold and he was drenched from his swim.

"Your life is forfeit, Sung."

"Yes, mistress."

"But that is too good a fate for you. I should have you flogged to death. Or pulled behind our ship all the way back to China, but there is no way of knowing when we will return because you did not get the jade crown."

"I will drown myself now, mistress."

"You will do no such thing," Lai Choi San said angrily. She glared at the prostrate man. "Rather than punish you, I will let you live with your guilt. You will not fail me again."

"No, Captain, I will not!"

Lai Choi San made a dismissive motion with her hand. Sung hurried away belowdecks, and she walked to the railing and stared at the ships docked along the Embarcadero. Beyond those ships in the city lay the crown of the Jade Emperor. She had failed to get it once. There would be no failure a second time.

6

Slocum stared at the Sum Yop headquarters building and shook his head in wonder. There was no way this side of hell he could get inside again. Even if he did, there was no way of knowing where the body of Ah Ming's father might have been stashed. He heaved a deep sigh. There was no way of knowing if the other tong had even moved their rival's body into the building or had dumped it into the bay.

Using Ah Ming as translator, he had questioned three of the On Leong hatchet men who had spied on their enemies. They had seen the old man's body in the street before being driven away by the huge army of killers that had poured from inside the headquarters. After that, no one belonging to the On Leong tong had seen Ah Ming's father.

Slocum wished he had brought a pair of binoculars to better study the guards on the roof. He caught sight of two or maybe three men patrolling there. They held the high ground. The next tallest building was a good story shorter and across the street. While the street was not broad, using a grappling hook and rope from another rooftop would be impossible. Scaling the sheer wall might be possible, but Slocum saw men loitering in the street who would raise an alarm. They might not be Sum Yop but they would certainly be curious why a white man was poking around with rope or ladders.

More dynamite would blow a decent-sized hole in the wall, but he had done that once. Going to the well twice with explosives would spell his end. Ah Ming had explained that the Sum Yop leader, Little Pete, was a cunning, sly man. From the touch of awe that mingled with the greater contempt when she spoke, Ah Ming considered Little Pete a worthy adversary.

Slipping back into shadow, Slocum hunted under a pile of garbage in the alley until he found a cellar window for the store directly across the street from the Sum Yop command post. Using the butt of his six-shooter, he knocked out the glass in the window and squeezed through the small opening. The cellar was musty and filled with cobwebs, but Slocum cared less about the owner's sanitary policies than he did about the drains.

He heard rats scurrying about and chittering frantically just below a drain grate in the floor. Memory of the rats nipping at his flesh came back to haunt him. Slocum swallowed his distaste—maybe even outright fear—and pulled up the grate. The stench from the sewer below gagged him. He pulled up his bandanna and used it to filter the air. When he dropped into the sluggishly flowing muck below, he was glad he was wearing high-top boots. There was at least a foot of sewage.

Following the tunnel to what he reckoned to be the center of the street, he quickly found himself in utter darkness. Knowing it was dangerous but having no other choice other than retreating, he lit a lucifer and held it up for light. The sudden flare might set off the gases rising from the sludge. He was lucky and did not blow himself up.

But his luck ended there. A quick examination showed that the sewer into the Sum Yop building had been bricked up. He kicked at the wall and discovered it was sturdier than the sewer pipe around it. After burning his fingers on three lucifers, he retreated through the cellar and back into the alley.

The Sum Yop headquarters across the street mocked him.

"Nothing's invincible," he told himself. In spite of his self-assurance, Slocum saw no way to breach its defenses. Even if he got in, how would he find a corpse? If he found it, how would he get it out?

And why the hell were the Sum Yop hatchet men intent on keeping a dead body from proper burial?

Slocum sat on a crate just inside the alley and glared at the Sum Yop building. He tried to figure how many men were inside and could not. The guards pacing along the street changed every few minutes, but there was no mistaking the fact that they were guards. Seldom had Slocum seen such alert sentries.

He shook himself off and knew he had to get cleaned up after the short sojourn into the sewers. With a single glance backward, he left behind the Sum Yops and headed for a bathhouse he knew just outside of Chinatown. At the moment, he'd had his fill of yellow faces all glaring at him with hatchets in their hands.

As he made his way through the street he noticed posters glued to walls and even wrapped around a lamppost. Slocum tugged at one and pulled it down.

BEHOLD THE SPLENDOR OF CHINA!
IMPERIAL JADE BROUGHT BACK BY
THE FOREMOST EXPLORER OF HIS DAY
SIR WILLIAM MACADAMS

The fine print told of his exploits in China and the South China Sea and conveyed the explorer's knowledge of those cultures so much that Slocum folded the broadside and stuck it into his pocket. He needed an expert who spoke his language. Sir William Macadams looked to be just the man.

Slocum felt better than he had in months. The bath had gotten off the worst of the grime, and he had paid an extra ten cents not to use the prior bather's water. That had been a wise decision. While he soaked in the hot water, Slocum had the proprietor wash his clothing and get the sewage off his boots. All that Slocum had retained while taking his bath was his gun and gun belt holding spare cartridges, which stayed close at hand.

He had bathed and gotten a bite to eat and actually thought the future looked brighter now that he had arrived at the small museum south of Mission Dolores near the edge of town. Colorful banners fluttered in the breeze and large posters proclaimed this to be the foremost display of imperial jade in the world. Slocum wondered about that, but exaggeration always made for a good story. More than once around a campfire he had spun tales that stretched the truth. Just a little.

Or more.

Walking up the broad steps, he went into the dank museum and waited a few seconds for his eyes to adjust. The day was cold and bright outside. The interior of the museum was illuminated by a dozen flickering gas lamps hung high on the walls. They hardly provided enough light to turn the place into a twilight.

Slocum immediately noticed the Specials lounging about. They made no effort to conceal who they were or that they were well armed. He wondered who would dare such men to see pieces of green rock—other than himself. And he was less interested in the jade artifacts than he was in getting Sir William to help him fathom the intricacies of the Chinese mind. Any help the British explorer could give might solve his problems with the Sum Yop and On Leong tongs.

"I'm looking for Sir William Macadams," Slocum said to a man dressed in a fancy uniform.

"Does Sir William know you were coming?"

Slocum considered his answer. If he said no, he would be turned away.

"He and I go back a ways. Of course he is expecting me. In fact, I'm late. I hope that doesn't put him out. He's a bit excitable."

"Don't I know it," the man muttered. "The other night didn't help, either."

"I should say not," Slocum said, wondering what had happened.

"Come along. I think he's in the curator's office. Hell, I know he is. He's been going over every single report ever filed in the museum."

"What's he looking for?"

"Heaven knows. He and his secretary are copying volumes."

"You make it sound as if they're up to no good."

The man's eyes went wide. He remembered he was talking to someone supposedly on good terms with the explorer.

"Oh, no, nothing like that. Here's the office. Go right in."

"Thanks," Slocum said.

He opened the door and froze. Suddenly glad he had asked for the violet water after his bath, he stared at the strawberry blonde seated behind the desk. The light cast her face in shadows, but Slocum thought she was about the prettiest woman he had seen in ages.

He swallowed hard. She was even prettier than Anne.

"May I help you?"

"Yes, ma'am, I'm looking for Sir William. You must be his secretary."

"I am. Tess Lawrence." She rose and thrust out her hand. Slocum did not know whether to kiss it or shake it from the way she presented it to him. He reckoned the limeys were big on grand gestures so he took it and kissed it. She recoiled as if he had burned her with his lips.

"I beg your pardon!"

"Isn't that how one greets an English lady?"

"I don't really know," Tess said. "I'm from Boston."

"You *are* Sir William's secretary?" He enjoyed the dismay on her lovely face. He had flustered her, and now she struggled to regain her poise.

"Who else might I be?"

"The gent in the uniform thought you were stealing all the museum's secrets, whatever they might be."

"We are doing no such thing! Sir William wanted to use the files as reference for future expeditions. That is all. He would never steal another's research ideas!"

"You might let the folks around here know that," Slocum said.

"What is your business with Sir William? He had nothing scheduled for this afternoon."

"Are you sure?"

"I make all his appointments and keep them in this book." She leaned forward slightly to place her palm on a small book with a floppy black cover.

Slocum pulled the book from under her hand, opened it, picked up a pencil from the desk and hastily scribbled his name.

"There. It's all official now. I'm supposed to see Sir William right about now."

"You are an impudent man," she said, but there was no sting in her words. If anything, she seemed as intrigued by Slocum as he was with her.

"Where is he? I can't believe he stepped out for even an instant."

"Why? Because these records are so fascinating?"

"Because I can't imagine any man wanting to be away from you longer than a minute or two. Maybe not even that long."

"Is that some Western charm?"

"Only if it gets me to see Sir William," Slocum said. Tess Lawrence enjoyed the banter more than he did. It was about time to see her employer and find out what the tong war was all about.

"I see," she said. "He will be back later."

"What happened the other night? It spooked the hired help."

"I . . . it was in the *Alta California*. Did you not see the story?"

"Been busy," Slocum said. Anything going on in a museum that reached a major newspaper had to be important doings.

Tess detailed the attempted robbery. He saw how reluctant she was to say anything more about the four men who had been arrested by the police.

"How many of them died during questioning?" Slocum watched her reaction. He had hit the bull's-eye. The San Francisco police were not known for their gentle ways. Such questioning as they were likely to have dished out had offended the Bostonian woman's civilized sensibilities.

"One escaped," she said. "He attacked a police captain and Sir William and escaped."

This surprised Slocum. Not many men were good enough or dangerous enough to break out of a San Francisco jail in plain view of a police captain.

"Sounds like the prisoner was a dangerous hombre," Slocum said.

"Yes, a real desperado. If that is the term." Tess looked worried now. "He was Chinese. Sir William thinks he was from the south of China and spoke Cantonese. And that he was a sailor from his manner of dress."

Slocum tensed. She was going into too much detail. He waited for what was sure to come. He was not disappointed.

"You appear to be a capable man, a true son of the range. Are you currently employed?"

"In a manner of speaking," Slocum answered. "I'm not being paid for it, though. It's a matter of repaying a debt."

"Is that why you want to see Sir William?"

He nodded.

"I can offer you two dollars a day if you accept a position with Sir William." Her lips thinned to a line, and the set to her jaw told Slocum she was determined. He also suspected she controlled the purse strings to Sir William's payroll.

"You thinking on hiring me as a bodyguard?"

"You seem quite capable." Tess averted her eyes and actually blushed. "You are well-built. And that six-shooter at your hip, well, it appears well used. You are a gunman, aren't you?"

"Nope, just a man trying to do the right thing. I don't kill people for money," Slocum said.

Her blue eyes locked on his. The determination in her

face hardened. "But you do kill people. If not for money, then for honor?"

"It has happened," Slocum allowed.

"I am not offering you a job to kill people but to protect Sir William. If it requires gunning down someone, you would not hesitate?"

"Don't know Sir William all that well to risk my life for him, even for two dollars a day," Slocum said. "Would I be protecting you, too?"

"Of course not," Tess said too quickly. "Who am I? No one would want to hurt me. I'm not a famous explorer."

Slocum heard the change in tone when she spoke of Sir William and suspected she was more than a little in love with the man.

"He must be something special," Slocum said.

"Oh, yes, he is. He—" Tess put her hand to her throat and looked past Slocum into the hallway. "You're back, Sir William. I was talking to this man about possible employment."

Slocum stepped to one side and let the Englishman come sweeping in, as if he were making a grand entrance on a huge stage before hundreds of people.

"I won't hire for my next expedition for a month or more. After the jade is sent for display in Boston. You know that, my dear."

"Miss Lawrence told me about the dustup the other night," Slocum said. Neither Sir William nor Tess corrected him. He was right. She was unmarried and from the worshipful look in her eyes, more than in love with Sir William. She was completely devoted to him.

"What a bother," Sir William said. He looked at Slocum for the first time. "I say, are you interested in jade artifacts dating from the Tang Dynasty?"

"That's close to what I wanted to palaver a mite with you about," Slocum said.

"You want to palaver? That's rich. Do come out into the display room, chap, and I'll show you the finest collection of dynasty jade ever shown in these United States."

He took Slocum's arm and guided him from the room. Slocum cast a quick look over his shoulder at Tess. She was torn between accompanying them and continuing her transcription. Duty finally won out, and she sat reluctantly to continue her work.

"Yes, yes, here. Take a look at that, my good man. The imperial crown. The crown of the Jade Emperor himself!"

Slocum stared at the intricately carved crown. There was a certain impressive quality about it he could not put his finger on. It had nothing to do with the head that must have been under the crown. Rather there was a sense of majesty about the crown itself.

"How did you come by something that ought to be on the head of the Chinese emperor?"

"This, uh, this was an artifact I found while digging in southern China," Sir William said. Slocum heard the lie.

"I read your broadside about the exhibit and how you collected all this." Slocum looked around at the cases in the center of the large room. The usual exhibit cases had been pushed back against the walls as if they did not matter.

"You doubt my word?"

"I don't hold it against you for wanting to show such gewgaws to folks here in this country. Did you take it off the head of the emperor himself?"

"Not exactly," Sir William said uneasily. "There might have been a shipment of the emperor's most cherished possessions that, uh, went astray. An observant man might notice and take advantage of inefficiency of governmental bureaucrats."

"So you stole all this from the ruler of an entire country."

"That is a crass way of phrasing it," Sir William said haughtily.

"You seem to know a lot about the Chinese and their ways," Slocum said. "Why would they kill each other over recovering a dead body?"

The sudden turn in the conversation nonplussed Sir William for a moment. But only for a moment. He launched into full professorial mode.

"You refer to the Chinese in this country? They consider themselves sojourners, temporary residents who will strike it rich and return to their home country one day. Those who die must be buried in Chinese soil, preferably in the town where they were born."

"So the whole damn body has to be returned to China? What if it isn't?"

"Unthinkable. The deceased's soul would be forever trapped in what they consider a barbaric land. That would be worse than any indignity they might suffer while alive. There is one thing, though. The body does not necessarily have to be returned to their homeland, but the bones do. Something religious, I think."

"So if one gent prevents the body of an enemy from being sent back for burial, he's doing about the worst he can?"

"Oh, yes, quite. I can believe that would happen. Do you know of such a case?"

"The Sum Yop tong has the body of the leader of the On Leong tong and won't give it up."

"That is a frightening notion. Such rivalry could spark a tong war that would decimate this city."

"That bad?"

"Ever so, ever so, my good man."

"What would you recommend be done? To get the body back?"

"If the Sum Yops are not inclined to release the corpse—or the bones—there is not a great deal any Westerner can do," Sir William said.

"If you were to give some advice . . ." Slocum began. He hesitated, then tilted his head to one side, listening hard. Something had changed in the museum. For a moment, he could not figure out what it was. Then he knew.

He threw his arms around Sir William and spun the explorer around and knocked him to the floor. At the same time, his hand flew to the ebony butt of his Colt Navy. Slocum drew and fanned off three quick shots toward the entrance to the display room.

The silver wheel spinning toward him missed by inches.

The hatchet man had released his weapon just as Slocum
fired. Bullets raced faster than the deadly ax, and Slocum's
aim was perfect. All three bullets tore through the tong
killer's chest.

The hatchet clattered against the floor behind Slocum as
he came out of his gunfighter's crouch.

"Sir William! Are you all right?" Tess Lawrence ran
from the back of the museum and skidded to a halt on her
knees beside the fallen explorer.

"Quite right, my dear. You might say right as rain, thanks
to this gentleman. You say you hired him? He earned his
day's pay, whatever that might be."

Sir William got to his feet. Tess brushed him off, but he
took no notice.

"Welcome to my employ." Sir William thrust out his
hand. This time there was no confusion. Slocum gripped it,
engaged in a small battle of wills as Sir William tried to
crush it and failed.

Slocum looked over at Tess, who beamed. He wondered
what she was thinking. It was probably that she had hired
the right man to protect her employer.

Slocum decided not to disagree, if that was what she
was thinking.

7

"Stay back," Slocum snapped. His six-gun still smoked, but he did not tuck it away in his cross-draw holster. Looking past Sir William revealed nothing out of the ordinary. Even the usual scurry of uniformed museum attendants did not occur. The Specials had disappeared as if they were nothing more than smoke on the wind.

He pushed past Tess Lawrence. The woman shot him another grateful look, then gripped Sir William's arm and began asking if he was all right. She had been more in danger. Slocum was not certain if the hatchet had been aimed at him or Sir William. It was time to find out.

Hurrying into the foyer, he looked around and immediately saw why the museum employees were not bustling about asking questions. Two lay dead just inside the door. Both had their heads split open by a single hatchet blow. Slocum tried to judge if one hatchet man had been responsible or if there had been others. He backed away, went to the dead man and knelt beside him. Laying his gun aside for a moment, Slocum rolled the tong killer over and began searching him. The quilt jacket and the trousers had no pockets to search. Inside the cotton shirt had been stuffed a single sheet of paper covered with Chinese curlicues.

Blood from at least two of the wounds Slocum had put into the man's chest soaked the page.

"I say, what do you have there?"

"I told you to stay back until I'm sure there's no more danger."

"Oh, by Saint George and all the dragons, the museum workers are dead, aren't they?"

"Deader than a doornail," Slocum said. He handed Sir William the page. "Can you read this?"

"It has a drop or two of blood obscuring some of the ideograms," Sir William said, holding the sheet up and peering at it. He saw two holes through the page as well as the blood. "You know that written Chinese is the same, no matter the dialect of the language?"

"So you can read it? Does it say who sent this killer?" Slocum poked the hatchet man. No response. He had died instantly from Slocum's rounds.

"I am a bit rusty. It might take a spot of work."

"It might be important," Slocum insisted.

"It might be a laundry list, also," Sir William countered. "They do not represent words by groups of letters, you understand. Rather, they draw pictures. There are thousands of ideograms to learn. No easy task."

"Surely, you know how to decipher it," Tess said, putting her hand on the explorer's shoulder.

Slocum saw the adoration in the woman's eyes. And felt a sudden irrational surge of jealousy. Why should he care what Tess thought of Sir William? The woman could choose whoever she wanted, and she had obviously set her sights on the Britisher.

"Well, yes, of course, my dear." The way Sir William spoke told Slocum that the sheet would be deciphered, possibly after long hours of hard work, but it would get done if only to maintain stature in his secretary's eyes.

Slocum finished his examination of the dead tong man, then grabbed his gun and went exploring through the long narrow corridors of the museum, alert for any sound. He worried that the Chinese assassins moved so quietly. In a way, this was their terrain. Slocum could stalk through woods as quietly as any Indian but could never hope to match a Celestial hunting a victim along the streets of San Francisco.

When he had made a quick pass through all the unlocked rooms, he returned. Tess pressed close to Sir William as they answered questions from a policeman. Slocum saw the man's three partners just outside the museum's main door. They looked as if they would bolt and run at any instant.

"No hatchet man anywhere I can see," Slocum said, sliding his six-shooter into its holster hard enough to get the policeman's attention.

"This is the one who killed the Celestial?"

"He saved Sir William's life!" blurted Tess.

Slocum still had not figured out if he had been the target for his involvement with Ah Ming and her On Leong tong. Just as easily, Sir William might have been the target of the inept attack.

"You recognize him?" Slocum asked.

"Whatya mean? I don't go 'round tryin' to identify the likes of them."

"What tong does he belong to?" Slocum asked patiently.

"From the look of 'im, he's a Sum Yop."

That still did not tell Slocum who the killer had been after. From what he had heard from Sir William, the jade on display had all been stolen, virtually off the head of the Chinese emperor himself. That might make him a target by the tongs, though the earlier attack that had worried Tess so had been committed by Chinese sailors. Slocum was at a loss to figure it all out. Mostly, he wanted to stay alive.

Collecting two dollars a day for keeping Sir William alive, too, was not so bad either, since it meant he had to stay close to Tess Lawrence.

"Do take this poor wight and dispose of him however is most efficient," Sir William said, looking with disdain at the dead Chinaman.

The copper whistled for his three fellow officers. Together

they got the Sum Yop killer out of the museum. As they left, the one Sir William had ordered about called, "Them other two. The white men. Them's your responsibility."

"I shall see to their burial," Sir William said stoutly. He struck his noble pose again. Slocum experienced a moment's pang when he thought it might have been for the best if the hatchet man had killed Sir William.

"I need to see about calling off the killers," Slocum said.

"Whatever do you mean, Mr. Slocum?" Tess's plucked eyebrows arched.

"That was a Sum Yop assassin. I think it's time for me to parley with their boss."

"You know him? You can find him?"

"Never met Little Pete," Slocum said, remembering the name from his talk with Ah Ming, "but I will."

"Do be careful." Tess took a step away from Sir William, as if she wanted to touch Slocum. Her employer stopped her in her tracks with a brusque order.

"My dear, I will need your help deciphering this sheet. Look up the ideograms in the dictionary as I give them to you. Come along now. Chop, chop, as the Celestials say."

"Yes, of course, Sir William." She hesitated, then flashed a shy smile at Slocum. Tess turned and hurried after the explorer, returning to the office.

Slocum wondered when the other two bodies would be taken care of. Sir William had assumed control of the entire museum by simply moving in. It was up to him to deal with such matters. Slocum hoped the explorer did not have to deal with another employee's corpse.

Slocum's.

It worked on the battlefield. Slocum hoped it worked with the Sum Yop tong. He waved a white handkerchief tied to a stick. Advancing slowly, he felt eyes watching him. Dozens of pairs of eyes. Any one of the men behind those eyes might have a rifle trained on him. If Little Pete decided, a trigger would be pulled and Slocum would be dead.

He stopped just outside the side entrance to the building. No hail of bullets met him.

"I want to talk to Little Pete!" His words echoed down the alleyway loud enough for anyone inside to hear. Waiting proved more difficult than summoning the courage to walk up with his white flag and six-gun holstered. By the count of heartbeats racing through his heart, Slocum reckoned he stood outside the door for better than ten minutes. After the first few, he knew there was no point in leaving. If Little Pete had wanted him dead, he would be.

That meant the tong leader only wanted him antsy. When he realized this, Slocum felt his heart slow down, and he became calmer than at any time facing the Sum Yops.

Finally his patience was rewarded. The door creaked open and a solitary figure appeared. He was of indeterminate age, though Slocum took him for at least forty. Hunched with age and shuffling his feet slightly, he might have been thirty years older, but Slocum did not think so. The man's dark eyes were bright and shining like glass orbs, and his hands were remarkably steady as they remained hidden within the dangling folds of his sleeves. Whether he clutched a hatchet or a six-shooter, Slocum could not say, but he was certain there was a weapon in one, if not both, hands.

"What do you want?"

"To speak with Little Pete. Are you Little Pete?"

"Would the magnificent leader of a powerful tong come out to meet with a worm such as you?"

"Pleased to meet you, Little Pete," Slocum said. He did not offer to shake hands. Little Pete had moved the barest amount and given Slocum a glimpse of the small pistol clutched in his right hand.

"You are a clever fellow, Slocum."

Slocum played poker with the best, but naming him as he did came as a shock. He knew his mask dropped for a brief instant, much to Little Pete's delight.

"You think I am stupid? You think that I do not know who blew up my humble building?"

"You were holding the leader of the On Leong tong prisoner."

"He is dead."

"Your men killed him."

"An unfortunate accident. These streets are so deadly," Little Pete said. "Anyone running when he should be walking is suspect."

"His daughter wants his body back."

"Ah Ming is a lovely woman," Little Pete said. "Lovely women think all they need to do is snap their fingers and whatever they desire will be given to them."

"What's the price?"

"Why do you involve yourself in Chinese matters, Slocum? Ah Ming saved your life. You got her father out of my building. Does this not make all even between you?"

"She wants his body," Slocum said. "Barring that, she wants his bones so they can be sent back to China for burial." Slocum saw that Little Pete was impressed by this. He had not expected Slocum to understand the importance of the bones. Silently, Slocum thanked Sir William's explanation. It might have turned the tide in his favor.

"Want, want, want. Always the beautiful women insist on what they cannot have."

Little Pete's face screwed up in a scowl. "You are her lap dog?"

"I'm doing what is honorable. Why aren't you?"

"Honor?" Little Pete spat. "What do you know of honor?"

"Maybe nothing. I do know everyone has a price. What is yours?"

"For the body? You would offer money for the body?"

Slocum remained silent. He got into a staring match with Little Pete that neither of them could win.

"You are direct, like all Westerners," Little Pete said. "If I say what I would normally, you will not understand."

"Then give it to me straight. Your price. What is it?"

"Jade," Little Pete said. "I want the jade in the museum."

"You tried to steal it the other night?" This surprised Slocum. He had been sure that Sir William had properly identified the men who had tried to rob him before as sailors.

"Bring me the jade."

"All of it? Or just something special?"

Little Pete smiled slightly. Slocum felt he had gone up in the tong leader's estimation again.

"The crown of the emperor. The Jade Emperor must regain his crown."

"You return it, you get to go home to China? Is that it?"

"You would not understand," Little Pete said haughtily. For a moment, Slocum heard Sir William in the tong leader. "Bring me the jade crown and I will give over to you the body you seek."

"Deal," Slocum said. Stealing a pile of jade was not going to be too hard. All he had to worry about was the exchange. Preventing Little Pete from double-crossing him, maybe trying to kill him, would be the hardest part. It would not take more than a half hour to get the body to the On Leongs and Ah Ming would release him from his debt of honor.

A smile came to Slocum's face, but it was not what Little Pete thought. He wondered how grateful Ah Ming might be for getting her pa's body back. As grateful as she had been before?

"You can't translate the paper?" Slocum did not try to hide his irritation. Sir William was his best hope of getting more information about the tong killer and his instructions. Slocum knew he could take the page to Ah Ming and let her read it, but he doubted she would give him the truth. Whatever hand she played, she held it too close for him to read.

"Whatever it is, I assure you this is not a laundry list, as you suggested earlier," Sir William said.

Slocum started to remind the explorer that he had not made any such suggestion but held his tongue. Tess glanced at him and smiled weakly. She knew. Because of her reaction, Slocum decided Sir William often made mistakes of this kind—or simply put his own failings off onto other shoulders.

"I will take it with me and ponder it far into the night," Sir William said. "Ta-ta." With that he was gone, leaving Slocum and Tess behind.

"I should be going, also," she said. Her weak smile disappeared. "He will decipher the note. Do you think it is important?"

"Could be," Slocum allowed. He had a good idea what the note actually said. It was likely to be a shopping list of all the jade Little Pete wanted stolen. His hatchet man had simply been too eager to please. If he had bided his time, he could have stolen everything for the tong leader without anyone getting hurt. Instead, he had bulled his way in, leaving a trail of dead bodies behind. Slocum had done Little Pete a favor by eliminating such a hotheaded killer.

"Good night, Mr. Slocum," Tess said. She clung to her small purse as if it were a lifeline and she were drowning.

"Would you like me to escort you to your hotel?"

"Oh," she said, brightening. Then the light faded. "Thank you for offering, but I will be all right. I should see that Sir William is situated for the night."

"He was going to work on the translation."

"He said that, but he will be in the bar downstairs at the hotel drinking that vile scotch whiskey of his."

Slocum started to make another suggestion, then held back. He had another chore to finish before he could think of asking Tess to accompany him to his quarters. But then, after he finished stealing the jade crown, she was not likely to give him the time of day, much less roll in the hay with him.

"Are you staying?" She looked at him with her innocent blue eyes. "There's no need."

"I want to be sure everything is locked up. With the two

museum staff dead, there's no one left to look after such things."

"Yes, of course." With that, Tess left. Her steps were slow and reluctant. Slocum wished he could hurry her along. The sooner he got to the robbery, the sooner he could get back the body of Ah Ming's father from the rival tong and get the hell out of San Francisco.

He walked to the large room where the display cases stretched like so many glass-topped coffins. Tess moved more quickly now and left the museum. Slocum told himself he should have gone with her.

He went to the case holding the emperor's crown. There was no doubt this was what Little Pete wanted. Slocum was a little surprised that the tong leader had not asked for all the jade. Carrying so much would have been difficult, but if you're asking for the moon, why not throw in the stars, too?

Slocum drew his knife, fiddled a bit and pried open the case. He wrapped the Jade Emperor's dull green stone crown in the black velvet it had rested on and tucked it under his arm.

Whistling tunelessly, he closed the case and made a final circuit of the deserted museum. No reason to let a second sneak thief in. When he was done, Slocum went to the front door and opened it a crack. He wanted to make sure Tess had not changed her mind and waited for him. All he heard were sounds from the distant harbor and a horse neighing some distance away. The museum was situated in the middle of a grassy area with trees around it. Slocum had learned patience as a sniper during the war. Sitting in the fork of a tree for long hours waiting for one shot had become second nature to him, but now he wanted the trade of a dead body for the jade crown completed.

Slipping out, he closed the door behind him. With long strides, he went out to the street and looked around again. A carriage loaded with three boisterous women rolled by on a cross street and then turned toward town. Otherwise, he was alone.

Slocum had barely started for Little Pete's headquarters when he heard a whistling sound. The impact on the back of his skull caused him to see stars as he pitched forward onto his face.

8

"You could have been killed!" Tess Lawrence was beside herself with anguish. All Slocum felt was the goose egg–sized lump on the back of his head.

"The crown is all that is missing," Sir William said glumly. "Of course they steal the most renowned piece of the collection. Without the jade crown, what is left? Nothing. Trifles. Bits and pieces of colored rock, nothing more."

"Oh, Sir William, that's not so," protested Tess, torn between Slocum and her employer. "The rest of the jade artifacts are superb! Everyone will want to see them. They'll flock to Boston from hundreds of miles."

"Doubtful," the explorer said, his mood even darker. He turned to Slocum. "What do you have to say for yourself, Mr. Slocum?"

"My head hurts like hell," Slocum said. "I should never have let anyone creep up on me like that."

"You are lucky you did not meet a fate similar to that of the museum employees," Sir William said. "These fiends will stop at nothing. To a tong killer, a human life means nothing. They are brutal and cruel." He wandered off, declaiming about the hatchet men.

Tess laid a gentle hand on Slocum's shoulder and looked deeply into his eyes.

"What? You see my guilt?" Slocum said. He felt both guilty and stupid. That was a terrible combination for him. Such carelessness usually got a man killed.

"I'm looking to see if you have a concussion. Your pupils seem to be of the same size and reactive to light."

"I'm fine," Slocum said. He shrugged her hand away. "I'll be even better when I recover the crown. It was my responsibility and it got stolen." He said nothing about his own intention to swipe it. In a way, having it taken from him while he was in the act of stealing it made his own guilt a little lighter. He had not actually *stolen* the Jade Emperor's crown. It would not have been legally stolen until he turned it over to Little Pete in exchange for the On Leong leader's body.

"Let the police tend to it, John," the blonde said softly. "These are dangerous men."

"I'm dangerous, too," he said in a level tone that frightened her. Tess's eyes widened, and she took a step away when she saw the promise of death that had come to his expression.

"I know that was why I hired you, but I never expected anything like this to happen. Tong killers and stolen artifacts. All I wanted was for you to protect Sir William."

"He has the look of a man who can take care of himself. Better than I can take care of myself," Slocum added bitterly. He recognized his tone for what it was. Self-pity. The world had dealt him terrible hands for more than a month. If he wanted to get out from under such a burden of bad luck, he had to stack the deck himself.

It might not come up with a royal flush but he could at least count on a full house.

"You rest, John. I think it would be all right for you to sleep, though you might want a physician to look at that lump first."

"Giving me the rest of the day off?"

Tess straightened and looked at him hard. "You rest," she insisted. "Don't go trying to find the thief."

Slocum only nodded. Even this small movement of his head sent a new jab of pain into his skull and neck. If he had gotten even a glimpse of his attacker, he might know where to start. He doubted the thief worked for Little Pete or the Sum Yop tong. Why steal something that was going to be handed over in a few minutes? Even if Little Pete was determined to keep the body of his foe, it made no sense to steal the jade crown the way it had been. Let Slocum show up with the crown, then kill him. Any Westerner was nothing more than a pimple on his yellow butt to Little Pete. What did honor matter?

Slocum left the museum and went back to the spot where he had been waylaid. He scoured the area for some clue. He was a damned good tracker, but the cobblestone street left no spoor for him to follow. Stride long and fury mounting, he headed for the Sum Yop headquarters. When he got there, he stood outside the door. He did not bother knocking. Little Pete knew he was here. Little Pete knew everything that went on around his little patch of Chinatown.

In only a few minutes, Little Pete shuffled out. Slocum noted that the Chinese limped on his other leg and had other inconsistencies in his supposed infirmities. It was all an act so Slocum would underestimate him.

"It was stolen," Slocum said without preamble.

"You stole it. Of course it was taken," Little Pete said.

"It was stolen from me. I was on my way here to turn it over when I was slugged."

"Ah," Little Pete said. His eyes darted about as he worked on this tidbit of information. "You do not think I am responsible for this attack on your person?"

"Who has it?" Slocum was blunt. He saw no reason to waste time bandying words. "There is no reason for you or your men to rob me. Ah Ming has no reason, either. I never told her or any of the On Leong about the swap. Even if she knew—"

"She does," Little Pete said softly.

"There's no reason for her to stop the exchange. You both get what you want, unless she desires the jade crown more than she does the return of her pa's body."

"Nothing matters more than the bones," Little Pete said solemnly. Slocum had already figured that to be true.

"Who stole it, then?"

Little Pete shuffled about. His hands remained hidden in the voluminous sleeves of his silk jacket. The soft sounds of silk moving reminded Slocum of wind in the tall pines. It was almost hypnotic, but the tong leader's quick movements were nothing like the invisible wind.

"An attempt was made before," Little Pete said.

"Nothing gets by you," Slocum said. "Who? Give me a name and I'll get the crown back. I want this matter to be ended. Now."

"There are rumors of a Chinese pirate who might be responsible," Little Pete said softly. Slocum perked up. The only reason the tong leader would speak in such a manner was to lure Slocum into deeper trouble.

"Does he have a name?"

"She is Lai Choi San, the most famous of the South China Sea pirates," Little Pete said.

"She?"

"Beautiful and treacherous. The only reason she would come to San Francisco from her usual haunts is to . . ." Little Pete let his words trail off so Slocum could supply the answer.

"The crown."

Little Pete bowed slightly.

"Where do I find her?"

"Where do you think?" Little Pete turned and went back into his headquarters. Slocum saw no one else but had the sensation of being watched as he stood alone in the alley.

"Where else?" Slocum snorted in disgust at his question. The only place a pirate would be was as plain as the nose on his face. He walked quickly to the Embarcadero. A sailor needed a boat.

"Lieutenant," Slocum called to a naval officer walking along scribbling furiously in a notebook. "Can I ask you a question?"

"Yes, sir," the officer said, giving Slocum a quick once-over. Seeing that Slocum was no sailor caused the lieutenant to dismiss him. Slocum did not care. All he wanted was confirmation of what ought to be obvious.

"Any ships from China leave on the morning tide?" If Lai Choi San had stolen the jade crown, there was no reason to remain in San Francisco. She would set sail immediately to return to China.

"There are ships coming and going all the time," he said, frowning. "Let me see. I've got the list of arrivals and departures here somewhere." He leafed through the pages of the notebook. "There was one bound for China that left yesterday morning. The next out will be the *Lissome Lass*, bound for Boston. Don't know when the *Lass* is set to sail. From the stores being secured, I'd say a day or two."

"What would a Chinese sail?"

The lieutenant stared more sharply at Slocum.

"You mean that junk that dropped anchor two days back? What's your interest in it?"

"It's still in the harbor? The one with a woman captain?"

"That's the one—the only one. I rowed past the junk right after it sailed through the Golden Gate and caught sight of the captain." He smiled wistfully. "I should sail under a captain that looked like her." The lieutenant straightened and slammed his book shut. "I suspect she keeps a tight ship. Very tight."

Slocum stared at the ships in the harbor. "Which one is she? The one captained by Lai Choi San?"

"You know quite a bit more than I'd have thought," the lieutenant said. He turned, squinted and then pointed. "That's the one. You can tell it's a different breed of ship entirely by the way it sits so high in the water at the stern."

Slocum's mind raced. If Lai Choi San had the jade, there was no reason to remain in port. Little Pete did not have the jade. Ah Ming had no reason to steal the crown and not immediately trade it for her father's bones. Slocum's spirits sank. San Francisco was a dangerous city. He might have been robbed by a common street thief.

"How long does it take a ship like that one to prepare for the trip to China? A junk?"

"As long as any other ocean-faring ship," the lieutenant said. "It would put on water and supplies. That could take anywhere from a day to a week, depending on what cargo it was loading. Never seen a junk before. It's bigger than I'd heard. It could take quite a spell provisioning it since the crew's at least as numerous as on a clipper ship."

Slocum reconsidered. Lai Choi San might have taken the jade crown after all. She had tried before. From Tess's account of the prisoners taken by the police and interrogated, they were Chinese sailors. Since the lieutenant knew of no other ships from the Celestial Kingdom in port, that left only the solitary junk.

"I think she might have stolen part of Sir William Macadams's exhibit over at the museum."

"Heard tell of some killings, but I thought nothing about it. I always have my hands full here."

"You responsible for maintaining the peace in the harbor?"

"That I am. Don't do much to prevent the shanghaiers plying their trade," the lieutenant admitted, "but I try to keep the captains buying the poor wights as honest as possible."

"Unless I miss my guess, that's not too honest, is it?"

"Not much." The lieutenant chuckled. "Most of them that get themselves shanghaied deserve it. A year at sea probably does them good."

"I have reason to believe Lai Choi San is responsible for the theft from Sir William and the murder of several men."

"That's all in the jurisdiction of the San Francisco police."

"But you patrol the harbor. You're a U.S. Naval officer who keeps things on the up-and-up on the water."

"I would like to get a look at that vessel," the lieutenant said thoughtfully. Memories of the lovely captain undoubtedly flashed through his mind.

Slocum wanted a better look at the junk's captain, too, if Lai Choi San was as good-looking as the lieutenant thought. Just seeing a female sea captain—any female captain, much less a pretty one—might be worth the effort to board and search the junk.

"If you're willing to sign an affidavit, I'll get my launch and enough marines to search the ship," the lieutenant said.

"It'd carry more weight if Sir William swore to the facts," Slocum said. "There won't be any trouble getting him to agree."

"To hell with that. You get me the papers later. I'll search the damned junk now!"

The lieutenant put his fingers in his mouth and whistled shrilly. A seaman scrambled up from below a pier.

"Sir?"

"Ready the launch. Tell Sergeant Lamont I want a detachment of marines on the double. We're going to search a boat."

"The junk, sir?"

The lieutenant glared at the seaman, who smirked, then saluted and disappeared. The officer had been thinking about paying a visit to Lai Choi San long before Slocum gave him reason.

"Mind if I go along? I can identify the stolen jade crown."

"How many jade crowns are there likely to be aboard even a Chinese ship?" the lieutenant asked. Then he laughed and slapped Slocum on the back. "If you've got a mind and the sea legs, come along. The bay is mighty choppy today."

They went to the end of a long pier where six armed marines and their sergeant waited for the lieutenant. Six more seamen came trotting up along the pier.

"Rowers, prepare," the lieutenant barked. He jumped into the long boat and paid Slocum no more attention. Slocum followed, not liking the rocking motion of the boat under him. Given the choice, he preferred horseback. He looked around, wondering if he should take a turn at an oar, but the bench seats were all filled.

"There, sir," whispered the marine sergeant, pointing to

a spot at the rear of the boat. "You got the look of infantry 'bout you."

Slocum nodded.

"CSA?"

Slocum nodded again.

"So was I. Tenth 'Bama Regulars. Becomin' a water soldier was the only way I could keep on with what I knowed best."

"Good for you, Sergeant," Slocum said. The lieutenant had already cast off the mooring lines, and his crew began rowing steadily, heading for the junk a mile out in the harbor. The farther from the dock the launch went, the rougher the sea. The rising and falling caused Slocum's belly to churn, and more than once he fought to keep from up-chucking. The sailors and marines watched him with some amusement, wanting the landlubber to disgrace himself.

He did not provide them with the show they desired. Instead, he swallowed hard and then pictured himself on a bucking bronc, unexpectedly tossing from side to side and then giving a straight-up lurch. When he did this, his queasy stomach settled and he began to enjoy the trip. Salt spray caused him to squint, and the wind that had blown through San Francisco, turning it downright cold, was freezing out on the water. He ignored that. He had survived frostbite.

That thought brought Anne to mind. He ignored the cold and the spray and stared ahead at the junk.

"What are they doing?" Slocum called to the lieutenant.

"Hailing us, I expect," the officer said. He waved his arms and yelled, "Ahoy. U.S. Navy. Come to inspect your ship!"

"Sergeant," Slocum said urgently. "What does it look like they're doing?"

"Lieutenant, sir," the sergeant yelled, getting to his feet and pulling his carbine around and putting it to his shoulder. "They're fixin' to fire on us!"

"They'd never do that. I identified ourselves as an official vessel."

"Then what's that five-pounder doin' on their stern?"

Slocum reached for his six-shooter but was out of range by too many yards. He saw a small brass cannon being lowered. Even at this distance the bore looked big enough for him to stick his head into.

"Desist," the officer yelled. "We're official—"

He got no further. The tongue of flame, the puff of smoke, the report were all secondary to the grapeshot fired at them. The lieutenant jerked around from a ragged gash left on his upper arm by a hot piece of lead. Two more of the lead pellets hammered into the bottom of the boat. Two seamen jumped to, bailing and cursing simultaneously.

"Fire!" The lieutenant pointed at the junk and repeated his order. "Fire on them! Return fire!"

Sergeant Lamont's marines did the best they could at this range. The launch rose and fell on every swell in the bay, throwing off their aim. Even if they had been on solid ground, Slocum wondered how many of them could make an accurate shot at this range. The junk, however, had no problem landing more of the grapeshot all around the boat. Splinters flew away and the launch began listing.

"Bail, damn you all, bail. We're takin' water!"

Slocum did not know who shouted the order. He obeyed. Using his hat, he began lifting water from the boat's bilge and tossing it overboard. Only four men continued rowing, and the lieutenant had them veering away from the junk to get out of range of its brass cannon. One more round of grape pelted them but did no damage.

"Those yellow swine," growled the sergeant. "I've half a mind to swim over there and cut their damn throats!"

"I'll join you," Slocum said. The old Southern soldier looked at Slocum for an instant, then laughed aloud.

"Damn me if I don't believe you would."

They bailed furiously while another seaman did what he could to patch the largest hole in the bottom of the boat.

Slocum took a final look over his shoulder as they neared the docks again, wetter and madder but in no danger of being drowned in the bay. He could not be sure at this range but thought he saw a woman dressed all in black watching.

If that was Lai Choi San, Slocum made a silent promise to not only retrieve the jade but to scuttle her ship. It was only fitting revenge for trying to kill him.

9

"Report, Lieutenant," snapped a man decked out in more gold braid than Slocum remembered seeing all through the war. He edged closer to the marine sergeant and whispered, "Is that the commodore?"

"Commands Fort Point and thinks he runs ever'thin'," Sergeant Lamont said, not bothering to hold down his voice. "Captain Johnson is in charge of the harbor patrol. He's laid up real bad right now with the gout, or so they say." Lamont chuckled. "Me and the men think he's got the clap, so the lieutenant's in charge."

Slocum watched as the naval lieutenant bearded the army colonel.

"Sir, the Chinese vessel fired upon us with no provocation."

"By damn! I'll blow them out of the water!"

"Fort Point's guns are not trained in that direction, sir."

"You young whippersnapper!" The colonel turned livid. "You do not tell me where to aim my cannon!"

"Sir, Captain Johnson has been over this with you," the lieutenant said, barely holding his own anger in check. "Aiming at vessels docked in San Francisco harbor is not wise. Your mission is to protect us from seaborne attack and to control the Golden Gate. Once a vessel is within the harbor, it is under the jurisdiction of the U.S. Navy."

"But they fired on you!"

"Sir, I will get the frigate and board them. The only reason they would fire upon an inspection team is because of illegal activities. I believe they are opium smugglers."

Slocum's eyebrows rose at that. He had never suspected such. The opium trafficking from the Orient was out of control because the navy did nothing to stop it. There were too many other crimes on the high seas to worry about, and from what Slocum had seen, the navy had little presence in San Francisco.

"You'll get a frigate," the colonel mocked. "Do you even know where your frigate is?"

"If you'll bend over, sir, I will check to see if it is where I suspect," the lieutenant said.

This produced a round of laughter from the marines. The colonel turned on them, saw they were wet and armed and in no mood to put up with him. He turned back to the lieutenant.

"Your insubordination will not go unnoticed, sir!"

"That'll be about the first thing under your purview that hasn't gone unnoticed, sir!" The lieutenant stood his ground well, Slocum thought. He was also liable to get court-martialed. It did not bother the officer unduly. With great deliberation he gave orders to his seamen to beach the boat and get to repairing the holes shot in it.

"You have a frigate nearby?" Slocum asked.

The lieutenant glared, then said, "You don't know. We had two. One was sunk during a storm a few months ago. This forces the remaining vessel to patrol up and down the coast, doing the work of two. If the frigate is not north of San Francisco, then it is south."

"I see," Slocum said. "What are you going to do about the junk?"

"There's not anything I can do until I can commandeer an armed vessel. Trying to board again using only the launch carrying marines with rifles is suicidal. That cannon would deliver even more death and destruction on us."

"You'll quarantine the junk?"

"No one gets on or off," the lieutenant vowed.

The officer was determined, but Slocum knew there were practical limits to what could be done. While being fired upon made the man mad, he also had to regulate other ships in the harbor. Slocum did a quick count and saw no fewer than fifteen. The time that could be spent cordoning off Lai Choi San's junk was minimal.

As the officer went about his business, Slocum stood and stared at the junk bobbing on the choppy bay. Lai Choi San must have the jade crown, but why wasn't she underway for the Orient? Even if she lacked sufficient food and water, she could put in at Hawaii to resupply for the final leg of the long trip.

"Are you waiting for something?" Slocum wondered aloud. As long as the junk remained at anchor where he could see it, there was a chance of recovering the jade crown. He didn't know how it could be done, but he would find a way.

"What use is the jade crown?" Ah Ming stared impassively at Slocum. "It is a fine tribute to the Jade Emperor, but this is not China."

"So you don't care that Lai Choi San has the jade crown?"

"I care that Little Pete has my father's body. You have not done well in retrieving it," Ah Ming said. She was slowly turning colder toward him. "I have given you incentives. You have not performed well in response."

"I tried to swap the jade for your pa," Slocum said. "Lai Choi San stole the jade crown, and that's all Little Pete wants."

"Little Pete is a liar," Ah Ming said, her anger rising now. "He is Sum Yop. He will not trade anything for my father's body. He wishes only to desecrate it. He shames all On Leong members. That is what he wants."

"Are you sure he hasn't disposed of the body? How hard would it be for him to just dump the body in the bay and let the sharks eat it?"

"He has the body," Ah Ming said flatly. "You must get it from him."

"You've made that clear," Slocum said.

"No, I have not," Ah Ming said. "I could not have made you understand or you would have returned what I seek most."

"Or I could have died." He saw that made no difference to the woman. If he died trying to snatch the body from Little Pete's headquarters, she would simply try another ploy. Knowing that he was expendable did not bother him as much as the notion that he had failed.

"To give you added reason to do as I have asked, to do as you have promised, you have one week to succeed."

"Or?" Slocum knew an ultimatum when he heard it.

"Those who think the Celestials never leave Chinatown are mistaken," she said. "We go freely everywhere in San Francisco. The shadows are our allies."

It was clear enough to Slocum that Ah Ming threatened him. If he failed, the On Leong hatchet men would kill him, no matter where he was in the city. In a fancy club on Union Hill, a Chinese waiter might poison him. Drink in a dive along the waterfront, and a coolie dockhand might drive a knife into him. Chinatown? Entering this part of the city voluntarily would be like a cow seeking out a slaughterhouse.

"I understand," Slocum said.

"I want my father's bones on the next ship sailing for the Flowery Kingdom. Your reward will be continued life."

Ah Ming turned and glided away as if she rolled on wheels rather than walked, leaving Slocum alone in the underground room. He went to the narrow tunnel outside and looked both ways. Nothing but darkness. With the hairs rising on the back of his neck, he turned in the direction he had come and walked slowly, carefully placing each foot in front of him. Once he smelled the pungent odor of opium, he wondered if the lieutenant had been right about Lai Choi San shipping in the sticky black tar opiate. Then he pushed all such thoughts from his mind. Standing outlined in bright daylight at the head of steep stairs, the hatchet man who often accompanied Ah Ming beckoned for him to hurry.

Slocum did, wondering if he would get a hatchet in the spine. He looked back once he was out of the underground maze. The On Leong tong killer had disappeared, either going down into the rabbit warren under Chinatown or slipping away somewhere else, possibly to trail Slocum. There was not a chance of a celluloid dog in hell that Slocum could spot the man, big though he was.

Slocum knew what a condemned man felt like now. One week. Ah Ming had given him that long to live if he did not return her father's bones. He wandered through the streets of Chinatown drawing stares. He wondered if they knew of Ah Ming's sentence or if they simply distrusted Westerners. Possibly a little of both produced the sudden silence and then the hushed whispers after he passed.

He took one last look at Little Pete's fortress building and finally headed back to the museum. He needed a few more details from Sir William before making another attempt to recover the jade from Lai Choi San.

"A most curious question, my dear boy."

Slocum wished Sir William would not call him "my dear boy," but that was the British explorer's manner of speaking. From all Slocum had seen, Sir William might not be able to remember names. He never called anyone by his name. Or her name. Slocum glanced over at Tess Lawrence, who watched Sir William closely.

"One I need answered, though, and you are the only expert around."

"Yes, quite. The surviving museum staff seems to have, what's the expression? Hightailed it? Beaten off in the tall grass?"

"Hightailed it," Slocum said, seeing Tess blush. After the deaths of the men on the staff, everyone else had either quit or gone on sabbatical until Sir William left. The owner of the museum had put advertisements in the paper asking for new staff but had been unable to find adequate personnel. Sir William had agreed to remain on the premises until the absent curator could be found.

"Tell me what a junk is like. Inside, outside, everything."

"One of the Chinese ships? That is a strange request, my dear boy."

Slocum forced himself not to clench his fists and hit the man for using that phrase again. He needed information. Sir William could not know that it would not recover the missing crown.

"Why do you want to know, Mr. Slocum?" Tess fluttered about, looking upset. She was lovely but Slocum thought she needed to take a bit more sun to do something about her flightiness. He knew she was unaccustomed to the morass of deaths and fights she had endured the past few days, but there was no call for her to be such a hothouse flower.

"I can't be certain, but I think the crown is on a junk out in the harbor."

"Ah, I see. Chinese sailors, junk, that's where the crown must be. Splendid deduction."

Slocum wondered if Sir William realized how the term *my dear boy* grated on him because he did not use it again, though it almost sprang to his lips.

"How do I get aboard without being seen? The junk fired on a naval launch this afternoon and put a few holes in it. Until a U.S. frigate returns to port, there's nothing the officials can do."

"So you intend to take matters into your own hands? Bravo! That's the spirit. I say, I can leave Miss Lawrence in charge here and come with you."

Slocum saw surprise blossom on Tess's face at the use of her name.

"It's better if I do this alone," Slocum said. "They're keeping a sharp eye out for boarders. From others I've asked, they are certain it is a pirate ship. The pirates would be expert at boarding other ships and repelling boarders trying to get onto their own."

"I see, yes. Well, I have sailed with some of the South China Sea pirates and observed their battle tactics. However, nothing I saw gives insight into sneaking aboard while they are in harbor." Sir William stroked his chin, then looked up at Slocum. "There might be a way. If you can come up on them from the stern, they might not be as likely to see you."

"The high part of the ship? The backside?" Slocum remembered how it had risen up, even more than on the heavy cargo ships in the harbor. He had not seen any window in the rear for a sentry.

"Yes, perhaps. Their lookout will be perched high in the rigging, up at the top of the sails. Since they are anchored, the sails will be furled. This gives the lookout a better view, but it also gives him more to do. He must look in all directions, and not having other ships sailing toward him, perhaps he will be more lax."

"I can hide in the blind spot at the stern?"

"Oh, yes, that would be capital, but you must get there first."

"Do you really want to risk this lone-wolf attack, Mr. Slocum? Your life is not worth the return of the jade crown."

"I beg to differ, my dear! It is worth many men's lives. I risked my own to get the crown. Why should he be deprived of similar adventure recovering it?"

Slocum was not going to argue the point. He did not look at this as some grand adventure. It was a chore. A duty. An obligation wrapped up in his honor. More than this, he knew if he failed, Ah Ming would set the On Leong tong killers on his trail.

"Twilight," Slocum said. "That'll be the best time to try."

"Tides," Sir William said. "Be wary of the tides. They are powerful in San Francisco Bay."

"I'll remember that," Slocum said. He was already planning on how best to row over to the junk and climb aboard.

Once there, finding the jade crown might be difficult, but it had to be easier than reaching the boat in the first place.

Shivering from the cold, wet spray blowing off the Pacific Ocean, Slocum hunkered down in the tiny rowboat he had rented. The sun dipped with amazing speed into the ocean beyond the Golden Gate. The setting sun only momentarily showed the origin of the name. The peaks on either side of the mouth of the bay shone like hills of gold. Then the sun was gone and only freezing wind remained.

It was time. Slocum shoved off from the shore and began rowing. He had to constantly reorient himself because of the strong currents that Sir William had warned of. The junk was nearly a mile off. Slocum thought he could cross that distance quickly. No lookout, no matter how observant, would see the tiny chip of a boat coming at the junk from the stern. He was cloaked in darkness and had all the time in the world to cross that watery mile.

After a half hour of rowing, his arms and back began to ache. Another fifteen minutes he was close to screaming in pain. The more he aimed for the junk, the more the tide swept him away. By the time he had covered half the distance, Slocum was fighting the ebbing current that threatened to suck him out into the vast Pacific Ocean. Darkness may have been his ally but the water itself was his fierce enemy.

Slocum took a few minutes to rub his hands and straighten his back. He saw how the tide swept him away from the junk now, toward the distant lighthouse just to the north of the bay's mouth.

He gritted his teeth, gripped the oars and began pulling with all his strength. Little by little he approached the junk, but when his strength began to fade from weariness, he lost ground fast.

Slocum knew no one aboard could see him in the dark water. More than once he had watched a slender white-clad figure come to the forecastle and look out toward San Francisco. Once he was sure whoever that might be had turned, leaned against the railing and stared out to sea—past him at the Pacific.

He was insulated from sight, but he could not get close enough to the junk to board it. He soon found himself rowing as hard as he could and losing position steadily. When he stopped rowing altogether, he realized he was being carried to the middle of the channel leading into the harbor.

Close to calling out for help, Slocum knew what his reception would be from the junk's crew. They had no compunction against firing on a naval vessel. They might make it a competition to shoot him out of the water.

Slocum was not sure when he gave up trying to reach the junk and began rowing furiously to get out of the channel and go toward the shoreline. There was no hope for him if he was carried out into the ocean. His hands blistered and his back at the point of snapping, he finally worked free of the main tide and let eddy currents carry him toward the rocky land. His rowboat smashed into the rocks and was turned to splinters, throwing him into the cold water.

Sputtering and thrashing about, he finally found bottom, got his feet under him and staggered ashore. He collapsed on a rock where he could stare at the dark outline of the distant junk.

Getting aboard had seemed easy enough. He had been wrong. Slocum realized he had also been wrong about other things. It was time to remedy his mistaken idea that he could ever recover the body of Ah Ming's father, and run like hell away from San Francisco.

10

Slocum trudged all the way through town and reached the museum just before dawn. He was shivering from the cold and badly needed to get into dry clothes. He had stashed his gear in a storage room in the museum. At this time of day, he reckoned he could get cleaned up, take his gear to the Wells Fargo station and get the hell out of town before Ah Ming realized he had gone. She might have spies in the stagecoach office, and if so, Slocum would have to take care of them.

An easier way might be to steal a horse and ride like the demons of hell were nipping at his heels—in a way they would be. It pained him to cut and run like this but getting the jade crown back from Lai Choi San had proven impossible. The navy frigate would be back sometime. It might show up before the junk sailed for China, but Slocum doubted it. There was no other way of boarding Lai Choi San's vessel and getting the jade crown needed to ransom the body of Ah Ming's father from the Sum Yops.

He tried to think back to discover where he had gone off the rails. All the way back to the Sierra Madres and barely surviving showed him no other course to follow. He had been a pawn in a huge game of fate. He might have avoided

San Francisco altogether, but he had been in this city before and liked it. Drinking away his sorrow had seemed reasonable enough at the time.

From there he had been bitten by rats, saved by the female leader of a secret Chinese society and generally used as a target by all and sundry. It was past time for him to hightail it.

"Beat off in the tall grass," Slocum muttered, grinning. Sir William presented another of the odd highlights of his stay in San Francisco that he saw no way of avoiding.

Slocum slipped into the museum and made his way through the silent cases in the main room, going directly for the corridor leading to the storage room where he had cached his gear. He had barely stepped into the large room when he heard a sharp intake of breath. His hand flashed to the butt of his six-shooter and he half turned, going into a crouch. He kept his six-gun in its holster when he saw a pale and drawn Tess Lawrence standing to one side of the room, a pad of paper in one hand and a pencil in the other.

"John, it's you. You scared me."

"What are you doing out here?" Slocum came out of the gunfighter's crouch and went to her. She had filled the top sheet of paper with long columns of names and numbers.

"I'm doing the inventory. We're getting ready to ship the collection to Boston. On a train."

She sounded defensive, but Slocum had other things to worry about. The hair on the back of his neck rippled constantly with imaginary hatchets cutting into his flesh. Ah Ming did not yet know he was abandoning the task of retrieving her pa's body, but word would get back to her fast.

"Didn't mean to interrupt, but you are working late."

"You look a mess," Tess said, stepping back a pace and giving him a once-over. "Have you been swimming in the bay?"

"Something like that," Slocum said. "I tried to get aboard the junk."

"You actually tried that? Oh." Tess put her hand to her mouth in fright. "I thought you were only considering it."

"I didn't get aboard and I didn't get the jade crown back from Lai Choi San." Slocum wondered at her reaction. She did not seem too surprised, but then Tess was smart. Anyone dripping saltwater onto the floor of the museum just before dawn probably had not been graced with much success.

"You aren't injured, are you?"

"I'm still in one piece. Wetter and wiser, but not hurt."

"Good. I worried that Sir William made it sound too easy to get onto that awful pirate's ship. She is quite infamous in the South China Sea, you know."

"If she's so infamous there, what's she doing here? What makes the jade crown so important to her?"

Tess shrugged. "I cannot say. It's valuable as an artifact, of course, as history of her people. She must have some reason to sail halfway around the world for it, though."

"Is it worth as much as all of this?" Slocum made a sweeping gesture with his arm and immediately regretted it. He sent droplets scattering all over the glass-topped cases.

"Oh, yes, I am sure it is," Tess said. "These are fine pieces, but there is only one jade crown."

Slocum started to say more, then realized time was quickly passing.

"I've got to get my gear," he said.

Tess looked as if she had seen a ghost.

"You're not leaving us, are you? Y-you can't be running off."

"I tried to get back the jade crown. There's no way I can get onto that ship. The navy couldn't do it. I can't. I'd rather be riding a pony chasing after strays."

"John, please. Don't go. We need you. I need you." She was almost stammering now. She clutched at his arm and looked deep into his eyes. "The crown is so important, but Sir William's life is more important. He needs your protection."

"What do you need?" Slocum asked.

"You," she said more boldly. Tess tipped her head back slightly and closed her eyes. Slocum should have walked away. He kissed her instead.

She threw her arms around his neck and pulled him down hard for a kiss whose passion mounted. The woman's intensity startled Slocum. She had been a meek little mouse, but something had changed. She pressed her body against him wantonly, wrapped a leg around his and began rubbing herself on his thigh like a cat stropping up against a table leg.

"I want you, John, I've wanted you from the moment I set eyes on you."

He tried to answer, but she shut off any protest by kissing him again. Her hands left their grip behind his neck and worked down, over his broad back and finally cupped his rock-hard butt. She pulled him in closer as she continued to move sinuously.

"You're getting all wet," he said.

"Yes, I am, because of you."

"I meant your clothes. I'm dripping all over the place."

"Then we'd best get you out of those wet clothes," she said, looking boldly at him. "Mine, too." She took his hand and pulled him along toward the curator's office where she had been working. Tess turned and came once more into Slocum's arms.

They kissed as their hands roved each other's body. Slocum was freed of his gun belt and shirt, and soon enough he had mastered the intricate fastenings of Tess's skirt. She stepped free, and he dropped to his knees and began burrowing under her petticoats, where he found warm, sleek legs.

"Oh, yes, John. Yes." She sighed.

He slid his hand upward under her petticoats toward the wet warmth nested between her legs. His hand brushed across her sex lips, and then his finger wiggled inward. He had to move fast to support her as she sagged down, weak in the knees.

He lifted her and swung her around to deposit her on the desk. Her arms flapped about, knocking books and papers to the floor so she could lean back. She lifted her legs, exposing herself lewdly to Slocum.

"See anything you like?" she asked needlessly.

"You have wonderful legs," Slocum said, stroking over the calves and working upward to her thighs. Her flesh trembled beneath his touch as he worked closer and closer to the blond nest he had been fingering before. She gasped when he bent over and pressed his face down and began licking.

His hands worked around her body to her fleshy buttocks. He kneaded them like lumps of dough until she was reduced to harsh panting, then worked higher. With dextrous fingers he worked off the woman's blouse and exposed her firm white breasts to the cool morning air.

She sagged back flat onto the desktop. Slocum worked from her bush up across her belly. His tongue dipped briefly into the well of her navel before slithering wetly even higher. When his face was firmly between the twin mounds of titflesh rising up from her chest, he began kissing and tonguing with furious strokes.

As she thrashed about, he reached down and gripped her thighs. This kept him in position to take her left breast entirely into his mouth.

"Oh, John, I . . . I—" He left her speechless when he began pushing the firm mound from his mouth using the tip of his tongue. He circled the aureola and pushed the lust-hardened nipple downward. When he was done with this breast, he jumped to the other and repeated the erotic torture.

"More, John, I want more." She tried to sit up as she reached down to find his hardened manhood. He gulped when her feverish fingers closed around his shaft and tugged insistently. His balls tightened, and he would have gotten off then and there if he had not worked hard to control himself.

"More?" he teased. "What more could you want, other than this?" He lifted her hips off the desk and slid her forward. The plum-tipped stalk bounced off her moist sex lips, paused a moment and then worked into her heated center.

"Yes, that, oh, you're so big in me. So big."

He slid another couple inches into her and reveled in the heat and wetness he found. She clamped down powerfully around him until he thought she would mash him flat. When she relaxed, he thrust forward and sank completely into her.

She let out tiny trapped animal noises now. Remaining within her was taking its toll on his control. He felt his balls churning and tumbling over and over as the pressure built within his loins. He felt like a boiler ready to explode. Withdrawing slowly, he tormented her and aroused her and made her scream out in stark pleasure.

When only the tip of his manhood remained within her, he paused, got some control back and then rushed in. Faster and faster he moved now, pistoning like a locomotive building up steam. The friction of his sensitive flesh against her female channel mounted until there was no turning back. He caught at her ass and lifted it so their crotches would grind together intimately. Hips rotating and thrusting, he drove even deeper into her seething soft interior.

"Yes, oh, yes, yes," she shrieked. She half rose off the desk, then fell back, arching her back and grinding herself into him. Slocum managed to draw back and thrust a few more times before he exploded like a stick of dynamite in her velvet-lined tunnel.

He spilled his seed into her greedy interior and then they both gave a final shudder and collapsed together. Slocum lay atop Tess on the desk for some time before her eyelids flickered and she looked at him. Her bright eyes were still blazing with lust.

"That was . . ."

"Good?" he supplied.

"The best ever," she said. "I never thought I could feel like that, like this, like—" She suddenly cut off the flow of words and turned away from him. Slocum straightened and began toying with her nipples. Both were still engorged with blood and sensitive. He knew because she gasped every time he tweaked or twisted them.

"Please, John. No more. I'm going to be sore."

"Sore?"

"You're so big," she said. "I'm not used to that."

Slocum started to say something about Sir William but held off. It was none of his business what Tess and Sir William did when they were together. She obviously had a crush on him, but Slocum could not tell if any of the feeling was reciprocated. Sir William bounced about in a world entirely his own. Letting anyone else in was not likely to happen.

As Slocum stepped back he realized he and Sir William shared that. Anne had melted his heart only to have hers frozen. To death.

"I'd better get dressed," he said.

"Are you still leaving? I wish you would stay," she said, sitting up on the desk. She put hands over her naked breasts but did nothing to conceal her privates. The honey-blond hair contrasted sharply with the dark wood desktop.

"I've got myself involved in more than you could believe," Slocum said. "If I stay, you'd be in danger." Seeing this had no effect on her, he added, "Sir William would be in constant danger, too. None of it would be his doing, either."

"You're in trouble with the tongs, aren't you? Which ones? The Sum Yop?"

"Sum Yop and On Leong," Slocum said. "Both would love to see me with a hatchet in the middle of my forehead."

"We can figure some way out of your trouble, John. We can. Sir William is a clever, knowledgeable man. And I want to do what I can to keep you here, too."

"For me?"

"For us," Tess said boldly. Her hands fell away, showing her naked boobs again. Slocum had to admit this was a powerful argument, but he knew that he had to think with his head and not parts of his lower anatomy.

"You promised. You're on the payroll."

"Fire me," he said.

Tess's face fell. She got off the desk and began dressing. "Be like that," she said bitterly. "This is what always happens. The men in my life are either scoundrels or only use me."

"Which is Sir William?"

She swung about angrily. Her cheeks were flushed and her hands balled into fists, as if she would hit him.

"Neither," she said. "He doesn't even know I exist."

"You might be wrong," Slocum said, knowing she was not. He had seen men like Sir William Macadams before. The adventure mattered more than anything else. The next horizon, around the next bend, over the hill rising before them, those counted more than life itself. No woman could compete with such potent lures. Again, Slocum knew. He and Sir William were alike in that, too.

"Oh, no, he's here early. I thought we had time!" Tess hurried to complete dressing. Slocum worked more slowly, but getting into his damp clothing proved difficult. He just slung his gun belt over his shoulder rather than taking time to strap it on when Sir William came barreling into the room.

"Good, good, you're both here. Glad to see troops eager for the battle."

"What battle's that?" Slocum asked.

"I've got a lead on where the jade crown might be," Sir William said triumphantly.

Tess gasped. Slocum looked at her. She had turned even paler than usual. Her porcelain complexion looked almost transparent.

"Who's got it?" Slocum asked.

"You were right to suspect the pirate out in the harbor, my good man," Sir William said. "Lai Choi San. She certainly tried to steal the crown the opening night."

Slocum started to point out that, while those would-be robbers were sailors, the other Celestials who had come into the museum were members of the Sum Yop tong. What connection could a pirate from three thousand miles away have with a local tong?

"I tried to get aboard her junk and couldn't do it," Slocum said.

"Yes, Sir William, he almost got himself killed. Dealing with this Lai Choi San is too dangerous. Let her keep the crown. Please."

Slocum stared at Tess now. She was not hearing Sir William at all. The man had spent a considerable amount of time and, possibly, money tracking down the jade crown. Because a Chinese pirate had the crown was not going to stop him from recovering it. If anything, it would make the repossession all the more exciting.

"Nonsense, my dear. Slocum and I will meet with Lai Choi San and sweet-talk her out of the crown. What could a pirate possibly want with a trinket if I can offer gold in exchange?"

Slocum's mind raced. Sir William was willing to ransom the crown. How could he be separated from it so Slocum could give it to Little Pete in return for Ah Ming's father? Leaving town was premature. He might satisfy everyone concerned—except Sir William—and leave San Francisco with his honor intact.

"When do we meet her?" Slocum asked. Again Tess sucked in her breath and looked as if she were going to be sick. He ignored her. "Give me a few minutes to change clothes, and I'll be ready."

"Capital, my dear boy, capital!"

The change of clothing meant little to him. Slocum wanted to be sure his Colt Navy was properly cleaned and oiled. Then accounts would be settled.

11

"How did you get in touch with her?" Slocum asked.

"It was not easy, but I found a gentleman—and I use the term loosely—who sells supplies to those who come into harbor and are desirous of avoiding legal entanglements."

"A black marketeer," Slocum said.

"Well, yes, that might be an apt description," Sir William said. He leaned back as the carriage clattered along the cobblestone streets, going past Portsmouth Square and toward the docks. He might be out taking the air for all the strain he showed. If anything, he treated this as a lark. Slocum knew differently.

"He sent a message to Lai Choi San?"

"I don't know how he contacted her. Imagine this, a female pirate captain. Chinese, to boot. Most peculiar, though the Celestials are peculiar people, all the time bowing and scraping, banging their heads against the floor in subservience and then cutting off your head with one of their damnable axes. Triads and tongs and secret societies, they have it all."

"How can you be sure this black marketeer actually contacted Lai Choi San? He might consider you worth kidnaping for a reward."

"Who would he ask? Pah!"

"Tess," Slocum said. "She would hand over all the remaining jade artifacts in exchange for your life."

"Then she would have to fork over all of my precious collection for the pair of us," Sir William said airily. "You are, after all, along to protect me. Whatever danger I find myself in, you'll be in it up to your fetlocks, too."

That did not make Slocum feel any better. He wished he had been the one arranging to meet Lai Choi San so he could guess how trustworthy the smuggler might be. Not very reliable was obvious. How much in the pocket of the tongs the man might be was another matter. The On Leong would want to help Slocum find the jade to get their precious leader's body returned. The Sum Yop might want to deal Slocum out of the game altogether. Little Pete would appreciate getting the jade crown and keeping the body of his enemy. That would be delicious revenge for whatever had occurred between the rival gangs.

"There! There he is! Our go-between. Driver, stop here. Now!"

The carriage rattled to a halt. Sir William had jumped out before it stopped rolling. Slocum was slower to follow. His eyes roamed about, taking in all he could. If this was a trap, he did not see it. The man stood alone in the street. No snipers on nearby rooftops appeared, and rushing from any of the open doorways would be difficult. Slocum decided the smuggler wanted as open a spot as the adventurer did if Sir William wanted to double-cross him. If Sir William even thought of such a thing.

"He'll go with us. Row us out in his boat," Sir William said.

"How much?" Slocum demanded. The smuggler got a shifty look and then grinned.

"You ain't like him. You look like you mean business."

"I say, old chap, we both mean business." Sir William was put out when the smuggler ignored him.

"I want a cut of the action," the smuggler said. "Word is

that somethin' real valuable got stolen. You and him, you're arrangin' with the lady pirate to get it out of the country."

Slocum said nothing. Let the man think what he wanted.

"Come on, then. We got a hard row ahead. The bay's a man killer 'less you know what you're doin'."

Slocum rubbed his blistered hands on his pants legs and tried not to groan as he moved. His back was stiff from the rowing the previous night. They went down to the docks where the smuggler pointed. Two men were already in a rowboat, one on each oar.

"Them's my boys. And this here's the way I signal Lai Choi San that I want to palaver." He shoved a small flag-pole into a holder and fumbled inside his coat to pull out a bright green and white silk flag. "There. Now we won't get fired on like that dumb-ass navy officer did." The smuggler laughed and jumped into the boat.

"This is high adventure, eh, my good man?"

"Fine adventure," Slocum said cautiously. He kept the smuggler in front of him where he could put a bullet into his gut if he tried anything. The man cheerfully ordered his two men to row.

They cast off and within minutes were like a cork bobbing in a pond. Slocum held on to the sides of the boat but his eyes fixed on the junk. Already the lookout had spotted them. Half a dozen men prowled restlessly along the deck. The activity stopped when a figure dressed in white appeared on the highest deck.

"There she is," the smuggler said. "That's Lai Choi San givin' us the once-over. She might not like you totin' that hogleg."

"Life is full of disappointments," Slocum said.

This made the smuggler a little uneasy, but he went back to joking with his men to keep their minds off the effort required to row through the choppy San Francisco Bay.

"If we have to, can you swim back to shore?" Slocum asked.

"What's that? I should say not. It's too far, and the water

is too cold. I have even heard that sharks come into the bay, though I have not seen any. What is wrong? You think we're going into a trap?"

Slocum shook his head. He had no idea what they were getting themselves into, but he would find out soon enough. The rowboat bumped hard against the side of the junk. Ropes fell from above and the two rowers quickly secured the boat. Like a rat going up a line, the smuggler scrambled up a rope and lightly vaulted over the railing. To Slocum's surprise, Sir William followed with almost as much grace. Grunting and feeling the pain in both back and hands, Slocum reached the deck after the others.

He stared in open admiration at Lai Choi San. She was just an inch shy of being beautiful. Dressed in white silk, blouse and trousers, she wore a woven hemp belt around her trim waist. From it hung a curiously broad-bladed sword and a dagger. On another woman, it might have been an affectation, an attempt at decoration. Slocum had no doubt that Lai Choi San used both and had killed repeatedly with them. She might be beautiful but there was no mercy in her dark eyes.

He could not help but compare her to Ah Ming. They were cut from the same cloth.

"You were at the museum," Sir William said. "You tried to steal the crown the night of the premier showing." He looked around and pointed. "Him, him and that one there. They were the brigands who tried to steal the jade."

"What do you want?" Lai Choi San made no pretense at civility. She glared at the smuggler, who looked sheepish as he shrugged.

"The crown, dear lady, that's what I want. I'm prepared to offer a fine reward, shall we call it, for the return."

Slocum saw instantly from Lai Choi San's expression that the pirate did not have the jade crown.

"I thought you came for me to buy it from you."

"However did you get such a mistaken notion?" Sir William asked.

"Him. He's playing both of you, one against the other,"

said Slocum. "Sir William is offering a pile of gold for the crown."

"He cannot have it for any price, even if I had it," Lai Choi San said.

"Of course you have it. You stole it!"

"Stole it! How did you get it? You robbed an imperial messenger."

"It was an abandoned artifact. I found it in an archaeological dig."

"The Jade Emperor will not be denied. That is his crown and has been on the royal brow for more than one thousand years. You stole it. You killed the guards and messenger and stole it. I demand its return. In the name of the Emperor, I—"

"Oh, be quiet, you tedious shrew," snapped Sir William.

Slocum saw that berating Lai Choi San aboard her own ship was not a smart thing to do. No captain would permit it, and the pirate queen maintained her control over a cutthroat crew by sheer force of personality—and an iron hand. Slocum rested his hand on the butt of his six-shooter. A dozen of the woman's crew were already slipping knives from sheaths at their belts.

"She doesn't have the crown," Slocum said. Sir William was not having any of it.

"You listen to me. I—"

"Now," Slocum said, grabbing the explorer's arm and pulling hard enough to unbalance him.

"Don't interrupt," Sir William said angrily. Red in the face, he was ready to explode.

Slocum looked around and saw that the smuggler had turned pale. His eyes darted around but always came back to the spot on the railing where the rope ladder hung. Below it in the rowboat were his two rowers. It would take only three quick steps for the smuggler to be over the railing and in his boat. Slocum moved to block the man's escape, hoping to force him to settle some of the dust kicked up by an angry Sir William.

It did not work that way. The man lunged, pushed hard

against Slocum and tried to vault the railing. Slocum tripped
him and whirled out of the way. Every one of Lai Choi San's
crew had their knives out and were advancing. Slocum
caught a glimpse of Sir William out of the corner of his eye
and saw that the man realized his mistake.

"You don't have the jade crown, do you?" Sir William
said in a weak voice.

Slocum seized the man and bodily threw him over the
railing. Sir William's feet hit the top rail and sent him tumbling through the air. Slocum heard a loud splash. He
backed away, eyes locked on Lai Choi San's.

She said nothing but did not have to. Her crew was acting according to her unspoken orders.

"I'll kill you," Slocum said.

"Wait!" Lai Choi San put up her hand. "You threaten
me?"

"Nope," Slocum said. "A threat's something that might
not happen. I just made a promise."

A flicker of amusement crossed her face. As quickly as
it came, it vanished.

Slocum did not hesitate. To do so would mean his
death. He turned and arched over the railing in a smooth
dive. He hit the icy water and felt his breath being sucked
away. Kicking hard, he fought to get back to the surface.
He came out sputtering. He tossed his head and got the
water from his eyes. Ten yards away the two men in the
black marketeer's boat were putting their backs into rowing. Thrashing through the water just behind paddled Sir
William. He yelled for the men to stop, but they only
rowed faster.

Slocum felt the warmth being sucked from his body by
the cold bay water. He started swimming and quickly overtook Sir William.

"We've got to stop the— Slocum!" Sir William pointed
and was dunked.

Gunfire caused Slocum to roll over in the water and
look high above at the junk's deck. Three crewmen used

old muskets to shoot at the fleeing men. For such ancient weapons, their accuracy was amazing. Both of the smuggler's henchmen jerked about and fell overboard. Slocum did not have to see their bodies to know they were dead.

"Sharks," Sir William gasped out. "The blood in the water will draw sharks!"

Slocum put his face down in the water and stroked as hard and fast as he could. Like an arrow he shot through the water and quickly reached the empty rowboat. He pulled himself up on the far side, peering over it at the junk. Lai Choi San stood with her snipers. Whatever she said, they lowered their muskets and backed off. Slocum heaved himself into the boat and lay in the bottom a moment, getting his breath back. Then he shivered hard.

"Help me, help me in, my good man," Sir William said. His shaking hand reached up out of the water. Slocum braced his feet, grabbed the adventurer's wrist and heaved. Sir William popped out of the water and crashed to the bottom of the boat, causing it to rock.

"Take an oar. Row," Slocum said, keeping his teeth from chattering only through force of will. "It means our lives."

Sir William took his place, then nodded. They stroked together. Slowly at first, then with increasing speed and power, they sent the boat skipping over the choppy water.

It was only after a few minutes of effort that Slocum realized they were going away from San Francisco and heading for the far side of the bay. Somehow, that mattered less than getting away alive. He looked up at the junk bobbing on the same waves that tormented him so in the smaller boat. The deck was empty save for a figure dressed in white.

Lai Choi San.

She watched but Slocum wondered what she was thinking. She could have blown them out of the water easily but had ordered her marksmen to stop firing.

"This is a bloody lot of work," said Sir William, panting.

"I know," Slocum said. It was the second time in as

many days that he had been forced to row for his life. The result each time had been the same. A tired back. More blisters on his hands. And failure.

This time felt different, though.

Lai Choi San disappeared from the deck. Slocum rowed just a little harder for the other side of the Golden Gate.

12

"They are out of range, Captain," complained Sung.

"No one asked your thoughts," Lai Choi San said coldly. She placed her hands on the railing and watched as Sir William and the other rowed furiously to get out of range. She had no compunction about killing the black marketeer and his two men, but the one with Sir William fascinated her. She had no time for fascinations, however. Lai Choi San turned to her first mate.

"I would go into San Francisco," she said. "I want you and three of the crew to accompany me."

"Only three, Captain?"

"Where I go there will be no need for more," she said. "Hurry, Sung, before you anger me."

The mate bobbed his head and backed away. Lai Choi San let out a soft sigh. Sung was a fool, but he was loyal. Since she had let him live after his failure, he was likely a devoted fool. Granting him continued life had been a boon she seldom gave, but Lai Choi San was nothing if not practical. Sung was an experienced seaman and had acquitted himself well on the journey from the Flowery Kingdom. She would need his skill going home.

"Going home," she said, a far-off look in her ebony

eyes. How she longed to see China again! She would again
be in her beloved homeland before the Jade Emperor. With
the stolen crown.

She sighed again. Sir William obviously did not have
the crown if he and his henchman had dared come to her
ship and offer a ransom for its return. Lai Choi San closed
her hands on the railing again. She would have set sail long
ago for China if the jade crown had come into her grasp. If
Sir William did not have it, that meant someone else did.
Recovering it would be the work of an afternoon.

Sung needlessly called to the men lowering the small
boat to indirectly tell his mistress they were ready. She
walked with measured step to the side of the junk, then
swung with the agility born of long practice onto a rope
and slid down lightly to the boat. Within minutes they were
rowing directly for the San Francisco docks.

Lai Choi San sat quietly in the prow, considering her
options for recovering the crown. All would fall into place
soon enough, if she applied the proper grease to the rails of
underworld commerce.

"A carriage, Captain?" Sung waited for her answer as she
climbed from the boat onto the dock. Her snow-white garb
remained unsullied by the slightest speck of dirt. Walking in
San Francisco would certainly soil her clothing.

"No," she said. "I want everyone to know I am coming
and have adequate time to prepare."

Sung bowed deeply, then pointed to the spots where he
wanted the crewmen to walk. Lai Choi San noted that he
was wise in his choices. No street thief would be able to
approach her, saving her the need for dispatching a worthless remnant of humanity herself. Head high, step stately,
Lai Choi San began her journey through San Francisco as
she headed for Dupont Gai and Chinatown. It took more
than an hour for her to arrive in front of the Sum Yop tong
headquarters.

A quick glance at the mortared front and the recent
patchwork covering an explosion convinced her to find

another way into the building. Without breaking stride, Lai Choi San continued to the side of the building and found the alley. Her quick eyes saw the way the dirt had been churned here, indicating many feet had come this way recently. She halted, did a precise turn to her right and faced the door. Aware that the Sum Yop members on the roof watched her every move, she did nothing.

Sung came and dropped to the ground in front of her, head bowed low.

"Mistress, should I break down the door? It is wrong to keep you waiting."

"It is wrong, but Little Pete does so," she said loudly. "Perhaps he is not home. Perhaps he does not care for what I can offer."

Sung wisely did not speak. He had done his part. Lai Choi San waited for the count of ten, then did her precise right turn, but before she could take even a single step, the door opened. Little Pete came out, bowing and scraping.

"Madame, welcome to my humble abode."

"You live here?" Lai Choi San could not keep the contempt from her voice, nor did she want to. "Perhaps I should seek others. The On Leong are not far from here."

"Please, madame, allow me to offer tea."

"From China?"

"From India," Little Pete said with only a hint of regret.

"You should have tea from China." She clapped her hands. One of her crewman hurried over, bowing. Both hands extended in front of him, he held out a small package for Little Pete. "It is a small gift, but perhaps it will show my earnest desire for friendship between us."

Little Pete bowed lower and accepted it. "Your friendship is a thing to be cultivated," he said cautiously. He backed away and ushered Lai Choi San inside.

She looked neither left nor right but missed nothing as they twisted through the maze of crates. Her nose wrinkled at the stench of dynamite but she said nothing. Little Pete bowed deeply and allowed her to enter a sumptuous room hung with fine silk curtains. Posh pillows were arranged on the floor in a semicircle around a low teakwood table already set with a tea set.

Lai Choi San sank down gracefully, knees on a pillow. Little Pete followed so he faced her across the teakwood table. They were alone in the room, but Lai Choi San felt eyes on her. Little Pete's hatchet men were watching, within a simple call's distance should their leader require their deadly services.

After exchanging a few pleasantries and Little Pete pouring the tea for her, Lai Choi San got down to the reason she had come.

"The crown is missing," she said. "The Jade Emperor will be most upset if he cannot wear it at the summer festival." She sipped at her tea and watched Little Pete closely for his reaction. Not even a flicker of interest betrayed him.

"He has never attended the summer festival without it. Nor have any of his predecessors. This would be a terrible loss of face," Little Pete said.

"We are agreed on this point," Lai Choi San said. She sipped again at the bitter tea. It was not even from India, she guessed. Ceylon, with its inferior product, was more likely. It was all she had expected from a minor tong leader in a foreign devils' city.

"What would the emperor give for the return of the jade crown?" Little Pete wondered aloud. His keen eyes fixed on hers.

"The emperor would be most appreciative," she said. "He would not want his far-flung servants to lack for rifles." She carefully put down the teacup. "His *loyal* servants, that is."

"I seek one day to return to the land of my birth," Little Pete said, "as do all born in the Celestial Kingdom. If I had this jade crown I would certainly be the joyous first to see that it was restored to the head most deserving of wearing it."

"Fifty rifles," Lai Choi San said, as if thinking aloud. "That would be a fair price for the jade crown."

"Rusted muskets are of no use," he replied.

"New rifles, modern weapons," she countered.

"What good are fifty rifles without ammunition?"

"Of course, you are right," she said graciously. "This is all nothing but idle talk. Guns for a relic dating to the Tang Dynasty." She watched him closely and saw the flare of greed.

"If I or any member of the Sum Yop find the crown, we would be honored to restore it to the emperor."

"Do you know who has it?" Being so blunt carried risks. Lai Choi San saw the briefest confusion on Little Pete's face. The Sum Yop did not have the jade crown.

"We shall make inquiries," the tong leader said.

"Make them quickly," Lai Choi San urged. She bowed slightly, then rose. She left the room without a backward glance at Little Pete. If anyone in San Francisco could find the jade, it was Little Pete. How long it would take him to retrieve the emperor's crown was another matter.

Lai Choi San hoped it would be soon. She did not mind Sir William hunting for the jade crown. He was a buffoon but the man with him was a different matter. If any of the foreign devils could find the emperor's lost crown, he might be the one.

"Where has she gone?" Little Pete lounged back on the cushions, sipping at his tea. How vile was the tea that Lai Choi San had given him. The pirate had no taste. She could at least have stolen a better quality, perhaps from Ceylon.

A burly hatchet man bowed deeply and said, "She returned immediately to the docks. She and her pirate scum are rowing back to the junk."

"So I was the only one she asked to recover the jade crown," mused Little Pete. "What does that tell me?" he muttered to himself, then put his teacup down on the table. His fingers drummed as he thought.

"No one else spoke to her?"

"Only her first mate. The one called Sung," answered Little Pete's henchman.

"She wants the Sum Yop to retrieve the jade crown, and

she does not know where it is. In exchange for the crown, she will give us fifty new rifles and ammunition. That is a trade worthy of an emperor."

The hatchet man remained silent, staring emotionlessly at his leader.

"The one named Slocum wants to deal with us, but he does not have the crown. The Britisher does not have it— now. The pirate does not have the jade crown in her possession, but all three want it."

"As does Ah Ming," the hatchet man said.

"Ah Ming wants it only to recover the bones of her father."

"Should I toss the body into the bay for the sharks?"

"No," Little Pete said, shaking his head. "Leave the bones in the vault. We might find ourselves in possession of the jade crown the pirate queen wants so badly through trade with the On Leong." He muttered to himself, then asked aloud, "Why does she want the crown? I detected desperation in her voice."

"Ah Ming?"

"No, no, you fool," snapped Little Pete. "The pirate. Lai Choi San. She is willing to do anything for the crown." He stretched out on the cushions and folded his hands over his protuberant belly. "She will give us rifles."

"We can use more guns," said his minion.

"We will take the rifles she offers, then."

"The Sum Yop have the crown?" The hatchet man's eyes widened in astonishment. "But—"

"Silence," Little Pete said. Any more from his henchman and he would grow mightily angry and no longer be responsible for his actions. "She does not know that we have no idea where the jade crown is. We will take the guns and send her on her way."

"She is very dangerous."

"The Sum Yop are not? You are more than a fool. You are an idiot! We *tell* her we have the crown. We take the guns, then send her on her way. What is she to do? How can one shipload of pirates stand against the might of the Sum Yop tong?"

"A boon, master," the hatchet man said, bowing deeply.
"What is it?"

"I want to kill her."

"No," Little Pete said carefully. "You may kill Sung. I want Lai Choi San for my own. Double-crossing her will be a pleasure, but nothing like what will follow." Little Pete laughed. His hatchet man merely grinned.

Lai Choi San tossed her head to one side to get salt spray from her face. She stared at the junk bobbing on the waves. How she hated the filthy hovels on the ground and loved the sea. Her ship was more than her home. It was her key to the entire world.

All she needed to make her world complete was still in China but would be released to her once she found the emperor's jade crown.

"Mistress," Sung said quietly. She did not bother to turn. The feel of wind and water against her skin was too invigorating after burrowing through the dusty warehouse the Sum Yops called their headquarters. "They will cheat you."

"More than that, Sung," she said. "Little Pete intends to steal the rifles. What I do not know is if he has the crown."

"You will deal with him, although he is a swindler? I do not understand."

"Of course you don't. Who else in San Francisco might find the jade crown? The On Leong want only one thing— the return of their leader's bones. If the crown were in their possession, Little Pete would soon receive it in trade. The other tongs have no interest in angering the emperor. No, Little Pete is the one most likely to find the crown, so he is the one we deal with."

"But he will double-cross you. You said so!"

"I know he will. He suspects I know, as well. If he doesn't, he is a greater fool than I believe."

"What do we do, mistress?" Sung sounded worried.

"There is a small chance Little Pete will obtain the crown and deal fairly with me."

"Then you will double-cross him?" Now Sung sounded hopeful.

"A tempting thought. It might be necessary. If I must deal honestly with him, I will need rifles."

The boat bumped against the side of the huge junk. Lai Choi San grabbed a ratline and climbed it with ease. Sung and the other three followed once they had secured the smaller boat.

Lai Choi San stood on the deck, eyes questing beyond the Golden Gate. *Gum Shan*, the Golden Mountain, her countrymen called this place. A land filled with barbarians and sojourners. It was not home. She must complete her mission and return to the Flowery Kingdom quickly or she would certainly go mad.

"Set sail," she called out. "We put to sea to find us something worthy of our talent as pirates!"

A cheer went up from the crew. They had languished in port long enough. It was time to ply their trade once more on the high seas.

Lai Choi San agreed.

13

Ah Ming stood on the dock, staring into the harbor. Outwardly calm, she seethed as she watched the junk unfurl triangular sails, catch wind and begin its journey through the Golden Gate. She watched until the colorful sails were out of sight. Only then did she turn and face her bodyguard.

"Kill him. He failed."

The hatchet man inclined his head in acknowledgment. Then he said in a curiously soft voice, "What of the emperor's crown?"

"It's aboard the junk," Ah Ming said. "Lai Choi San is taking it back to China. I care nothing about that. It belongs to the emperor and should rest on his head."

"The body," her bodyguard said.

"My father's bones will never be returned. Little Pete is a vile bandit. May the Kama Lords take his soul to the lowest levels of Hell and torture him for eternity."

"You wish to attack the Sum Yops?"

"Kill John Slocum first. He is the enemy of all On Leong members. Then we will see to an assault on Little Pete," Ah Ming said. The man bowed even more deeply, stepped away a pace and then hurried off. She turned and looked out to sea. No track of Lai Choi San's junk remained now, not even a wake in the choppy water.

She had hoped Slocum would accomplish what she was hesitant to do. A tong war could last for years with hundreds killed. So be it.

"I say, it was a bloody good trip back to the museum," Sir William Macadams declared. Slocum was less sure of that. His body ached, and every joint protested his every move. His hands were blistered from rowing and his feet were swelled from so much hiking.

They had made landfall near Tiburon. Even with the lure of ten dollars offered by Sir William, they had been unable to find anyone willing to drive them around the bay back into San Francisco. After a very long walk, they had reached the ferry and taken it to the Embarcadero. Only then had they found a carriage driver who would take a chance they would pay after they reached the museum.

"You stay," the driver said when they both got down. "One of you, get the money. The other stays here."

"Go on," Slocum said. He saw that the driver was uneasy with the choice of who was to remain behind. Though he had been drenched, almost drowned like a rat and dried out so that his salt-caked clothes clung to him, he was obviously the more dangerous of the pair. Slocum knew his saltwater-drenched six-shooter would probably not fire if he threw down on the driver, but the man could not know that.

"Here you are, my good man," Sir William said, bustling back with a handful of scrip thrust in front of him. "We appreciate your courage in taking a risk on us."

"Thank you, sir," the driver said skeptically. He leafed through the paper money one bill at a time studying which bank had issued it. A slow smile came to his face. Slocum knew the bills were all drawn on a solvent local bank.

"What do we do now?" Sir William asked.

"I don't know where the jade crown is," Slocum said. "Little Pete does not have it, nor does Lai Choi San."

"The other woman. The tong leader's daughter. What of her?"

"Ah Ming wants her father's body returned more than she would want a piece of jade. It's a religious matter."

"Ah, yes, the return of the bones for burial in hallowed ground." Sir William looked around, then shrugged. "Nothing sacred for the Celestials in this country."

He returned to the museum, in seeming good humor. Slocum trailed behind, in a foul mood. The encounter with Lai Choi San had left a bad taste in his mouth. Three men had died for no reason. He still could not figure out why the pirate had not ordered her men to shoot him and Sir William out of the water. It had been a decision solely on her part. That Slocum was certain of, seeing how she spoke with her marksmen on the upper deck of the junk. He was not sorry she had called them off but only wondered why.

To torment me even more, he decided. His hands were like pieces of cured leather from long hours roping cattle and still they had blistered from the oars. He was fed up with San Francisco and anything having to do with the sea. It was time for him to seek out the serenity of the desert. Or the plains. Or the mountains. Anywhere that wasn't a city.

As he went into the museum, though, like a dog with a bone, he still worried at the mystery of the crown's location. If anyone in the town wanted to get rid of an artifact, Little Pete—or Ah Ming—would have heard of it immediately. No thief would keep such a trinket. Even the locoweeds wandering the streets of this town were not likely to hang on to it, although the emperor of the North might.

"What happened?" Tess came running out of the main room and stopped to stare at Sir William and Slocum. "You both look as if you were drowned and washed ashore somewhere."

"That's close enough to the truth," Slocum said. He remembered he had intended to fetch his gear and get the hell out of town when Tess had stopped him before. The idea of leaving San Francisco was even stronger now that he had decided he did not know who had the jade crown.

Whoever had stolen it from him might be one of the museum patrons who had taken a fancy to it. Just because the society people on the opening night were richer than he had any chance of becoming did not mean they weren't thieves.

Slocum snorted in disgust. If anything, most of them had gained their riches by being crooks. Or worse. The railroads had been built using coolie labor, with the workers' pay seldom more than a bowl of rice a day. He had seen the dockworkers. More were Chinese than white. The town ran on the backs of the Celestials. While all that might be true, it did not tell him who had the crown.

It was definitely time for him to hightail it.

"What are you going to do, Sir William?" Tess was distraught.

"Prepare what remains of the exhibit for transport. If I don't find the jade crown myself, then the display will have to endure without it," he said airily. "A new expedition might be in order, too. That crown was unique, but there might be others of more historical significance for me to uncover."

"You took that one off a courier," Tess said uneasily.

"I discovered it. It was a legitimate artifact lost to the ages."

Slocum wanted no part of their discussion. From the hints Sir William had dropped, he might have stolen the crown off the Chinese emperor's head and then claimed it was an archaeological treasure "lost to the ages." The British explorer had a way of viewing the world through a very narrow spyglass. If he saw something that interested him, nothing else existed until he possessed it. Not for the first time, Slocum wondered why Sir William ignored the most beautiful trophy of all—Tess Lawrence.

Leaving them, he made his way through the maze of corridors until he reached the storage room where he had stashed his gear. He quickly changed his clothes, noting that those he put on were hardly better than those he took off. The only difference was the new set had been drying.

With Tess's and Sir William's voices echoing through

the deserted museum, Slocum sat on a stool and cleaned his Colt Navy. Saltwater would destroy the precision mechanism. The next time he had to draw might require some accurate shooting. Having the six-gun jam or the ammo misfire would be his downfall.

" 'He drew, he misfired, he died,' " Slocum quoted quietly as he ran his cleaning rod in and out of the barrel before attending to the six chambers in the cylinder. "Not the kind of epitaph I want. Better to have it read, 'He killed six but there were seven.' " Satisfied with the action and the new rounds he slid into the cylinder, he spent a few minutes working on the holster, rubbing in saddle soap and making sure the leather would not catch if he had to draw fast.

Done with his cleaning chores, he slung the cross-draw holster around his waist again, then picked up his gear. He stopped in the doorway when he heard sounds that should not be echoing through the museum. Dropping his gear, he drew his pistol and went hunting.

Sir William and Tess had returned to the curator's office to continue their argument. He was surprised that the woman put up such a spirited dispute to the egomaniacal explorer's ideas.

Then he heard the soft sound of silk sliding across silk. Or perhaps a Celestial's slipper on the hardwood floor. Slocum moved like a puff of wind through the corridor and saw the hatchet man crouched near the entrance to the main room. When the Chinaman shifted his weight slightly, Slocum saw two hatchets in his hands. This killer meant business. Slocum aimed carefully, then cocked his six-gun.

He yelped when the wood handle of a thrown hatchet banged into his hand, forcing him to drop his gun. Ignoring the pain, he spun and caught at a burly wrist bringing a second ax down on his head. Slocum quickly discovered the Celestial was stronger than he was. He stepped into the man, then spun around while still holding the hatchet man's wrist. Slocum tripped him and wrested the ax away.

By this time the first killer had responded. Jumping to his feet, he silently came at Slocum, the two hatchets weaving a deadly pattern in front of him. Slocum feinted, then hit the floor and rolled, coming up with a fallen hatchet. He could never hope to match the man's skill with the deadly blades—and he did not try. He threw it directly at the hatchet man's face.

Quick swipes of the two flashing hatchets knocked it away, but Slocum had bought himself enough time to kick at the tong killer on the floor and knock him away from where he tried to grab Slocum's Colt Navy.

Slocum retrieved his gun, fired three times, then brought the muzzle around to fire two more. The Celestial with the pair of hatchets died. The other was slammed back and lay propped against a wall, bleeding from two bullets just above his heart.

"I say, what's going on?" cried Sir William.

"Keep Tess in the office. Lock her in, if you have to. The tong's sent men to kill me. Maybe you, too."

"Little Pete? The Sum Yops?"

Slocum had been with both tongs enough to see subtle differences. There must be some badge or pin or other identifying mark to let the casual passerby in the street know who he was dealing with, but Slocum could not see the insignia. He had seen the man he had gunned down in Ah Ming's underground maze.

"The On Leong," Slocum said. "My time's run out."

"What time is that?"

"I'll tell you later," Slocum said, never intending to do anything of the sort. He did not want to admit his motives for recovering the jade crown had nothing to do with keeping Sir William's exhibition complete.

"I can be of great help," the explorer said, irritated. "I am an expert on these people."

"For once, do as I say and we might all get out of this without having our hair parted down the middle by one of those hatchets."

Slocum reloaded as he headed for the main door. He had to see if Ah Ming had sent more than this pair to kill him.

She hadn't.

Exhausted, Slocum lay on his belly watching the mouth of the alley. He tried not to cry out when rats ran around him, sniffing and occasionally nipping at him. Memory of the rat pit made him want to run. Memory of the four hatchet men he had killed during the day kept him still and silent.

A solitary man walked past the opening of the alley, hesitated, looked down into the gloom as if hunting for Slocum, then walked on. Coming to Chinatown had been foolish, but Slocum knew the only way he was going to get out of San Francisco alive was to dicker with Ah Ming. She had issued the death warrant for him and no one else could issue a stay of execution. Going to Little Pete would produce nothing but a swift knife in the ribs. If Little Pete thought he could weaken the On Leong by killing Slocum, he would. Both tong leaders had come to the conclusion that Slocum had.

Nobody knew who had the jade crown.

The sound came to him like wind in the tall pines. A distant whisper, nothing more. He tensed, then rolled onto his back. His six-shooter pointed directly at Ah Ming. She had come up from the far end of the alley, making a sound to alert him only at the last instant.

"You move like an Apache," he said, trying to compliment her.

"They are savages. I move like a Chinese."

"I've been hunting for you all day, but your hatchet men have other ideas. Why did you send them to kill me?"

She stared at him and the gun in his hand without a trace of fear. He could end her life with only a small pressure on the trigger, but he wouldn't. She had found him. That meant she wanted to palaver, too.

"You failed. The jade crown is gone."

"You don't know that," he said. Then a tiny piece fell into place. "Lai Choi San doesn't have it. She just left."

"Without the crown? I do not believe this is so," Ah Ming said.

"Little Pete doesn't have it," Slocum said. "He's still willing to trade your pa's body for it."

"He is a liar," she said with rancor.

"I'm not. I promised to find the jade crown so I could trade with Little Pete."

"Why are you so sure Lai Choi San does not have it and yet is on her way back to China?"

Slocum knew Ah Ming would find it hard to believe, but he tried. "I play poker. Some of it is luck, the way the cards fall. Part of it is knowing the odds. Most of it is reading the fellow across the table to figure out if he's bluffing or has something worth betting. Lai Choi San does not have the crown, but she wants it real bad."

"You can be so sure? By looking hard at her?"

"I can," Slocum said with more confidence than he felt.

"Why did she leave the harbor?"

"I don't have any idea," Slocum said. He holstered his pistol and stood. If she had wanted to kill him, their conversation would not have gone on this long.

"Why do you seek me? To order me to call off my *boo how doy*?"

"The hatchet men? No, I just want the time we had agreed upon. Till the end of the week."

"Little Pete will throw my father into the bay by then."

"Talk to him. Tell him I'm bringing the crown, but it's out of the city."

"He will not believe it."

"Tell him Lai Choi San has the crown."

Ah Ming stood a little straighter and her hands went into the huge sleeves of her dress. Like Little Pete, she carried weapons there. He was within seconds of a knife or a pistol being used on him.

"It's a lie, but you said he was a liar. There's no harm in lying to a man like him."

"What will you do to find the emperor's crown?"

She had Slocum there. He had no idea how to track the valuable artifact through San Francisco's criminal underground. If no one in Chinatown had it, that meant one of the other gangs must. The Sydney Ducks had been disbanded years ago, but there were any number of successors that controlled crime outside Chinatown. He had to find his way among them.

Even as this thought crossed his mind, he knew in his gut that it would do no good. Still, he had to say something, try something.

"Until the end of the week, Mr. Slocum," Ah Ming said. She stepped back, turned and in the time it took Slocum to blink, she disappeared. He strained to hear her slippers moving on the littered alley. Only the scampering rats and the sound of a building settling reached his keen ears.

He heaved a deep sigh. He had won himself a little more time. Not enough to actually find the jade crown, but enough to figure out who had stolen it from him. Slocum set out to begin his search in earnest.

Allies, Slocum thought. That was what he needed. Trying to find the crown by himself would never work—he had done nothing but fail so far. He needed more eyes and ears, more feet hitting the pavement and even knives and guns to back him up. Sir William was out of the question. The way he had so foolishly antagonized Lai Choi San told Slocum the arrogant Brit was too used to getting his own way to know when to be quiet. The tongs were not to be trusted. Slocum knew that Little Pete's reputation for having the temperament of a stepped-on sidewinder was well deserved. Ah Ming was hardly better. She was driven to get her father's body back and devil take the hindmost.

That did not leave him a whole bunch of people to recruit.

He stopped climbing when he reached the summit of Sutro Peak. Dawn was breaking. He had, at most, three more days to locate the jade crown. With the sunlight of a new day warming his back, he slowly scanned the coastline going southward for any vessels. A smile came to his lips when he saw the triangular parti-colored sails of a junk.

That had to be Lai Choi San sailing not two miles down the coast. She had left the harbor but not to return to China with her emperor's crown. The pirate sought something in that direction, and Slocum had a good idea what it might be. He had spent an hour in the harbormaster's office sneaking a peek whenever he could at the list of ships due into port soon. Only one had been of interest—or would have been of interest to Lai Choi San.

Knowing she would not go too far, Slocum began the long walk down the west-facing side of the hill, heading for the rocky shore. How he was going to get onto the pirate junk was something he could work out later.

And after he got aboard, *then* he could figure out how to recruit Lai Choi San to help him.

14

"This is certainly a balls-up affair," Sir William said. "Beg your pardon, my dear. I don't mean to use such language in front of a lady, but everything has completely turned upside down, don't you see?"

"Yes, it has, Sir William," Tess said. She chewed at her lower lip as she looked around the main display room in the museum. There were a dozen display cases laden with jade. They all mocked her. No matter how hard she tried, she could not avoid looking at the one where the jade crown had been. It was only a small void in the collection but it might have been big enough to drive a stagecoach through.

"I cannot cope with this. I simply cannot do it anymore. My nerves are all jangled. You do it."

"What?" Tess's eyes widened. "You want *me* to see to the packing and final arrangements for transportation of the collection?"

"You can do it, my dear. You are most capable."

"But you said you would tend to it personally, that no one else could make even the simplest of plans without your approval."

"I am hereby granting you full authority to do all that. I

must not be bothered with minutiae. There are so many other things to occupy me." Sir William struck his pose, hand over his heart and the other reaching for the sky. "Recovering the fifteen-hundred-year-old crown of the emperor of China is foremost."

"I'm dumbstruck, Sir William," she said. "I have no idea where to begin."

"Don't underestimate yourself," he said sternly. "Do things step by step. Pack the jade in excelsior inside crates. Arrange for it to be placed aboard a transcontinental train so it arrives safely in Boston. You have already made arrangements for the exhibition in that fine city, have you not?"

"Why, yes, of course, just as I arranged for this museum."

"See? You are capable enough."

"It's a grand responsibility," she said, her blue eyes glowing with inner fire. "This is a valuable collection."

"Very valuable, considering the blood and toil it took to gather it. Now," he said, "we both have things to do. I want the collection on the train by the day after tomorrow. How long do you think it will take to arrive?"

"Are you riding with it, Sir William?"

"If I find the jade crown, yes. Otherwise, I will remain in San Francisco until that matter is put to rest. You can accompany the collection and wet-nurse them, so to speak." For a moment his eyes dropped to Tess's ample bosom. She blushed at the thought that he might finally look upon her as a woman and not an animated clotheshorse. The instant passed.

"You'd meet me in Boston?" Tess studied the man closely for a clue to his real intentions.

"Yes, yes, of course. I would not miss the opening night for anything." He paused, pursed his lips, then said, "Except recovering the emperor's crown, that is. Never have I seen such a fine example of Oriental art. The quality of the carving, the color of the jade, all perfect. One might say it is a museum piece fit for an emperor." He laughed at his small joke.

"Where are you going to hunt for the crown?" Tess asked. "Do you have any ideas?"

"In spite of what that Slocum chap says, I am certain the pirate has it. Lai Choi San is her name. She ogled the crown and coveted it the opening night. She must have it. I'm going to the harbor and inquire after her."

"Very well, Sir William," Tess said. "I certainly have my work cut out for me." She rubbed her hands together in anticipation of crating so many fine jade artifacts.

"You're forgetting something, my dear."

"What?" Tess jumped guiltily.

"I will write you a check for, oh, a thousand pounds so you can pay for the workmen, the material and, naturally, the cost of shipment on the railroad."

"Of course," Tess said, slumping in relief. "I thought you meant something else."

"Whatever it might have been, you will think of it on your own. You're a clever lass. Yes, yes, quite clever."

"That I am," Tess said softly. Sir William bustled off to write her the check as she walked slowly from one display case to the next, mentally packing each piece. This was something she had not dared hope for. Ultimate authority in transporting the entire collection!

Tess Lawrence got to work.

"The ship just sailed and you have no notion where it is headed? That's outrageous, sir!" bellowed Sir William.

"I keep track of the cargo for what excise taxes we can levy," Captain Johnson said, forcing himself to keep his temper. "There's too many smaller vessels going in and out, fishing boats and the like, for me to keep track of them all."

"This was a Chinese junk!"

"I received the report from my lieutenant," Johnson said. "You were the one who talked him into trying to board that vessel?"

"I convinced him to do his duty, that's what," Sir William said. "You were nowhere to be found."

"I was on medical leave," the captain said. He hobbled around the counter and sat heavily in a chair, his leg thrust out in front of him. "This time of year, my gout gets so painful I can hardly put in a half day's duty."

"Then the U.S. Navy should replace you," Sir William said tactlessly.

"I ought to keelhaul you for insubordination. I can do that during the half day I'm not laid up moaning in pain."

"Use boiled tea leaves on it. And eat cherries," Sir William said.

"What? Are you a doctor?"

"I have been in all corners of the world. Those remedies work on gout."

"Do tell," the naval captain said, rubbing his leg. "I'll give it a try. It has to be better than that bitter potion the doctor's been giving me."

"The junk," Sir William urged. "It left suddenly. Are other vessels due into port?"

"Only one. A cargo ship from down south." Captain Johnson got to his feet and hobbled to his desk. A few seconds of page flipping brought him to the one he wanted. His bushy eyebrows arched and he looked back at Sir William. "You have interest in the *Nathan*?"

"I have never heard of this vessel until this moment. My interest is in what that pirate stole from me. She has it on board. A valuable artifact."

"She? Pirate?"

"Lai Choi San is a notorious pirate from the South China Sea. She came here to steal my incredibly valuable collection of jade artifacts. They are valuable not only in a monetary sense but also from the knowledge the academic world can glean from—"

"The *Nathan* is carrying five hundred rifles, ammunition and four new cannons for Fort Point. It's a military arms shipment."

"Just the thing a pirate like Lai Choi San would sniff out. She's like a hound dog on the seas, I tell you, Captain.

Nothing gets past her. She has stolen the finest piece of my jade collection, and now she is going after your guns."

"Not mine, the army's," Captain Johnson said glumly. "Colonel Fisher will not be pleased if his replacement armament is stolen on the high seas, though."

"The lieutenant mentioned that you have a frigate. Send it out after the junk."

"I cannot contact the ship's captain. I am supposed to have two frigates but—"

"Yes, yes, I've heard all that. You are trapped behind a desk and can do nothing?"

"I can telegraph down the coast and see if I can contact the *Nathan* at a port along the way. A warning might be sufficient to allow the captain to fight off a pirate attack." Captain Johnson sounded skeptical. Pirates in these waters were nonexistent. The patrolling frigates had driven off what few wreckers there were along the coast. An occasional Russian ship ventured toward the Farallones and the egg farmers there got upset. The frigate would chase the Russian sealing ships away. That was as close to piracy as he had seen in the five years he had been posted here.

"What other ships are due to lift anchor soon?" Sir William asked.

"Only one. A Cape schooner bound for New York. The *Portobello* sails with the tide."

"At sundown or dawn tomorrow?"

"Is there anything else I can do for you?" Captain Johnson asked. His face twisted in pain as he tried to put weight on his gouty foot.

"I see you are off for the rest of the day. Cherries and tea leaves, old man. That's the spirit." Sir William left the naval station and walked to the end of the dock. His eyes fixed on the emptiness where Lai Choi San had anchored. He heaved a sigh. Without naval cooperation, the pirate would go unpunished and his jade crown would be lost forever.

Disconsolate, he turned and walked slowly down the Embarcadero, unaware of eyes following his every step.

"No, no, be careful!" cried Tess Lawrence. She hurried to hold the door for the workers moving the crate filled with jade artifacts. "Don't bang it around so."

"It's gonna get bunged up somethin' good if you're movin' it any distance. Where are we takin' this stuff?"

"Load everything onto your wagon first. There're only two more boxes." Tess wrung her hands as the men moved the crates from the main room of the museum to the waiting wagon. She cringed as they heaved the final crate up into the wagon bed. It landed with a distinct *thud*. She relaxed. There had not been a breaking sound accompanying it.

She had worked all afternoon packing the crates. Excelsior filled every nook of each crate and she had stuffed carefully wrapped items into the wood shavings. Not trusting another to do the work, she had wielded hammer and nail herself to close each crate. Then she had sealed cracks where she could with melted candle wax. Already she saw some of the wax cracking off the crate that had been dropped so unceremoniously.

"Where we goin'? I remember hearing the British gent say somethin' 'bout the train station."

"Train? No, how did you get that idea?" Tess said too quickly. Her heart hammered fiercely.

"Just what I'd heard. Where, then?"

"To the docks. To the *Portobello* loading area."

"That one of them schooners?"

"Yes," she said, not wanting to go into detail with a mere workman. "I'll ride in the back with the crates. Please put my trunk and other luggage into the wagon, also."

"Whatever you say."

The man grunted as he heaved the trunk in. Tess could hardly slide it, and he lifted it with only a small display of strain. Her valise quickly followed. She hugged it close to her chest as the wagon began moving through the darkened streets. She hoped they were not too late. Sir William's being away had convinced her of this last-minute change in plans. He *had* wanted the collection sent on the train.

A small smile curled her lips. He had wanted so many things, and now he was not going to get any of them.

"Do you have to hit every pothole in the street?" she complained. She clung to her valise. In it were all the papers for shipping the jade to New York City—and the rest of the ticketing. To lose any of it now meant explanations she simply did not want to give Sir William.

She rested her hand on one crate and looked at the others. They would survive the sea voyage well. The wax made them almost impervious to the water seepage bound to occur on any long trip around Cape Horn. The excelsior cushioned shocks to prevent cracking of the jade. And there were only four crates. Few enough to keep track of but enough to make her ridiculously rich.

"That the one? That there sailin' ship?" The workman pointed to a tall-masted ship.

Tess had no idea if it was the right one but she realized the man could not read. She peered about, then saw a man working with a thick sheaf of papers.

"A moment. Wait right here." She jumped down, turned and glared at the driver to make certain he would not drive off with the precious jade collection. Only then did she go to the man with the papers.

"Evening, ma'am," the man said.

"Are you in charge of cargo for the *Portobello*?"

"That I am. You got another load?"

"Yes, right here." She fumbled in the valise and found the necessary bills of lading. Tess passed them over.

"Have your men unload where they are. I'll get the dock wallopers to get it aboard. You sailin' with us, too, ma'am?"

"I reckon so," she said.

The man smiled ear to ear, showing two gaps where teeth had been knocked out. "Then this might be about the best trip we've had in years. You're an asset, that's for certain sure."

"Thank you," she said.

"Will your husband be joining you on the trip?"

"I . . . yes, he will," Tess said, hoping she sounded positive enough to dispel any suspicion.

"We'll be sailin' with the morning tide. Be aboard the good ship *Porto*, as we affectionately call 'er, by five a.m."

"I had hoped to stay in my berth overnight," Tess said. She looked around, sure someone watched her.

"Ma'am, you're gonna be sick of that cabin 'fore we reach New York. Spend the time on land."

"Then I cannot stay in the berth?"

"Nope," he said. "We got a small problem we're takin' care of. Fumigatin', you see."

"Bugs?"

"Them, too. Seems the ship's cat got fat and lazy and the rats sorta took over once we got to port. But that won't be no problem when we get under way," he assured her.

"No, of course not." Tess looked around, increasingly nervous now. She was certain someone stared at her, but she could not find where they were.

"Five sharp, ma'am, or we leave without you."

"My crates . . ." She took an involuntary step when four sailors came down the gangplank and hefted the boxes with practiced ease.

"Stowin' 'em in the cargo hold, ma'am. Don't you worry your pretty head none. My boys are the best on the San Francisco–New York run."

"Yes, of course, how silly of me." She saw that the driver and workman who had unloaded the crates from the wagon waited impatiently. She started for them, only to be stopped by the ship's mate.

"Your bill of lading, ma'am. For the cargo." He held out a sheet of paper.

"Oh, yes, thank you." She smiled weakly and went to pay her workers. They touched the bills of their caps, hopped back into the wagon and drove off with a clatter, leaving her alone on the dock.

She pulled her valise closer to her for comfort. She found none.

"Find somewhere to spend the night," she said aloud to

convince herself she could do it. "There must be a nearby hotel where . . . where I won't be seen."

She started walking, only to hear a steady *click-click* of boots against the cobblestones behind her. Every time she spun to confront whoever followed, she saw nothing. Tess screamed when she rounded a corner and ran full into a man who stepped out.

Strong arms circled her and pulled her close. She caught the scent of filth, of dirt and whiskey.

"Let me go!" she cried, trying to force herself away. The man was too strong.

"Is that any way to act with the man who is going to ride you like a prize filly all night long?"

She stopped fighting and looked up into the man's unkempt, bearded face.

"Jason!"

"Who else, princess?"

"You have it? Where is it?"

Jason Stark laughed and spun her around.

"The crown's where nobody can find it. You got the rest of the jade? I saw you with men unloading a wagon."

Tess laughed and stood on tiptoe to kiss him.

"I have it all. Sir William left for the day and never came back. I had hoped to steal a few of the smaller pieces, but with him gone, I packed it all up. It's aboard the *Portobello* right now!"

"So that British fool's going to be at the railroad station, thinking his precious gewgaws are on the way to Boston?"

"And we'll be on the *Portobello* going around the Horn to New York."

"With the jade," Stark said.

"With the jade *and* the emperor of China's jade crown," Tess said. "Now where are you going to make love to me until the ship sails? I want to see the place."

"Like hell. You want to get down to doing the dirty deed," Stark said, laughing. He put his arm around her. "This way, princess. I might even let you wear the crown—if you take off all the rest of your clothes."

"Oh, Jason, you're such a joker."

"Who says I'm joking? You'd look great naked as a jaybird 'cept for the crown."

Together they went off, whispering to each other what outrageous things they would do that night.

Behind them, unblinking eyes followed their every step.

15

"It's nothing but a plow horse," Slocum complained. "You can't expect me to pay twenty-five dollars for this broke down old mare." He looked over the horse. Its teeth were good, gums pink and eyes clear. Otherwise, there was hardly anything about the horse worth a second glance—other than he needed to ride faster down the coast than he could walk.

"Well," said the farmer, rubbing his chin. "I had this old nag for quite a spell. Like one of the family."

"I'm not offering to buy your wife," Slocum said. "Just the horse."

"Truth to tell, I'd as soon give up my wife as this horse. She's not as likely to kick me. Twenty dollars."

"Sold," Slocum said. He patted the horse's neck and got a sour look in return. He pulled out the money he had been paid by Sir William to act as his guard and handed it over. The farmer counted it twice, then nodded brusquely.

"Get on out of here, 'fore the wife sees you takin' the horse. Like I said, the horse is like one of the family."

Slocum put a hackamore on the horse and then swung up to ride bareback. He never gave the farmer a second glance. He had been right about the horse. It was broken but for the plow. The mare danced about under him and then settled down, resolved to make the best of carrying a man on its back rather than being hitched to a yoke and plow.

Slocum got the horse to a trot and kept up the pace as he found the coast road. His feet ached and his back hurt, but it felt good to once more be astride a horse. He strained to catch a glimpse of the ocean. Lai Choi San had been sailing slowly. The winds had turned against the pirate captain the last time Slocum had glimpsed her ship.

But the more he rode the more desolate he became. Nothing but endless steel gray ocean stretched as far as he could see—and not a sail interrupted the endless vista. By close to sundown he rode into a small town. A sign battered by wind and salt spray revealed this was San Grigorio. To Slocum it meant only a place to rest.

As he rode slowly down the middle of the main street, people came out to stare at him. He doubted being a stranger was any part of the attraction he provided. Not many men rode without saddles or decent bridle. He waved to a few of the men, who turned away and grumbled. In a few minutes he had become just another face and ceased to be newsworthy.

Dismounting, Slocum swung the rope around a hitching post and went into the saloon. The crowded gin mill was already filling with men finished with their day's work. He stopped when he heard one man, wearing a green visor and sleeve protectors say, "Damnedest 'gram I ever got. From the navy commander up in San Francisco."

Slocum moved to stand closer to the telegrapher. He smelled pungent acid and saw many small holes burned in the man's shirtfront and pants from tending the lead-acid batteries needed to move messages up and down the coast.

Slocum signaled that he wanted a beer. He sipped at the warm, bitter brew slowly and leaned toward the telegrapher to hear more. He got an earful.

"Captain name of Johnson wants a signal sent to his frigate."

"He don't know where it is?" asked another patron.

"Reckon not. If we see his frigate we're supposed to send a wire up to naval headquarters and try to semaphore a warning."

"Warning?" Slocum could not hold his tongue. The locals turned and stared at him as if he had three heads. "What kind of warning? It must be something that's mighty dangerous for everyone."

"Nope. Wants the ship commander to know there's a Chinese boat with some stolen goods on it."

"Do tell," Slocum said, taking a deeper draft of his beer. It left a metallic taste in his mouth.

"Not sure what's aboard the chink ship," the telegrapher went on, "but I never heard of such a thing. A boat that's sailed all the way from China and don't look like anything else in these waters."

"I saw that ship," the barkeep said excitedly. He put down his polishing rag and leaned closer. "Earlier on today. I thought it looked funny. Had three-sided sails. One was flapping real strange."

"Suppose I ought to tell that Captain Johnson?"

"Costs money to send telegrams, don't it? You ought to make 'em pay. Them's the gummint. They got more money 'n any of us."

"Going south?" Slocum asked the barkeep. The man's bushy eyebrows wiggled, seemingly alive and on their own.

"Yup. You some kind of lawman? You after the thieves on that boat?"

Slocum shook his head. He finished his beer and left, aware that the telegrapher and his small group of friends watched him. Out in the street, he looked around. The sun had set and turned the air cold as a breeze blew off the ocean. He shivered, hitched up his gun belt and then mounted his plow horse.

"A while longer, old girl," he promised the mare. The horse snorted and began plodding along. No matter what Slocum did, he could not get more speed from the horse.

It turned out he did not need a racehorse to overtake Lai

Choi San's junk. Sometime before midnight he drew rein and stared into a small cove. Bobbing on the gentle waves there lay Lai Choi San's junk. Slocum could not make out the crew aboard, but he heard the singsong calls of one pirate to another.

Slocum dropped to the ground and considered what to do. This was the best chance he was likely to get. If he tethered his horse too securely, it might starve.

"Go on, you're on your own," Slocum said, taking off the hackamore. He gave the mare a swat on the rump. The horse neighed, tried to rear, thought better of such effort and walked away. Slocum knew someone would find the horse eventually. In this part of the country the only danger lay in mountain lions deciding this was a tasty meal on the hoof.

Pushing that from his mind, Slocum studied the terrain, then began a slow descent down the rocky sides of the hill. He tumbled and slid but eventually got to the shoreline. Not a hundred feet away toiled a dozen Chinese pirates. They sawed at a long tree trunk, taking off the limbs. Slocum wondered if one of the ship's spars had broken, and they worked to replace it.

With so many of the crew ashore, Slocum knew he stood a better chance of reaching the junk and searching it to settle once and for all the matter of whether Lai Choi San had the jade crown. The telegram message making its way down the coast told Slocum that the naval commander back at San Francisco thought the pirate had the stolen artifact. Slocum was a good poker player and read people well, even Celestial pirate captains. He doubted Lai Choi San had the jade.

He was the only one. Sir William thought she had it. So did the U.S. Navy.

Slocum slipped away from the crew, going around the dark shoreline until he reached a spot where the junk bobbed not fifty yards away. Grunting, tugging, rolling, Slocum got a fallen log into the water. He worried it would be too rotted to float, but his fears proved groundless as it caught on the waves and rode high. As far as his approach went, this was the easy part. Flipping belly-down on the log, Slocum aimed it toward the junk and began paddling.

His arms ached after only a few strokes, but he kept moving. When he came within a few yards of the ship, he tensed. Craning his neck around, he watched the sentry walking slowly along the deck. The junk rode high in the water—it had not taken on much in the way of supplies. That told Slocum Lai Choi San did not intend to head back to the Celestial Kingdom. In his mind, this was another point in favor of his belief that she did not have the jade crown.

The lookout stopped to peer in Slocum's direction. Slocum froze. Keeping astride the log proved difficult—it kept trying to turn under him and throw him into the water. Slocum lowered himself and clung to the log, sure he would get a musket ball in the back at any instant.

When he heard the steady pacing begin again, he paddled closer until the log butted into the junk's hull. The dull thump was muffled by the lapping of waves. Slocum grabbed and caught a rope dangling down. He took the rough cord in his hands and winced. Blisters still bedeviled him. He took a deep breath, steeled himself against the pain and began climbing. With Lai Choi San posting sentries even in a deserted cove, discipline aboard the junk had to be great. She ran a ship as ordered as any U.S. Navy vessel.

With a kick, he swung over the railing and landed on the deck. His boots, wet from the trip from the shore, slid out from under him. He sat heavily. Cursing his clumsiness ended fast when he realized this had saved him from discovery. Another lookout on the poop deck came over and leaned against a railing. He had heard something. Calling out to the other guard produced a quick, staccato exchange that ended with both men going back to their posts. Slocum was not even suspected as being aboard.

He got his feet under him and made his way slowly toward the aft where hatches opened down into the bowels of the junk and another led off the deck into what must be Lai Choi San's quarters. Six-shooter drawn, Slocum opened the hatch and peeked inside. The small, neat room was empty. Wherever she had gone, Lai Choi San was not at home.

Slocum ducked inside and looked around. The tiny cabin was filled with charts and maps and arcane navigational equipment. Slocum recognized a compass and spyglass. Otherwise, the geared devices were a mystery to him. He quickly went through drawers looking for the crown. He found only a small jade ring. It was a different color, a deeper green than anything he could remember Sir William having in his exhibit. Slocum returned it to the drawer where he had found it, but he searched thoroughly for any kind of secret hiding spot.

He found nothing, as he expected. Lai Choi San did not have the jade crown. He knew she might have it hidden somewhere else aboard the ship, but he doubted it. She was a pirate and had a crew of pirates. Anything she wanted to keep would be here, in this cabin, where she could keep an eye on it.

His boots sucking with the water in them at every step, Slocum knew he could not be quiet enough to explore the rest of the ship. When he bent over a desk littered with documents, all written in Chinese, he stared out the window until he got his bearings. Locating the crew working in the cove was easy enough. From the way they bustled about at the shore, he figured they would be returning soon. It was time for him to get off the junk and back to land where he belonged.

Slocum slipped from the cabin and went to the railing. The line he had used to climb was gone. He leaned far enough over the railing to see that the log he had paddled out on was still close to the ship.

A sixth sense warned him of attack. He ducked and turned as the deck lookout rushed him. Slocum got his arms around the man's hips and lifted. Twisting, he tossed the pirate over the side.

Slocum cursed when he heard the loud splash the sailor made when he hit the water.

The other lookout on the upper deck yelled something in Chinese that had to be an alert. Slocum started to jump over the side and take his chances when he saw that the pirate he had dumped into the drink had clambered onto the log and sat astride it. From the silvery glint in his hand, the pirate had drawn a knife. Slocum would have to fight for the log.

There was not time.

Two pirates came onto the deck from below. Slocum knew he could gun them down, but what would he do then? Fight the rest of the crew? Hiding was the only thought in his head. He took a step toward Lai Choi San's cabin, then knew he would never reach it. Even if he did, he would be trapped. The windows in the captain's quarters were too small for him to squeeze through.

Without breaking stride, Slocum reached up, grabbed a dangling ratline and pulled himself upward. He swung out enough to lock a leg around the lowest spar. Sinking down flat, he tried to look like part of the shop's rigging.

For a brief instant he thought he had succeeded. Half a dozen sailors came on deck and went to the rail, yelling down to their comrade in the water. Slocum wished he could understand what they were saying. He spoke reasonably good Spanish and got by in half a dozen Indian tongues, but Chinese was totally alien to him. They could be laughing at the man in the water, deriding him for being so damn clumsy.

Or they could be plotting to come after the invader on their ship. Slocum just did not know.

He edged along the spar with the intent of going to the far side of the ship and then lowering himself into the water. That meant a dangerous swim ashore in frigid water, but it was safer than staying where he was. Inching along like a caterpillar, reaching out, pulling himself up and then extending flat again, he made his way to the center mast. He had just reached it when someone spotted him.

"Aieee!"

The cry from below was chilling. Slocum threw his arms around the huge center mast and pulled himself up. A splinter flew off the mast in front of his face. The slug whined off into the night, but another quickly followed. And another and another. He agilely whirled around, putting the thick wood post between him and the pirates shooting at him. They all used single-shot pistols—muzzle loaders, which saved him. While they were busy reloading, he made his way carefully along the spar to the far end, intending to dive off.

He looked down and decided that was not a good idea. Two pirates climbed ropes dangling at the end of the spar to cut him off. He touched the pistol in his holster, then knew he might not be able to shoot either of the men in the dark, much less both.

Spinning, almost losing his balance, he turned, went back to the center mast and got around it, intending to dive off and swim the shorter distance back to shore. In the dark waves, the sailors might not be able to spot him. Wobbling a little as he moved, he reached the end of the spar. Below him still straddling the log sat the pirate he had tossed overboard. A decent dive would take Slocum well past him.

He glanced behind and saw that the two pirates on the ropes had reached the spar. They ran along as if they were on solid ground rather than fifteen feet above the deck. Slocum bent down to make his dive when he felt cold metal press against his arm.

A thrown knife cut through his sleeve and pinned his arm to the spar. He reached to pull the knife out and another pinned his free arm. Slocum twisted and yanked to tear the cloth.

From below came a mocking voice. "Do not try to escape, Mr. Slocum. I am quite accurate with my knives, as you can tell."

Lai Choi San stood with another knife ready to throw. He had no doubt she was the one who had pinned him— and that another throw would gut him.

Slocum simply slid down and straddled the spar, both arms fastened to the wood by Lai Choi San's knives. She could have killed him with either toss. The only problem he saw was that she might have a more diabolical and tortuous death waiting for him.

16

The two Chinese pirates on the spar pulled the knives free and then kicked Slocum off. He fell through the air, trying to hold back a scream and failing. He landed heavily on the deck. He raised his head and saw white linen pants. Looking upward even more, he passed the quilted jacket and finally stared directly into Lai Choi San's eyes. They were cold and Slocum knew he could expect no mercy.

"You got me," he said, getting up. A foot on his shoulder shoved him back to the deck.

"Remain where you are," the pirate captain said fiercely. "I will cut off your ears and feed them to you if you disobey me."

Slocum did not doubt Lai Choi San was capable of that. He felt feathery touches as a sailor searched him. His Colt Navy was lifted from its holster so smoothly he barely felt it being taken. The bare foot remained on his shoulder, holding him in the proper position to pay homage to the captain of a Chinese vessel. Slocum seethed but could not get free.

"You searched my cabin," Lai Choi San accused.

Slocum saw no reason to dispute it. He nodded.

"What were you looking for?"

"Jade."

Slocum reeled as she reached down, knocked off his hat and grabbed a handful of hair. She pulled his head back at a painful angle.

"What did you find?"

"Nothing but a jade ring."

Slocum swallowed hard when he felt the sharp edge of her blade against his throat.

"Did you take it?"

"I left it. It wasn't what I was looking for."

"What did you want?" Lai Choi San pulled the blade from his flesh. He felt a tiny trickle of blood from a nick she had given him near the pulsing artery at this throat.

"The emperor's crown," he said. Even if he were so inclined, he saw no reason to lie. "If you've got it, you hid it well."

"You knew I did not have it. You are not a stupid man."

"Everyone else thinks you have it," Slocum said. "I ran out of possibilities." He tried to shrug but found himself shoved back down hard to the deck. He was beginning to get angry.

"I want it, but I do not have it," Lai Choi San said. Slocum heard the honesty in her soft words.

"Who does have it?"

Lai Choi San said nothing. Slocum chanced a quick glance up and saw a thoughtful expression on her face. Somehow, she was finding out that little tidbit—and Slocum had failed.

"What are you going to do with me?"

"You search for the jade crown to give back to Sir William?"

Slocum hesitated. He had been lying to everybody about his real intentions. The time to start telling the truth was at hand. After all, he had nothing to lose.

"I was going to give it to Little Pete."

"The Sum Yop leader? Why?"

Slocum felt a surge of confidence now. He had surprised the pirate captain.

"I owe a debt to Ah Ming. Giving the jade crown to Little Pete will erase the debt."

Lai Choi San remained silent as she turned this over in her mind.

"You owe me a debt. You have violated the rules of my ship. To remove this debt of honor, you will work as one of the crew."

The heavy foot slammed him flat, then disappeared. Slocum got to his feet and stared into Lai Choi San's impassive face.

"You will be at the orders of any crew member," she said. "You will be the lowest of the low." Lai Choi San stepped back and spoke rapidly in Chinese. Then she turned her back on Slocum and went to her cabin. When she stood in the doorway, she glanced back over her shoulder, a slight smile turning up the corners of her mouth. With that, she disappeared. The door slammed hard behind her like some peal of doom for Slocum.

"Go. Work," ordered a sailor. The others laughed. Some things were universal, and mocking whoever was on the bottom rung of the ladder was one of them. Slocum balled his fists, then relaxed. Lai Choi San had caught him fair and square. He would work at whatever task they set for him until he could jump ship and get back to dry land. He had avoided San Francisco shanghaiers. He wouldn't let a Chinese captain, even one as pretty as Lai Choi San, impress him into her crew.

The sailors pushed and shoved him around until he got the idea that he was supposed to be scraping the deck and cleaning it. Through the night he worked until he was woozy. The crew ashore brought the new spar on board. As far as Slocum could tell, it was not for repair but replacement, should it be needed. From his position on hands and knees with a horsehair brush scrubbing the planking, he watched as the Celestials secured the spar on the deck. Some went aloft and examined the topmost crossbeam. From all the shouting and yammering, the ones on the deck began shortening the beam they had brought aboard.

By the time sunlight poked above the land, Slocum was so tired he could hardly lift his arms. It quickly became apparent, after a single bowl of rice shared with the others, that his workday was just beginning. When they saw he could tie knots, he was put to work with the rope used in the rigging. By the time the sun was fully up, Slocum wondered why they were not sailing. The junk was in tip-top shape, from what he could tell. The crew moved around restlessly, looking for trouble and occasionally finding it. Twice Lai Choi San stopped fights.

Slocum had seen the same problems in garrison-duty soldiers. They were keyed for one thing: fighting. These men sailed and fought. When their primary mission was denied them, they sought outlets—usually trying to do the things they were trained for.

Another hour passed. Slocum worked on the top deck where the captain would stand when the ship was at sea. He patched some rot on the rudder arm and was taking his time looking as if he was finished to give himself a rest. The usual tormentors in the crew were all distracted from poking and prodding him to great work when the lookout high on the center mast shouted and pointed.

A burly Celestial waved to them from the shore, then dived into the water and swam quickly. When he came aboard, shaking water off like a wet dog, the others gathered around. All of them called out what had to be questions. They fell silent and parted for their captain.

Slocum got a good look at the newcomer for the first time. He wondered where Lai Choi San's first mate had been and what he had to say. With head bowed, Sung spoke for some time. Lai Choi San nodded occasionally, then waved her arm and pointed out to sea.

A great cheer went up. The garrison duty was past. The sailors clambered into the rigging and began unfurling the triangular, parti-colored sails.

The woman came to the top deck and ignored Slocum. He continued his nonwork on the rudder until she brushed him away. Her quick, knowing eyes looked at what he had done. She nodded once. Slocum knew that if he had tried to sabotage the junk, he would be hanging from the top yardarm, a rope around his neck.

As it was, he merely continued as the ship's slave.

Sung came and stood just behind his mistress, head still bowed. Slocum wondered what terrible thing the man had done to work so hard at sucking up to Lai Choi San. She continued to snap out what Slocum took to be questions and Sung answered briefly. The only word Slocum understood was *Portobello*. When he had made his way along the Embarcadero, he had seen a sailing ship of that name.

Slocum grasped the railing to keep from being tossed overboard when the junk lurched under full sail. The wind caught the canvas and propelled the ship with surprising speed. For a moment Slocum wondered why he had not let the sudden jerk carry him off the ship. With the junk moving as swiftly as it was, Lai Choi San would never return for him. Whatever information Sung had brought lit a fire under her.

"You are used to ships, Mr. Slocum?" came the unexpected question.

"Once or twice," he said, "I was on a Mississippi riverboat."

"That is an inland river?"

"A big one," he said. "More than a mile across in places."

Lai Choi San chuckled. "You think that is a big river? You should see the Yangtze. It is wider than ten *li*. The current is swift, also, carrying the life of China with it."

"Are you going back to China soon?"

"You fear we sail now for the Flowery Kingdom with you?" She shook her head sadly. "If only that were possible."

"What your mate told you will make it happen soon, won't it?"

The woman spun and stared at him. Then she laughed. It was not a friendly laugh.

"You are more observant than I thought, Mr. Slocum. You are a dangerous man—in your way."

"What's aboard the *Portobello* that you want?"

This time she spun on him and laid a sharp-edged knife against his throat.

"If I thought you knew anything about this, I would kill you." He did not flinch. She took the knife away but did not sheath it. "At the first sign of treachery, you will be killed. Sung will kill you. He has wanted to do so from the moment you and Sir William came aboard the ship in San Francisco."

From the corner of his eye Slocum saw how the huge, hulking first mate tensed at the name "Sir William." Things began to fall into place.

"He was supposed to steal the jade on the night of the exhibition opening and failed."

"Do not be too clever for your own good," she warned.

Slocum saw nothing to lose. She would kill him on a whim. He had missed his chance of falling overboard and getting back to land. Like it or not, he had made his decision to see this through, wherever it led.

Sung grabbed him by the arm and shoved him down the steps to the main deck where he was put to work again, this time making certain the decking was properly tarred and sealed. Slocum knew they could have forced him below-decks to work on the hand-operated bilge pumps. Here he was in the open air and could look around as the junk sailed. After careful observation of the way the land moved in relation to the ship, Slocum figured that they were sailing northward along the coast, heading back toward San Francisco. It took only this single fact to lead him to Lai Choi San's battle plan.

The pirate ship would intercept the *Portobello* and steal whatever was aboard. From all Lai Choi San had said, she wanted only one thing: her emperor's jade crown. How the crown had gotten aboard the sailing ship or who had stolen it were mysteries that Slocum did not need to solve. It was enough to know where the crown was.

Long before the *Portobello* was sighted by the lookout high in the rigging, Slocum had worked out a plan so he would be the one who recovered the jade crown. Returning

to San Francisco would be easy enough once he got off the
junk. A quick trade with Little Pete would get him Ah
Ming's father. Then, with his debts all erased, he could
hightail it. Desert was fine. Or mountains, in spite of the
winter storms. Anywhere that was not a San Francisco
filled with scheming Celestials.

The junk veered sharply, causing him to lose his balance. He caught himself on the railing, amid a wall of water crashing down. He flinched but held on tight. Getting
drowned now was not in the cards since he had gone
through too much getting to this point.

The *Portobello* saw the junk tacking toward it but did
not change course. The Cape schooners hugged the coast
all the way, only venturing into empty sea when they
reached Colombia and headed directly for the East Coast,
stopping over in Cuba. Such ships were used to considerable
traffic all around them, but the *Portobello* captain recognized the danger immediately. Semaphore signals flashed
that Slocum could not read. He doubted Lai Choi San could,
either. Nothing mattered to her now but getting close enough
to board.

The pirates not engaged in working the sails all flocked
to the starboard side, knives and swords ready. The few
who carried pistols were armed with single-shot black
powder weapons. Slocum itched for his six-gun, but he had
no idea where Lai Choi San had put it. For all he knew, she
had tossed it over the side.

"Ahoy, steer clear of us!" yelled a mate in the prow of
the *Portobello*. "We have right-of-way!"

Lai Choi San snapped one final order and then fell silent.
Slocum felt the expectation of battle building among the
crew. They had done this before. This was what they
lived—and died—for.

"Veer off!"

The junk arrowed directly for the other ship, then turned
and seemed to skid against the water, coming up side by
side in a maneuver Slocum found both fascinating and
adroit. Lai Choi San's sailors were expert. The ships hardly

bumped when the pirates threw grappling hooks over the other ship's railings.

Slocum saw the *Portobello* crew rushing on deck and dropping from the rigging, reaching for belaying pins and other weapons. Compared to the junk's crew, they were woefully unarmed.

"Repel boarders," screamed the ship's captain. Slocum wondered if he had ever been in combat, much less attacked by pirates. He doubted it. The *Portobello's* captain shouted contradictory orders and caused more confusion among his crew than the swarm of Celestial pirates now attacking him.

"To the cargo hold," Lai Choi San said. "I will not leave you aboard my ship, Mr. Slocum. You would find a way to scuttle it."

"Mighty long walk to shore, if I did that." He obeyed the woman when she pulled out a knife and prodded him with it.

Judging distances and the up-and-down motion of the two ships on the waves, Slocum jumped. He miscalculated enough so that he lost his balance and went tumbling. Lai Choi San followed. She landed lightly on her feet and immediately drove her knife tip into a *Portobello* crewman's eye. The man screamed in agony and whirled away. Lai Choi San took two quick steps behind him and slashed his throat. She stepped over his fallen body without so much as a glance.

Slocum got to his feet. Slipping in blood, he made his way to the stern where the captain's and passengers' cabins stood with doors open. If the jade crown was aboard, it would be there and not in the hold. A quick glance into the captain's cabin showed total disarray. Slocum rummaged about but saw nothing of the jade crown. He backed out and bumped into the captain. The man's eyes were wide and unseeing because of the complete fear clutching at him.

"Where is the jade crown?" Slocum demanded of the man.

"We're being attacked by pirates. Pirates!" The captain turned and charged off, shouting incoherently. Slocum started after him, then stopped. The man would be no good even if he did catch him. Fear seized him completely.

Slocum poked his head into another cabin. A familiar trunk stood open. He hurried to it and began yanking women's clothing out. The more furiously he worked, the more Slocum seethed.

Tess Lawrence was aboard. These were her clothes. When the trunk was empty, he examined it for secret compartments. Nothing. The search of the rest of the cabin was done quickly and produced similar results. Nothing. Not even a small piece of jade.

Slocum charged from the cabin and crashed into two seamen holding Lai Choi San. He bowled them over, letting the Chinese captain jerk free.

"Look out!" Slocum cried. One sailor pulled out a small pistol and cocked it. Slocum launched himself, grabbed the man's arm and dragged it down so the bullet went into the deck. Not stopping, Slocum swung a long, looping haymaker that drove his fist all the way to his forearm into the man's belly. The sailor gasped, turned green and passed out.

Slocum got his balance back in time to see Lai Choi San finish cutting the other sailor's throat. Again she killed without any hint of remorse.

Sung yelled to her. She turned her back to Slocum, giving him the chance to end her life. On the deck lay the unconscious sailor's pistol. He swept it up, cocked, aimed and fired.

Lai Choi San glanced over her shoulder at him, then up to the poop deck. Slocum had expertly drilled another sailor attempting to kill her. This time she smiled. A little. Then she walked away, as if this were nothing but a Sunday stroll to stop at an open hatch. She pointed, grated out commands, then stepped away as her pirates pulled four crates out of the hold.

Slocum read the destination stenciled on the sides: NEW YORK CITY. He wondered what was going on. Sir William had said his jade would be exhibited in Boston. Shrugging off this minor discrepancy, Slocum started to look for Tess.

"Back to the junk if you desire a long life, Mr. Slocum," ordered Lai Choi San. "We have company."

"What's that?" He turned to see a long column of black smoke rising from empty ocean.

"A steam frigate. If you remain, you will be tried for piracy. I have heard they hang offenders from the yardarm after only a brief trial at sea."

Lai Choi San jumped to the railing, gauged the distance and leaped back onto her ship.

Slocum knew she was right. Unless he killed every last surviving sailor aboard the *Portobello*, he would be charged and convicted of piracy. What decided him was Sung struggling with Tess Lawrence. The woman fought hard, but the Celestial sailor was too strong for her. He made the leap back onto the junk with her tucked under one arm.

Finding a dry spot amid the puddles of blood, Slocum dug in his toes, ran and then made a powerful jump at the now-separating ships. He kicked hard and managed to grab the railing of the junk as the last grapple was cut free. The *Portobello* rapidly fell astern.

He clung to the railing, toes kicking against the slick side of the junk until a powerful hand reached down and seized his arms. Sung pulled Slocum into the junk and dropped him like he would a fish. Slocum kicked about for a moment, then got to his feet.

Sung was gone. The first mate already shouted orders to the men in the rigging who expertly unfurled all their sails.

"We cannot outrun a steam-powered vessel," Lai Choi San said to Slocum, "but perhaps we will not have to fight. Their smoke remains black."

"What's that mean?"

The frigate had come closer. Slocum guessed the U.S. Navy vessel was less than a mile away. Although the range was far too great, the frigate fired its forward gun. The shell fell woefully short, but it was only intended to be a cautionary shot. "Surrender or die" was the plain message carried by the small geyser where the shell exploded.

"They waste ammunition," Lai Choi San said almost gleefully.

"You said they'd catch us. They've got heavier guns, bigger than your cannon." Slocum pointed to the brass cannon at the stern. Two sailors stood by it. Slocum remembered all too well how effective it had been against the navy launch back in San Francisco Bay. There, however, the range had been short and there was no chance of return fire.

"The smoke, Mr. Slocum, the black smoke. It tells the story."

"You can outrun a steam frigate?"

"Yes," the pirate said softly.

Slocum watched nervously as the frigate steamed closer and closer. The junk sailed along, skimming the water with the wind catching the sails and forcing them to billow to their fullest, but the steam-driven ship overtook them and angled to cut off the junk's escape to the north.

Slocum stiffened when he heard a loud explosion. The frigate's smokestacks vented a huge puff of black smoke and then . . . nothing. The junk kept moving with the wind and soon left the frigate behind, dead in the water.

"The smoke should have been white," Lai Choi San said. "There was a problem with their boilers. The harder they pushed their engines, the closer to disaster they sailed." She laughed. "It will be days before they can repair a ruptured boiler." Lai Choi San sobered. "By then I will be ready to sail for China."

She pointed to the crates on deck.

Slocum felt the jade crown slipping from his fingers. Ah Ming's father's bones might never be returned to her by the Sum Yop tong. Lai Choi San's victory was his failure.

17

"Come into my cabin, Mr. Slocum," the pirate captain said. She half turned and pointed, as if she were ordering a small child about.

He cast a quick look at the crates, then shrugged it off. He would have to find some way of getting the jade crown out of those boxes, but it had to wait until he had dealt with Lai Choi San. That looked to be a dilemma. She was the absolute ruler in his small floating kingdom, with an army of cutthroats to do her bidding. The only real chance Slocum had for being rescued lay behind him, helpless on the high seas with a ruptured boiler.

Lai Choi San closed the door behind him. Slocum noticed that she also slid a locking bolt into place. She brushed past him as she went to the stack of papers on her desk. She began idly leafing through them.

"Why did you do it?"

"What?" The question took Slocum by surprise.

"Aboard the sailing ship, why did you save my life?"

"I remember doing it twice, now that you mention it." Slocum tried to figure out where she would have stashed his six-shooter. The obvious places were all closed. Drawers and small cabinets were secured against the rocking motion of the junk. If he began hunting, she would know instantly. The knives sheathed at her belt were not for decoration. More than he cared to remember, Lai Choi San had shown that.

"Yes, twice. The question remains unanswered. Why did you save my life? Twice?"

"A lovely woman like you dying seemed to be a waste," he said. He surprised himself when he realized there was more than a nugget of truth in his words.

"I am a pirate who enslaved you. I made you do demeaning tasks."

"No work's demeaning, if you get paid for it," Slocum said.

"You think you will be paid for scraping decks and dipping your hands into tar to seal leaks?"

"That needed doing. Wouldn't another of your crew been doing those very things if I hadn't been here?"

"Yes," she said, sounding a little perplexed. "You are a complicated man, Mr. Slocum. I do not understand you."

"That's all right. Nobody understands much of what goes on in the world." He slipped around the cabin, sharp green eyes hunting for either his six-shooter or another weapon.

"I want your opinion of this," she said, turning. She held a sheet of paper in her hand, but other than a few of the Chinese ideograms the page was almost entirely covered with a picture. For a moment, Slocum couldn't figure out what it was. Then he grinned when he made out the tangle of arms and legs.

"A couple folks who enjoy each other's company, I'd say. It's hard to tell what's going on with all that clothing in the way, though."

"It does not have to be in the way," Lai Choi San said. She handed him the erotic drawing, then began unfastening the frogs holding her tunic closed. Slocum looked from the drawing to the real thing. Bit by bit her pale flesh appeared. With a shrug of her shoulders, Lai Choi San got rid of the quilted tunic and stood naked to the waist in front of him.

"The picture's nowhere as good as the real thing," he said, tossing the drawing aside and stepping closer. Lai Choi San waited for him, not moving a muscle. He reached out and ran his fingers lightly up her right arm. He felt the flesh quivering under his touch.

He gripped her shoulder and pulled her closer. She took a small step. He ran his hand from her shoulder around and down so he pressed his palm into one of her apple-sized breasts. This produced a small moan from her. When he similarly covered her other tit with his hand, Lai Choi San closed her eyes and let out a long sigh.

Slocum squeezed down gently. He felt the dark nubs of her nipples begin to throb with desire. He crushed down, and this brought the first real response from her. She stepped even closer so her breasts were mashed flat. She put her arms around his neck and drew him down. He thought she wanted to kiss him. Instead, Lai Choi San guided his face down between her breasts.

He kissed tender flesh. She moaned louder now. He moved his hands around behind her as his mouth began working all over those tasty mounds. He licked and kissed and then nipped gently as he reached the summit of one breast. Sucking the nip between his lips, he felt it throbbing and pulsing with every beat of her heart. A quick stab of his tongue forced the nipple down into the softness below. Lai Choi San moved closer, trying to get more of her into his mouth.

Slocum's tongue whirled about like a prairie tornado, then drifted lower. He found the deep well of her navel and sucked there for a moment before driving his tongue inward. Moving around, he found the ties holding her trousers on and unfastened them. Using only his lips and tongue, he pushed them off her slender hips until they fell to the deck. Between her legs nestled a tiny puff of pubic hair more like a bottle brush than what he was used to finding.

The pirate captain parted her stance and opened herself to him. He pressed his face into her and licked along the slit until he tasted salty juices leaking outward. Slocum looked up at her. The woman's face was tense with sexual need.

"Show me how to get into the position on the paper," he said.

She said nothing as she pushed him away. Slocum lost his balance and sat on the deck, his feet flat on the floor and his knees bent. As he started to straighten, she stepped over his body and lowered herself. Slocum saw how they might fit together.

"Get my jeans off," he said.

She already worked to accomplish that feat. He had to lift himself up so she could slide his pants over his hips, but when she did his erection jutted upward. She sank down quickly, her knees on the floor as she spread wide for his entry.

Slocum gasped as she came down upon him. There was no hesitation. One instant he was out in the cold, the next he was surrounded by hot, wet female. When he was entirely within her, she put her hands behind her on his upraised knees and rocked back. Slocum thought she was going to break him off inside her. He sat up and put his arms around her waist for support.

The rocking motion of the ship helped them get into the proper rhythm. Lai Choi San rocked with one tempo, Slocum another and the ship added a third. He slipped in and out of her tightness only an inch, but the motion was more than enough to excite him. She began tensing and relaxing her powerful inner muscles around him, squeezing and kneading and making him feel as if her hand worked knowingly on him.

"You're good," he gasped out. He stared into her lovely face. Lai Choi San said nothing. Her eyes were closed, and her lips thinned to a line as she concentrated on the sensations rippling through her.

Slocum closed his own eyes and focused on what was going on. Their motions were intensely arousing. A white-hot core blazed within his loins, then spread slowly like spilled kerosene with a match tossed into it.

Slocum pulled himself up and forced his face between

her breasts. He felt as if they were bent into a pretzel, but what a rush of sensation every time they moved! He fought to hold back the fierce tide rising within his loins. He felt her body quivering as she moved faster around him. He forced his hips off the deck as she began twisting from side to side. Coupled with the up-and-down toss of the ship, Slocum was no longer able to restrain himself. He let out a low, guttural groan and pumped fiercely into her.

She was more subdued. Lai Choi San gasped, then bit her lower lip. He knew she was getting off but hardly a sound escaped her lips. Then they sank back to the deck, both spent from their exertions.

"How was it?" Slocum asked.

"There are many pages in that book," Lai Choi San said, a tiny smile curling her lips.

"You're a surprising woman. Pirate and ship's captain and—"

Before Slocum could finish, a harsh rapping came at the locked cabin door. He could not understand the rapid stream of Chinese, but he caught the gist of it. Slocum flopped back on the floor as Lai Choi San lithely rose and stepped away from him. She dressed quickly. Slocum wanted to watch but knew when she opened the door, he had better have all his clothes on. He grabbed his pants, rocked back on his shoulders and pulled them on, both legs at the same time. He rolled onto hands and knees, then came to his feet. Quick fingers finished the buttons on his fly and got the rest of his clothes into respectable shape. It was not so much for him that he dressed quickly as for Lai Choi San. She had to maintain discipline aboard the ship. If it got out she was trying out every erotic drawing in a thick book with a foreign devil hardly above a slave in status, it would harm her standing as captain of the junk.

She did not even look in his direction as she settled her quilted jacket, then opened the door. Sung stood outside, looking worried. He twisted his head about to get a look into the room, but by now Slocum stood docilely, no threat to Lai Choi San or anyone else.

Sung rattled on for almost a minute. Lai Choi San only nodded once before sending him on his way.

"What is it?"

She looked at him with expressionless eyes. Slocum could not believe they had made love only minutes before and she looked so impassive now.

"The crates are ready to open. The crown must be in one of them."

Slocum had nothing to say. He wanted that crown for reasons that Lai Choi San probably understood but would never allow to happen. She had her own uses for the crown and cared nothing about Ah Ming wanting her father's bones returned to China.

Slocum trailed her outside onto the deck. Four crates had been lined up. The crew hovered about the wood crates, pry bars in hand. Lai Choi San nodded once and four men set to ripping open the crates.

Lai Choi San walked over and looked into the first crate to be opened. She began rummaging through the excelsior and removed several pieces of jade that had been displayed at the museum. She treated each piece with reverence, but her obvious apprehension mounted as she emptied the second and third cases and had not found the jade crown. Slocum stared into the fourth crate, as if he could see through solid wood and locate the crown.

She worked methodically and soon had taken out everything within this crate, too.

"Where is the crown?"

"Not here," Slocum said, answering because she had spoken in English. He was the only one likely to understand.

"You do not know where it is. I watched your face. You thought it was in one of these crates."

"Only because you did," Slocum said. "I'm proving to be a lousy tracker. I lost the trail some time ago." He said nothing about being the one to lose the jade crown. The lump on the back of his head still throbbed where he had gotten clubbed.

"Get her on deck," Lai Choi San snapped.

For a moment, Slocum did not understand who the woman meant. Then he remembered. Tess Lawrence had been aboard the *Portobello* to watch over the crates around the Cape to Sir William's exhibition back East.

"This is the jade from the museum—what remained after the jade crown was stolen," Slocum said. "She can't know what happened to it."

Lai Choi San spun from Slocum and spoke rapid-fire Chinese to Sung. The first mate replied in the same rapid fashion. The pirate captain turned back to Slocum.

"Sung says he watched as the woman and her lover took the crown aboard the ship. He was unable to steal it, so he did the right thing. He rode down the coast until he saw my ship, then told of the crown being aboard."

"But it wasn't," Slocum protested. He was confused about the part of Tess having a lover and having the jade crown. If he had been able to talk to Sung directly, he was sure the mistakes could be cleared up. The only one Tess had ever shown any affection toward—other than the single time with Slocum in the curator's office—was Sir William. And he had no time for her.

"It was."

"You said she boarded the *Portobello* with her lover. Sir William?"

"No, not the pompous ass who stole the crown from my emperor," Lai Choi San. "Another."

Slocum tried to remember seeing Tess with another man. While she had spoken to many during the course of the exhibit at the museum, there had been no one who had produced that spark of sensuality he had found when they had made love on the curator's desk. She had been harried and all business and a lot of other things, but never sexual.

Except toward Sir William. Slocum still wondered if the British explorer had any idea that Tess had set her cap for him.

"Bring her on deck. I want the crown!" Lai Choi San screamed in English, but her crew understood. Sung hurried to drop into the hold. In a few minutes he returned, carrying a bound Tess over his shoulder like a sack of suet. She struggled, kicking and trying to get away but he was too strong and her bonds were too tight.

Sung dropped her unceremoniously onto the deck at Lai Choi San's feet. The pirate captain glared down at her captive.

"Where is it?"

"What are you talking about?"

"The emperor's crown. You stole it, you and your lover. I want it or you will pay dearly!"

Slocum watched as Tess wiggled about and got her feet under her. With her hands tied behind her back, she wasn't as steady as she might have been. The pitch and roll of the junk added to her woe. She almost got to her feet when a particularly strong swell unbalanced her again. No one offered to help her rise, and Slocum held back. She had not seen him yet.

When Tess finally got up, she thrust her face into Lai Choi San's.

"Go to hell!"

"You are wrong," Lai Choi San said softly. Slocum had never heard such menace in a woman's voice before. "You are the one who will experience hell." She snapped her fingers. Sung and two others grabbed Tess and spun her about.

A large hook had been fastened to a rope dangling from the lowest yardarm. Slocum had seen hooks like this used in slaughterhouses to hold sides of beef. He started to speak, then realized Lai Choi San did not intend to impale Tess on the hook. In a way, her intentions were even crueler. The hook slid under the ropes binding her wrists. At Sung's order, two men tugged on the other end of the rope.

Tess let out a squeal of surprise, quickly followed by one of stark pain as her feet left the deck. She dangled inches above it. Her entire weight was supported by her wrists. The pressure on her shoulders had to be excruciating from the way she had turned pale with shock.

Slowly turning, she swung back to face Lai Choi San.

"You will remain this way until you tell me where the jade crown is."

"No, never," spat Tess. Slocum admired her courage. Once she told Lai Choi San what she wanted to know, there was no reason for the pirate captain to let her live. As she twisted back and forth, Slocum came into her view. Her eyes went wide. Then she spat at him. "You—you—traitor!"

"She sees you for what you are, Mr. Slocum," Lai Choi San said, grinning wickedly.

Slocum did not answer. The pirate knew how to manipulate people. With one sentence she had turned Tess against him by confirming the bound woman's suspicions. Even more, she had added to Tess's sense of isolation. She would find no allies aboard the junk.

"How could you?" Tess tried to kick at him but the movement sent new lances of pain into her shoulders and upper body. She swallowed hard to keep from showing it. She failed.

"If you do not tell me what I want to know, you will be tortured."

"Will be? Will be?" cried Tess. "What are you doing to me now?"

"Preparing you." Lai Choi San walked over and ran the back of her hand over Tess's cheek. "You are so fair. The sun never touches your lovely, smooth skin." Lai Choi San whipped out a knife and slashed. Tess's blouse parted all the way to the waist. More quick moves completely cut the garment from her body so she was naked to the waist.

Slocum saw the Chinese sailors nudging one another and trying not to smirk. He wondered if they had been promised Tess after she told Lai Choi San what she wanted to know.

"The sun will burn your flesh. All of it," Lai Choi San said, pressing the tip of her knife into Tess's nipple until a drop of blood formed. "You will find it quite painful. You will beg for death but will be denied. Until you tell me where you hid the emperor's crown."

Tess clamped her mouth tightly shut and glared at her

tormenter. Lai Choi San stepped away, then barked orders
in Chinese. The crew rushed to obey. She turned, stopped
and looked at Slocum with cold eyes.

"Get to work. The upper deck needs scrubbing." Then
she disappeared into her cabin.

"You son of a bitch!" Tess shouted at him. "How could
you throw in with them? They're pirates!"

Slocum felt eyes on him. Sung watched, as did several
of the crew. They might not speak English but he believed
they understood it well enough to report to Lai Choi San if
he said anything that might give Tess comfort. He walked
away, the woman screaming curses at him. When her voice
turned hoarse, she stopped yelling and began sobbing.

As he worked scrubbing the upper deck, Slocum
watched Tess swing to and fro in her misery. Occasionally
a crewman would come by and touch her. She flinched
away, but there was nothing more she could do. Slocum
seethed at the indignity heaped on her, but he had to bide
his time. He knew Lai Choi San watched him as closely—
more closely—to see what he would do.

The one thing in Tess's favor were the heavy clouds
moving in from the ocean. A storm was building and cut
off the sunlight, saving her from slow roasting. Still, being
half naked on a ship this late in the autumn turned her flesh
blue from cold. Burn or freeze. Neither was a decent fate.

Even as that idea crossed Slocum's mind, he harkened
back to his ill-fated crossing of the Sierras. Freezing to
death. Not a fit way to die by accident. It was certainly no
way to die intentionally.

He scrubbed harder on the deck and waited.

Dinner was the usual bowl of rice. This time the crew
sat on deck, using their chopsticks to slide the gummy rice
into their mouths, but their eyes were fixed on Tess.

Slocum used the diversion the woman afforded to slip
into Lai Choi San's cabin. He had thought hard about the
layout and where she might have put his holster and six-
shooter. A cabinet opened to reveal not only his six-gun but
several others. Slocum emptied the other pistols, then

made sure his own was ready for action. It was twilight outside, and the junk moved closer to the land, hunting for a harbor to weather out the storm.

He left the captain's cabin and hung his pistol in his holster over the railing. It would be exposed to the salt spray lashing against the landward side of the junk but would not be noticed by the crew in the dark. Slocum sat and watched as Tess swung like the pendulum in a Regulator clock. Every swing put that much more strain on her wrists and arms, but there was nothing he could do about it at the moment.

The night turned blacker than the inside of a coal sack when the storm hit. Rain pelted the deck and tossed the ship about. At times, Tess was swung so far that she was over the water. This gave Slocum an idea. Rescuing her would be dangerous, but he doubted either of them had long to live if they stayed aboard the pirate ship.

Lai Choi San came from the hold barking orders. Crewmen scampered into the rigging with surprising skill. The wind and rain did not bother them at all as they furled the sails and made them fast. Lai Choi San called again. Sung ran up. She pointed to Tess, then gestured. Slocum decided she wanted to know where her pet deck scrubber had gotten off to. He hunkered down in the shadow near the railing.

Both the captain and her first mate disappeared into the hold, giving Slocum what might be his only chance to save Tess. If the Chinese pirates found him, they would lock him up—or worse. Slocum grabbed his six-shooter and holster, strapped it around his waist and pulled out the small blunt knife he had used to scrape the decks.

Tess did not see him approaching, but the men in the rigging did. They yelled out a warning to Sung.

Slocum drew his six-shooter as he strode forward, aimed and fired point-blank, hitting the man in the middle of the chest. For a split second, Slocum thought he had missed. Then the first mate dropped to his knees and clutched at the wound. There was no turning back now. If Slocum failed, he was a dead man.

Even if he succeeded in carrying out his harebrained

plan, he might die. At least that death would happen while making a bid for freedom.

Slocum jumped to the railing, then leaped over, grabbing the rope above Tess.

"What're you doing?"

"Save your breath. You're going to need it." He pressed close to the half-naked woman as the tossing ship sent them gyrating around wildly. He began sawing at the rope with the blunt scraping knife. Strand by strand the thick rope parted, but Slocum had to be exactly right when he cut the final strands.

He wrapped his left arm around Tess's waist, then slashed down savagely as the junk rolled to the side.

Tess let out a scream as the rope parted and they plunged downward, past the railing and directly into the churning water.

They hit the water. The cold drove the breath from Slocum's lungs. He felt Tess react to the sudden icy immersion and suck in water. Kicking hard, he got them to the surface. She sputtered and retched to get the water from her lungs.

Slocum immediately saw the flaw in his plan. Tess was still bound with her hands behind her, and he was weighted down by the six-shooter around his waist. A wave rose above them and smashed down with a power that should never have existed in the world.

Once more Slocum and Tess were driven underwater. This time, Slocum had no strength left.

18

Slocum lashed out with the knife still clutched in his hand. Tess yelped and he knew she was still alive, but a wave washed over them again, carrying them around and around for what stretched to an eternity. When they broke the surface again, Slocum was gasping for air. He stabbed out again, this time finding the ropes holding her wrists together. A powerful slash. Then the blade slipped from his fingers and he dropped it into the churning sea.

"Try to get free," he shouted in her ear. He clung to her fiercely, but the strength was flowing from him like the very water pouring from above. He felt Tess strain and then nothing.

"My arms. Free," she gasped out. "But they're dead. I can't feel anything with my hands."

"Relax and lie back," Slocum said. "I'll pull you along." He hoped he was not making a promise he could not keep. With powerful kicks, he got himself under her so he could partially support her weight. With his left arm still curled around her, he began kicking and stroking with his right arm. Not sure what direction he went, he only rode with the waves.

They both let out loud cries of fear when the ocean rose

under them and tossed them high into the air. Slocum landed with impressive force, Tess atop him. For a few seconds he lay stunned. Then the wave swept over him again, trying to pull him back into its watery bosom.

"Land, we're on land. Gotta get farther inland." Slocum tugged and pulled what was little more than dead weight. He felt Tess trying to help, but there was no strength left in her.

He stubbed his toe and fell heavily, taking her with him. This time when the pursuing wave clawed wetly at them, it found no purchase.

"We made it," he said. "We made it!"

Tess shivered violently. Slocum kept his arm around her until he could muster enough force of will to stand. Even then he was as weak as a kitten. Together they managed to walk a dozen yards into the shelter of tall trees. Here, protected from the blast of the wind and the worst of the spray from the surf, they sank down.

"I'll build a fire," he said. "You're going to die of . . . chill." Slocum stared at Tess Lawrence. The woman had shrunken into a fraction of her usual vital self. Her teeth chattered, and her skin was blue from exposure. *Anne* came unbidden to his mind. He had lost one woman to freezing. He would not lose another.

"H-how're y-you going to build a fire?"

Slocum fumbled in his pocket and came out with the tin holding his lucifers. He might be drenched but the matches would be dry in their watertight tin. A few minutes later he had collected enough firewood and brush to start a small fire. It sputtered and hissed and burned quickly. He hastened to add larger twigs and then finally a dried limb the size of his wrist.

The heat was welcome but not enough. He built the fire higher and hotter until Tess stopped shivering so much. She huddled near the heat and looked up at him.

"I'm naked," she said.

"Halfway," he allowed.

"Isn't there something you can do?"

"Not right now. My own clothes are sopping wet." Slocum took off his shirt and wrung it out. He tried to dry it for her but did not get very far.

"The hell with it. Hold me. I need you to hold me or I'm going to die," she said.

Slocum realized she was right. He piled more wood nearby, then sat with Tess, his arms around her, his wet shirt covering them both. Eventually the heat dried the shirt and afforded them a little more comfort. Sometime in the night, Tess nodded off. Slocum forced himself to remain awake to feed the fire. Without it they both might die from exposure.

This time it was different. By morning, he was stiff and cold but both of them were still alive.

"You saved me. Why?"

"I couldn't let Lai Choi San torture you to death," he said.

"You'd thrown in with them. You and the pirates. I don't understand."

"I was their prisoner, too. I just had a little more freedom to move around."

"I'm so confused," Tess said. Slocum fed the fire until it blazed again. While she sat and soaked up the warmth, he went hunting and clubbed a pair of squirrels for breakfast. Although Tess's nose wrinkled at the sight of the scrawny animals, she ate most of them after Slocum had done as good a job cooking as he could over such a hot fire.

Only then did he ask, "Lai Choi San's first mate said you had the jade crown with you on the ship. How'd you get it back?"

From the way she averted her eyes and stared into the fire, Slocum knew part of the answer.

"You stole it," he said. "You and your boyfriend."

"How'd you know about Jason?" Tess looked up at him, frightened. "Does everyone know everything?"

"I don't know squat," Slocum admitted. "That's what I heard. Was it Jason who slugged me and stole the crown?"

Tess nodded.

"So you two were in cahoots to steal the jade crown from Sir William all the time?"

"Not exactly. The idea didn't spring full-blown like Minerva from the head of Zeus. A small seed of an idea just sprouted and grew until I knew we could get away with it."

"After Lai Choi San's pirates tried to steal it at the opening of the exhibition?"

"If we could place the blame somewhere else, we could get away scot-free," Tess said. "When Sir William left everything about the shipping in my hands, I thought we might be able to steal the entire collection."

"I saw the crates. They were marked as being shipped to New York."

"Jason is from there. He said he knew men who could pay huge amounts of money for Chinese jade. But the crown was the best of the pieces. Worth a fortune."

"A small fortune or a big one?"

"Huge," Tess confided. "It is a Tang Dynasty artifact, dating from AD 600."

"Instead of sending it all by train to Boston, you were going with it to New York. Sir William would never have found you."

"That was what I thought. Jason had other ideas, apparently. The whore's son!"

Tess began shaking again, this time from anger. Slocum draped his shirt over her bare shoulders. The cold morning air slipped across his own bare chest, but he was better able to tolerate it than the woman. Moreover, modesty dictated that she be covered.

"Why wasn't the crown in the crates? Lai Choi San isn't one to miss something she wants so bad."

"Jason, he, oh, I hate him!"

"He double-crossed you?"

"He put me aboard the *Portobello*. I knew what was in the crates. I thought I had the box in our cabin with the jade crown. He slipped off the ship seconds before we sailed. I didn't realize that he had gone until I looked in the box and found only a brick. When I searched, one of the sailors told me he had seen Jason standing on the dock."

"With the crown."

"Yes, with the damned crown. I could have killed him, but we were already through the Golden Gate and setting course down the coast."

"That's about the time the pirates attacked."

"They can keep the rest of the jade artifacts. Those are really minor pieces. Oh, worth something, but only a fraction what the crown is." Tess looked up at him. "John, help me get the crown from him. Do that and you can have anything you want." Tess let his shirt slip open to expose one breast in obvious display of what his reward might be.

"What if I wanted the crown instead?"

"I—" Tess clamped her mouth shut and glared into the flames for a moment. "Take the crown. Take it, if you can kill him. I want Jason to suffer for what he's done to me."

"Lied? Stolen the crown? Or left you for the pirates?"

"All of that. I loved him. Add cheating on me to the list of reasons I want him dead."

"What about your feelings for Sir William?"

"I never . . ." Her voice trailed off. "Nothing gets past you, does it? I fell in love with him, but he didn't know I even existed. He couldn't even remember my name."

Slocum was not so sure. It just wasn't Sir William's way to show affection when he was distracted by a fabulous archaeological find like the jade and the emperor's crown. No man was likely to ignore Tess's being around. Slocum had not.

"What's your friend Jason likely to do with the crown?"

"He's not my friend." She flared, then settled down a mite. "He must have someone in San Francisco willing to buy it. If he doesn't, I suppose he'll take it back to New York."

"That means he'd go by stagecoach or railroad," Slocum said. "The *Portobello* was the only ship scheduled for the Cape Horn trip in the next few days."

"He might just leave town with it," Tess said.

Slocum thought on it. That did not ring true. He said so.

"You're right, John. It would be burning a hole in his pocket. He would want money for it, no matter what. Jason has no interest in beautiful things."

"That why he let you go?"

Tess looked up sharply and started to speak. Then her face softened.

"I don't know if you mean it or are just using me."

"You're free to go," Slocum said. He grinned and added, "Don't take my shirt, if you do go."

Tess laughed. Some of her old fire returned and turned her into a beautiful woman again, in spite of looking like a drowned rat. Her salt-caked hair hung stiffly and wind had burned her cheeks. From what Slocum could tell, Lai Choi San's intended torture of letting her sunburn had not been too effective, thanks to the storm. The woman's tender skin was again rosy with health and not at all frostbitten.

"Kiss it and make it well?" Tess saw how he was looking at her and bared her breast again.

"Later," he said. "Right now we have to get to San Francisco before your friend hightails it."

"He's not my friend!" She saw he was only joshing her and settled down.

Slocum wondered if the plow horse had wandered far—or if they were anywhere near where he had let it go free. It would be worth a few minutes to explore. If the horse was nowhere to be seen, there were other ways back to San Francisco.

"Thanks for the ride," Slocum called to the driver of the heavily laden wagon. Search as he might, he could find no trace of the plow horse he had bought in San Grigorio. After an hour hunting, Slocum could not even figure out where along the California coast they had landed. It might be north or south of the cove where Lai Choi San had put in to wait for Sung to bring her word of the jade crown. Instead of following the coastline, Slocum had convinced Tess to hike inland.

After getting over a sizable hill, they had spotted a road. Within thirty minutes he had flagged down a wagon loaded with foodstuffs heading for San Francisco and given the driver a cock-and-bull story about Tess being robbed and his horse dying under him as he chased the road agents responsible. The man had given Tess a spare blanket and let them ride into town.

When Slocum recognized some streets near Portsmouth Square, he decided it was time for them to strike out on their own.

"My pleasure," the driver said, giving Tess one last fond look. Slocum saw how she dropped to the cobblestone, letting the blanket flop open just a mite to give him his reward for being such a Good Samaritan. Slocum knew the thoughts running through the man's mind at that instant, and they had nothing to do with lending a helping hand to those in need.

The wagon rumbled on, leaving them on the sidewalk near a hissing gas lamp.

"What do we do now?" she asked.

Slocum did not want to mention that he was likely to have the On Leong tong swinging their hatchets for his head again, if they spotted him. He had lost track of time and did not know if he had gone over Ah Ming's deadline. Even if he still had time, he had no reason to seek out any of the Chinese gangs.

"We need money, we need clothes, we need someone to help us," he said.

"No, John. I couldn't!"

Their eyes locked, her blue ones wide with denial and his green ones cold with need. Neither wanted to answer questions Sir William was likely to have, but there was no one else they could turn to. Reluctantly, they started walking for the museum.

19

Sir William Macadams paced back and forth until he'd worn a dull path on the wood floor. The curator's office seemed more of a prison to him than ever. He was a man of action. He should be out on the trail of adventure, not worrying about trivial things.

Out in the museum he heard the click of soles on the floor. His heart leaped as he took a step toward the door. Then he remembered the troubles he had encountered and reversed his course, going to the desk drawer and pulling out a small pistol. He tucked it into his pocket since he was not certain he faced a challenge yet.

The office door opened a fraction of an inch.

"Who's there?" he demanded. Visions of tong killers waving about hatchets filled his vivid imagination but no one entered. "I say, who's there. Answer or be damned!"

"I prefer to stay on this side of the door," came a muffled voice.

"What nonsense is this? Show yourself, man." He drew the pistol but was hesitant about using it without some obvious threat to his person.

"Let's say I got me som'thin' you want. You got som'thin' I want, so we can do some horse trading."

"I don't need a horse. Either speak plainly or get out of here. I have serious matters on my mind that must be resolved soon." Sir William worried more and more about Tess and how she had simply vanished. Had he angered her? Or had he inadvertently told her to do something, and she foolishly acted without making him repeat it? He had checked the railroad depot and not found anyone who had either sold her a ticket to Boston or authorized shipment of the jade exhibition.

In spite of this, she was gone and so were all the pieces of jade that had been on display in the museum.

"Curse this place," Sir William grumbled. "I wish I'd never come to San Francisco!"

"Well, I kin make it a little better for you," the hidden man said. "Give me a thousand dollars, and I'll see you get your purty green stone bauble back."

"What are you going on about?" Sir William lifted the pistol and aimed it at the small opening through which the man delivered his ultimatum.

"I got the jade crown. If you want it back, gimme a thousand dollars."

"That's extortion, sir!"

"Call it what you like. I think on it as two businessmen conductin' business. I got what you want, and you got what I want. Each of us comes out ahead."

Sir William fired the small caliber pistol at the door. It tore away a hunk of wood and sent splinters flying everywhere. He cocked the pistol for a second shot.

"You crazy old coot! Kill me and you'll never find the jade. I got it hid real good. And you got to pay two thousand dollars now fer takin' a potshot at me!"

"Make it five thousand, then!" Sir William fired again. This time the man slammed the door. Ears ringing from the report, Sir William rushed to the door and flung it wide open. He pointed the small pistol this way and that but the corridor was empty.

Hearing running footsteps in the main room, Sir William hurried to follow. He caught sight of a shabbily dressed man darting into the foyer. The slamming of the outer door signaled the man's ultimate departure.

"Good riddance," Sir William said. He had no time for such foolishness. He had an assistant to find and jade to recover. He returned to the curator's office and his well-worn path to begin pacing again. It helped him think.

Jason Stark ducked as the first bullet slammed into the door. By the time Sir William had fired a second time, Stark was running like a scalded dog. The Britisher was crazy to pass up the chance to buy back the jade crown. Where would he ever find anything like it again? Stark had taken it around to his usual fences and all had turned him down. No one wanted to touch anything that might get the tong killers down on them.

Stark had tried to convince more than one of the dealers in stolen property that the hatchet men would not be interested, but all had said the same thing: stolen jade meant tong interest. Not a one of them even talked to Stark after saying that.

It had been a clever idea trying to sell the crown back to the man he had stolen it from, but Stark had not expected Sir William to be so quick on the trigger.

"Burn in hell, you damn fool," Stark muttered as he walked quickly along the road leading past the museum. "You won't ever see that damn crown again. I'll find somebody who's not scared to even look at it!"

As he mumbled to himself, an idea began to form. If none of the fences wanted to handle hot jade because of the tongs, why not try selling the jade crown directly to the tongs? He was good at making up stories. He could tell them he found it and only wanted a small reward. A couple hundred dollars would do. He didn't want to keep something that belonged to another people.

"Yeah, that sounds 'bout right," Stark said out loud. "I'm a fine, upstandin' citizen and only want to do the right thing. Returnin' it to them chinks is what I will do. A couple hunnerd dollars is better than gettin' shot at by a crazy Brit."

Stark slowed when he left Union Square and circuitously approached Dupont Gai, the main thoroughfare through the heart of Chinatown. He knew all the thieves and pickpockets in San Francisco. He knew the men who trafficked in black-market goods and bought stolen merchandise. But they were all white men. He had never set foot into Chinatown. All the stories of silent killers lifting the tops of the heads of anyone they didn't like came rushing back.

He almost retraced his steps, then found resolve. He needed the money. If Sir William was not going to pay him—and none of his usual cronies would, either—that left only one place to sell the jade crown. How hard could it be finding a tong? They were supposed to have their members all over the place. All he needed to do was make a few discreet inquiries and bang! He would make the deal.

Summoning up his courage, he walked into the section of town he had avoided since coming to San Francisco more than a month earlier. He faded back into a doorway when he saw a furtive Chinaman moving with obviously murderous intent down an alleyway. Intrigued and afraid, Stark watched as a hatchet appeared in the man's bony hand. Stark swallowed hard as the hatchet was sent spinning. From his vantage Stark could not see the victim, but he heard the hideous cry of pain, followed by a dull *thud*. He imagined the body collapsing to the dirty street.

The hatchet man ran past Stark without giving him so much as a glance. Stark pressed even harder against the door when he heard running feet. Passing him, hot on the trail of the hatchet man, came four Chinese. They spoke rapidly in their own language and split up when the got to Dupont Gai. All four sported wickedly long, sharp knives.

Unexpectedly, the door Stark leaned against opened, sending him tumbling to the floor inside the shop. He looked up at a young Chinaman.

"What's goin' on out there? Those guys're killin' ever'one!"

"Tong war," the Chinaman said. "You go. Leave. Not safe here."

"I need to find somebody," Stark said.

"No, you go. Hurry. Now!"

The young man took Stark's hand and pulled him up only to give him a shove out into the street. Stark stood there, looking around wildly. He was certain the hatchet men would come after him and split his head wide open. Pressing his hand against his coat pocket was not reassuring. He carried a slungshot there. Otherwise, he wasn't armed. No knife or six-shooter. Then Stark wondered what good even a Gatling gun would be against the yellow phantoms drifting through the streets intent on killing.

Courage almost gone, Stark started to get back into the sections of San Francisco he knew best. The dives along the Embarcadero were dangerous, but he understood what the rules were. The Sydney Ducks had been replaced by other, more brutal gangs, but Stark got along all right with them. The worst in his world were the police and the Specials, but they could be bought off. He had yet to find even a squad of Specials who would not respond to a few dollars each.

For that kind of money he could hire them to kill anybody he wanted. But here? He was in a different country— a different world.

Stark started to leave the Chinese community behind, then slowed and finally stopped. Nobody he knew wanted the jade crown. What good was stealing it if he could not get money for it? He'd look like a damned fool wearing it. Besides, it was heavy and was too small to fit his head. He had gone through a lot to get that crown to give up on selling it.

Stark shook his head ruefully. The ease of gulling Tess Lawrence had made him think everything would go smoothly. She had expected him to sail off to New York with her, sell the jade and then they would live happily together in some nice little whitewashed house with a yard in front and, after a few years, a gaggle of kids running around. Jason Stark had his goals set higher than that, although Tess was quite a piece of ass. A moment of guilt passed for how he had used her.

"She wanted it, she did," he said. Stark turned and started back into Chinatown. "And who am I to let her sacrifice mean nothin'?"

He hitched up his pants and put his hand on the slungshot in his pocket. Those knives and hatchets were not going to bother him none. He was too much a man for that. He was the one who stole the jade crown that all the Chinese wanted. At least he figured they would want it, what with all the jade trinkets on display in the store windows.

Stark strutted along the street, keeping his eyes peeled for any sign of a man who might be a tong member. When he saw a pair of them on a street corner, making little effort to hide the symbols of their position—the hatchets—he boldly walked over to them.

"You gents know where I kin palaver with one of the big bosses?"

"Big boss?"

"Your big boss. I want to talk to him," Stark said. He became a little uneasy as the two exchanged looks, then began yammering in their singsong talk. "Speak English so's I know what you're sayin'," he demanded. "You don't, then I go find another big boss to make my offer to."

"On Leong?" asked one.

"Don't know what you just said," Stark said. For some reason this calmed them.

"We take you to Little Pete. He big boss of Sum Yop tong."

"Just the man I want to see. Little Pete. A little name for a big boss, huh?" Stark laughed at his own joke, then let his chuckle die down when neither of the Chinamen so much as smiled. He followed them, basking in the attention he got. The people peered fearfully, and Stark loved the feeling that they were afraid of him. He never thought for an instant it might be the men guiding him through the winding streets of Chinatown that engendered the fear.

"Here," said one, pointing to a two-story building that had seen better days. If he had not seen men walking along the roof carrying rifles, he would have thought it

was deserted. The front had been blown out and crudely
repaired. From the scent of fresh mortar, Stark knew that
the new masonry was less than a week old.

"Can't hardly go through solid walls," he complained.
He wondered if the two men were joshing him.

"Not here. There." The larger of the pair, who towered
above Stark, pointed to an alley.

Stark walked to the corner of the building and looked
down. He saw a solitary man standing, arms crossed over
his chest, guarding a door.

"Much obliged," Stark said to his two guides. "If you
ask the big boss real nice, he might let you touch it."

The two hatchet men exchanged glances, then turned
uncomprehending stares on Stark. He laughed. They
would all know soon enough what he was offering. Hell, let
the boys on the front line wear the jade crown for a second
or two. That ought to make them feel real special.

"I'm here to see the big boss," Stark declared. The man
in front of the door did not move a muscle. There was not
even a twitch of an eyelid or throb of a vein. The man
might have been cut from pale yellow stone.

"Little Pete? I want to talk to Little Pete." This got him
more than a twitch. The man reached out, grabbed Stark by
the lapels of his coat and yanked him forward. Surprised,
he grabbed for the slungshot in his pocket. Stark pulled it
out and swung. The heavy lead-filled bag hit the man's
forearm. He did not even flinch.

Stark yelped when he was lifted off his feet and shoved
through the door that someone inside the old warehouse
had opened. Stark staggered and fought to keep from landing on his butt. The door slammed shut. Through the dust
and dark he saw a hatchet man sporting two of the wicked
hand axes.

"You were expectin' me, were you? That's good. Real
good. Uh, I'll just go this way. Little Pete wants to talk to
me, he does."

Stark found himself herded through the maze to a small
clearing made from stacks of crates. Seated on a low stool

was a man he took to be Little Pete. He was dressed better than the others and sipped at tea.

"Howdy," Stark said. "You must be Little Pete."

"Why do you interrupt my tea?"

"That's no way to talk to a man who's got what you want." Stark felt buoyed by the knowledge that he had the jade crown. He went and took the tiny porcelain cup that Little Pete had placed on a low table and knocked back the contents. He spat it out. "That tastes like shit. You need to get yourself some decent whiskey."

Little Pete said nothing. His emotionless eyes fixed on Stark until the man turned a little edgy.

"Look, I got the crown. The jade crown."

"The emperor's?" For the first time, Little Pete showed a flicker of emotion.

"Yup, the one that the crazy Englishman had on display with the rest of the jade gewgaws."

"How did you come by this . . . artifact?"

"No reason to go into details. Let's say Sir William don't care to buy it from me. He's such a poor loser, too. Now, you, I see you got the look of a wise man 'bout you. I'm willin' to part with the crown for, oh, call it two thousand dollars."

"So little?"

Stark licked his lips and wondered if he had made a big mistake. The chink thought the jade crown was worth more.

"Just for you, two thousand," Stark said, deciding not to press his luck. He was asking twice what Sir William had balked at.

"I would see the crown," Little Pete said.

"No way, no sir, not like that. We got to be sure this is on the up-and-up, you know?"

"I will not pay without seeing the emperor's crown," Little Pete said. "If you cannot show it to me, there is no need to continue." He clapped his hands. From the shadows came three of the biggest Chinamen Jason Stark had ever seen. He was not a tall man; they were. Each was almost a full head taller and all outweighed him by fifty pounds. None of it looked to be fat, either.

"Hold your horses, my good man. I said I won't deal on those terms. But we can come to a meetin' of the minds, so to speak."

Little Pete tilted his head slightly, silently urging Stark to continue.

"We meet, see. We meet in some neutral spot. I got the crown so you can look it over. But you bring the money with you. Gold coins or bullion would be good, though I'll take scrip. When we're all satisfied, you and me, we swap. You get the jade crown and I get the money. How's that?"

"The time of meeting?"

"This evening," Stark said, his mind racing. He had not thought this far in advance.

"I must have the crown now," Little Pete said. "So, the meeting where you tell me the location of the crown is now."

Stark frowned. He did not follow what the tong leader meant. Then he did. Strong hands grabbed him and lifted him off the floor.

"Hey, no strong-arm stuff. I ain't tellin' you shit!"

"You have not been introduced to the ways of the Orient. We will begin with sharp knives. Then move to needles," Little Pete said, grinning wickedly. "If you have not told me what I desire, heated branding irons are good. I like them most of all."

"Hold your horses, wait, let me go!"

Stark screamed as a knife was pressed into his kidney. He kicked feebly and then screamed even louder when a second knife slashed along his lowest rib, then moved to the next and next. His coat quickly became a bloody rag.

"I'll tell you what you want. Don't, damn you, that hurts!"

"You give up so easily?" Little Pete sounded disappointed. "I had hoped for more."

"You're a madman!"

"Some say that," Little Pete agreed amicably. "You will say that after a few hours of excruciating torture." He gestured toward a back room.

Stark kicked harder. The knife points kept coming, no matter how he twisted.

"I . . . I'll show you where it is. I got the crown hid real good. Stop, just stop. You're killin' me with the knives!"

"We have hardly begun," Little Pete said. "Very well. Show us the crown." He grinned even more fiendishly and added, "I hope it is not there. It has been so long since I have enjoyed a good torture."

Stark babbled in terror. Why had he thought he could ever deal with these crazy, bloodthirsty chinks?

20

"Captain, the ship is coming again. White smoke. Steam!"

Lai Choi San lifted her spyglass and studied the navy frigate. Her lips thinned to a line. How could this happen? Her mind raced as she considered the possibilities. There were two boilers in the frigate. Only one had blown, leaving the second functioning and capable of driving the ship after hers.

She peered through the squall that wrapped both ships. Without sail, she was in perilous straits. The steam-powered frigate could plow on, no matter what the weather.

"Fix our stern cannon," she ordered.

"The range is too great," Sung said. He had bandages wrapped about his chest, making him into a mummy. His voice whistled when he talked and occasional pink flecks came from his mouth. Lai Choi San doubted he had long to live, yet he insisted on getting up to help defend the ship. She only hoped he did not die at an inopportune time and put the entire ship in jeopardy.

"We must let it come closer," she said. "They will not expect cannon fire. Our first shot must count."

"As we have done before?" Sung asked. A tiny smile crept to his lips. "The way we did against the British cargo ship?"

"It wasn't armed," Lai Choi San said. "We had to lure it close to put a hole in its hull." She lowered the spyglass and wiped rain from her face. These were the times she felt most alive.

In danger and with . . . him. But he was not here, and she must grab what thrills she could.

"Rudder, hard to port," she bellowed. The two men on the rudder put their backs into the effort, swinging the ship by force of will as much as by muscle to heel over. This put the frigate in the precise spot she wanted in another minute or two.

"It still steams toward us," Sung said. He spat blood now. Slocum's bullet had nicked a lung. He gripped the railing and watched closely as the gunners prepared the brass cannon. "Use sold shot. There is no mast to bring down with chain."

Stripped to the waist and glistening in the cold rain, the men worked frantically to determine elevation, distance and estimate the powder for the shot. Lai Choi San paid them no attention. They were the best gunner mates she had ever found—impressed, in one man's case. He had become as loyal as any other of her crew once the benefits of being a pirate became clear. Why starve on a fishing junk when you could prosper by robbing other ships?

"Fire at the frigate's midsection," she said. Her heart raced. The pounding waves, the storm pelting her with rain, the approaching danger, it all came together in a heady mixture more intoxicating than any rice wine. Lai Choi San grabbed the railing to steady herself when the cannon fired.

"Direct hit!" cried Sung.

Lai Choi San said nothing. She lifted the spyglass again and watched gouts of fire explode upward. The shot had crashed into the smokestack of the one functioning boiler and ripped it away. The back pressure from the suddenly removed stack sent a shockwave downward that must have blown the rivets out of the good boiler. If not, it certainly popped the pressure valves. That was as good as destroying the engine. They would have to rebuild a head of steam.

"Sung, quarter sail. Get us away before they fire on us. I would return to San Francisco."

"The crown?"

"We have not recovered it yet," she said with a touch of anger coming to her words.

"The bitch from the *Portobello* must have—"

"No, Sung, she did not know where it was. She was only being stubborn. Another day or two of torture would have revealed her ignorance. She thought she had it, but she did not. Slocum did not have it. Sir William does not have it. Somewhere in the city someone has our emperor's crown."

"How will you find it?"

Lai Choi San laughed now. "Knowing who does not have it reduces the number of people we must kill to find it," she said. "Hurry, Sung. I see the other ship's captain ordering his men to fire upon us with their rifles. We are still in no position for him to bring his heavier guns to bear. We must remain out of range."

A rifle bullet whined through the air above her head. Lai Choi San did not flinch. She had been under fire too many times for that. She turned and watched as her crew lowered the topmost sails. She felt the junk surge as a gust of wind caught the canvas. If she had unfurled all the sails, the mast would have snapped from the wind. Her speed was not what she would have liked but it was still faster than the frigate. Escape was all that mattered now.

Escape and finding her emperor's crown so she could . . .

"Repair what you can," she said to her second mate. Li bowed deeply. "Wrap Sung's body in canvas. When we are back in China we will give him a proper burial."

"As the mistress orders, so shall it be," Li said, bowing even more deeply.

She looked up at the tattered upper sails. Ruining them to get away from the frigate had been necessary. Considering the ferocity of the wind, not much damage had occurred, but finding a protected cove to ride out the storm would have been the prudent course. Time wore on her, though, and she doubted the frigate's captain would have allowed her out of a cove should he have discovered her.

"You and you," she said, pointing to crew who were standing and watching the repair work. "Row me to the docks."

"Mistress," called Li. "Will you need guards? These two are callow youths, not true fighters."

"So?" she asked of the youngsters.

Both bowed and one said, "We will die for you, Captain!"

"They will do," Lai Choi San said. In a low voice, she told the pair, "See that you are armed with both knives and pistols."

They hurried off to get their weapons. Lai Choi San stared across the turbulent bay to the docks and the city beyond. Gaslights were being lit along the San Francisco streets. She could not abide the smell of the burning gas, but then that was the least of her discomforts in the city. The entire place stank. Not only were the streets filthy, so were the inhabitants. Not one in a hundred had bathed recently.

"Barbarians," she said in a low voice. Then her two crewmen returned. She hopped into the boat and let them row, one at each oar. As they approached the docks, she worked out a plan for hunting down the possessor of the jade crown. It had only been mildly humorous telling Sung where she did not need to look. That left only those in Chinatown to question.

As the boat touched the dock, she grabbed the mooring ropes and quickly fastened it. She had worked as a sailor much of her life. Such menial chores were not beneath her, although she commanded a ship of her own. One day, she would have a fleet of junks at her beck and call. They would be the terror of the South China Sea and even the Dragon Lords would kowtow to her.

"One on each side, three paces back," she said to her crewmen-turned-bodyguards. She had little faith that they would conquer should a serious challenge be delivered, but they would fight nobly and die similarly.

She avoided the functionaries at dockside. They would only impede her questioning. She had no cargo to load or unload. Only when she had the crown would she think about hoisting anchor and sailing across the Pacific for home. Even then, she might not need much in the way of supplies to reach Hawaii where she could take on more water and food for the real journey.

The closer Lai Choi San got to the section of town where her people lived, the uneasier she became. She had seen the ravages of wars between the Triads in China. The tongs had turned the people into rabbits scurrying for their burrows. Only once did her two bodyguards move up when a hatchet man approached. Lai Choi San motioned them back, advanced and then called out, "Do the Sum Yop fight everyone else?"

She had recognized the approaching hatchet man as Sum Yop by the small insignia on his hat.

"The Sum Yop need no allies," came the reply.

"I would speak with Little Pete."

She had no idea what caused the attack. The hatchet man looked calm, but her words sparked him to whip out a long-bladed knife and lunge forward. She drew her pistol and fired—the hammer fell on an empty cylinder. Before she could make a second attempt, both her guards had driven their knives into the hatchet man's torso. The killer sank to the cobblestone street and flopped facedown.

"He is On Leong," her guard said after a quick examination of the body. "Not Sum Yop."

"So they impersonate each other to add to the killing." She shook her head, then tended to her pistol. The cylinder had been unloaded. "Slocum," she said, remembering how he had shot Sung with his own six-shooter. "He must have unloaded the other pistols." She turned to her guards and ordered them to check their weapons. As she had suspected, both six-guns were similarly empty.

"What shall we do, Mistress?"

"Use your knives. We will avoid meeting anyone from now on. I will go to the Sum Yop headquarters and see Little Pete. Stay out of sight."

She did not wait to see if the men obeyed. She knew

they would. Lai Choi San hurried through the winding streets and was panting by the time she climbed a hill and came to the front of the Sum Yop building. What had to be extraordinary activity held the entire block. Sentries paced along the roof and more than a half dozen hatchet men prowled the street.

She motioned for her two bodyguards to remain behind as she edged forward, silent as a shadow.

The mouth of the alley where the entrance into the Sum Yop headquarters was as close as she could get without being challenged. Lai Choi San crouched down in a doorway, partly hidden by darkness. Her dark eyes fixed on the door as it opened and Sum Yop killers came spilling out. Six, eight, ten of them. Behind this phalanx of death strutted Little Pete. For such a small army to venture out during a tong war, a major attack had to be underway.

Or so she thought until she saw the man being dragged between two more Sum Yops. Lai Choi San caught a glimpse of the man's pale face. He was Occidental. She pressed harder against the door and tried to make herself into as small a target as possible when the knot of hatchet men came toward her.

"You might save yourself additional pain," Little Pete said, apparently talking to himself. Lai Choi San saw the prisoner jerk erect. Fear etched his face. She saw blood on his coat and he walked with a limp whenever his guards prodded him with their knives.

"I tell ya, I won't give it up easy. You got to pay."

"The price will be your miserable life. That has been decided." Little Pete stopped and looked up and down the street. From nowhere came a dozen more Sum Yops. They formed a wedge in front of him while the others who had emerged from the headquarters with him fanned out on either side and trailed to protect his flanks. Only the two men holding their prisoner remained close to Little Pete. A casual observer might think the Sum Yop leader was out for a solitary stroll.

"Want more. Kill me 'n you'll never find it."

"Very well," Little Pete said. "There might be a few dollars exchanged. Does that ease your mind?"

"Surely does," the man said. "Let's get on with it."

"Yes, the sooner you show me, the sooner you can spend your reward," Little Pete said.

Lai Choi San wondered if the Occidental was stupid to not hear the obvious contempt in Little Pete's words. Once he was squeezed dry of information, the man was going to be shark food.

She watched as the men walked away from her. In her gut, Lai Choi San knew what it was Little Pete went to retrieve.

What could it be but the emperor's crown!

21

"They have it," Lai Choi San said.

"What is this, Mistress?"

"Never mind," she snapped at her guard. "They are going to get it. We must not let them keep it."

"There is no way we can fight so many. We will die."

"You worry about death in my service?" she asked coldly.

"No, Mistress, not at all," one guard hurriedly explained. "If we die, you do not get whatever it is you seek. That would be wrong."

Lai Choi San cursed volubly. The man was right. She needed her entire crew, and even then there might not be enough. Little Pete had most of his killers around him. How the foolish Occidental could not understand his life was forfeit the instant he turned over the crown—and it *had* to be the jade crown they were after—was a mystery unless the man was completely stupid. If so, how did he get the crown from Sir William?

She broke into a run, not following Little Pete but angling away out of Sum Yop territory. It took her only a few minutes to find another hatchet man standing guard at a street corner.

"You, On Leong," she called. "I want to speak with your

leader. It is of utmost importance." Lai Choi San worried that the man would recoil at the idea of a woman issuing such orders. To her surprise, he bowed slightly and pointed to a darkened doorway.

"What's down there?"

"The On Leong leader," he said simply.

Lai Choi San cautiously went to the doorway and saw that it led to stairs going downward into the ground. She inhaled deeply and knew this was no trick. The fragrance of incense mingled with fine tea and even a hint of opium. These were all things she expected, and they refreshed rather than tired her like the overall scent of San Francisco.

She started down the steps, only to hesitate and look back. Both of her guards had knives at their throats.

"They do not go with you," said the On Leong she had spoken to.

Lai Choi San never looked behind her again as she plunged into the dark winding corridors under the Chinatown streets. She had a good sense of direction. At sea none was a better navigator, whether by dead reckoning or by the stars, but she quickly lost all sense of direction. All she knew was that the corridor stretched in front of her. At the occasional junction, a silent hatchet man pointed in the proper direction. The deeper into the labyrinth she went, the more she realized she could never fight her way out. Not only were those men guarding such an escape, she had to figure out what corridors in the maze to take.

Lai Choi San abandoned all hope of leaving alive without the help of the On Leong leader.

She suddenly found herself in a dimly lit room. Compared to the murk of the corridor, she felt as if a spotlight shone on her. A woman dressed in an emerald green silk dress knelt on a cushion. At hand were delicately painted porcelain teacups and a steaming pot of tea.

Bowing, she entered.

"I seek the esteemed leader of the On Leong."

"I am Ah Ming," the woman said.

"You lead the tong?" Lai Choi San tried not to sound surprised.

"You captain a pirate ship?"

"You are well informed," Lai Choi San said. She knelt when Ah Ming gestured for her to do so. She took the tea and sipped. It was good tea. Indian.

"I am the leader of the tong because my father has been killed by the Sum Yop. They hold his body. I want it back. My efforts have proven futile so far. Whatever you desire, I will grant you if you can get my father's bones back for transport to China."

Lai Choi San did not want to be direct and let this woman know what she really sought, but time was crushing her. She knew Little Pete went to get the jade crown. If the other tong leader held it, he would never relinquish it.

Lai Choi San told her story simply, finishing, "I must have the crown for ransom."

"I have no desire to possess the crown," Ah Ming said. "We find ourselves on the same road but with different destinations. My father's body is all I desire returned."

"And all I desire is the jade crown of the emperor."

"You are sure Little Pete is out of his headquarters?"

"He and two dozen men left with the Occidental."

"Describe him!"

Lai Choi San's eyes narrowed suspiciously at this. The identity of the Occidental mattered greatly to Ah Ming. She described the shabby man the best she could from her brief glimpse of him. Ah Ming relaxed visibly.

"I would fight Little Pete and the Sum Yop as they fetch the crown, but my men will instead attack their headquarters. This might be my best opportunity to recover my father's body."

"I understand," Lai Choi San said. She had not anticipated this. "Please guide me to the street so I might try to get the crown for our emperor."

"Three of you against ten times that number?" Ah Ming sounded surprised and a little amused.

"I will do what I must. As you know, I am a pirate. My trade might prove useful after Little Pete has the crown."

"So it might," Ah Ming said. She clapped her hands and gave instructions to a burly hatchet man. Lai Choi San rose and bowed.

"My thanks," she said.

"Thank you for this information. May you recover what you desire most," said Ah Ming.

Lai Choi San left the room and was startled to see that stairs upward only a few yards away brought her back to where her two men sat and talked amiably with the On Leong hatchet men.

"Hurry, hurry, we must not lose them."

"The *boo how doy* say Little Pete and his men are going to the docks."

Lai Choi San looked at the On Leong, bowed slightly in their direction, then got her bodyguards on their feet and running to keep up with her. She had no idea how she would accomplish the theft, but it had to be done quickly before Little Pete returned to his headquarters. If Ah Ming attacked to recover her father's body, the tumult would be too great to endure.

Out of breath, they reached the Embarcadero. It took only a few minutes to eavesdrop on workers along the way to know that Little Pete and his men had passed by recently. The passage of so many Sum Yops stirred fear to boiling. Lai Choi San followed the route, only to hear gunfire.

At first there were only a few shots, then there came a fusillade that sent echoes rolling along the Embarcadero. She had heard less noise during a pitched sea battle with all ships firing cannon.

Coming to a halt, she saw a skirmish line of marines advancing, rifles lowered.

"Stay back," called an officer. "There's a right good battle going on."

"Who?" The question slipped from her lips before she could restrain herself. She knew who the marines fought.

She needed to know about Little Pete and his Occidental prisoner who might know where the jade crown was.

"Some of them tong bastards got into a dustup. Captain Johnson called out the marines to take care of the situation. Nothing to worry over, if you stay away."

The sound of gunfire increased. White clouds of gun smoke drifted in her direction. Her nostrils flared at the familiar odor. She had been born to battle, and she was being kept from this one. Lai Choi San gestured to her two guards. They advanced, only to be forcibly turned back by marines with bayonets fixed.

Lai Choi San saw how the soldiers reacted and used this against them to slip around the end of their line. They dealt with her men. She hurried past into the choking white clouds still billowing from the fight. Volley after volley was fired, to be met with ragged return fire. She guessed that the tong killers were running out of ammunition. Facing so many well-armed marines in direct battle was not the way any tong fought. Theirs was the sudden death, the hidden killer, not direct confrontation.

Her heart almost stopped when she saw Little Pete and the Occidental pressed back against a warehouse wall. Little Pete's hatchet men fought in front of him, but one by one they were being cut down by the persistent marksmanship of the marines.

"That's the spirit, boys," came a loud call. "Give them what for!"

Lai Choi San stood on tiptoe to see who cheered on the soldiers. Her eyes narrowed when she saw Sir William. The British explorer stood near a naval officer, who glared at the man. How he had come to be with the marines was something she wondered at but knew it meant nothing in the long run. She concentrated on Little Pete and his prisoner. They were most likely to know where the jade crown was hidden. Since they had come to the docks, it must be hidden nearby, unless the Occidental lied.

While this buoyed her spirits, it did nothing to actually

regain the crown for her emperor. The docks were wide open and something as small as the crown could be hidden anywhere, in a crate, buried in the dirt, even concealed with nothing more than a rag thrown over it.

The gunfire became sporadic and the naval officer with Sir William shouted, "Surrender and we'll let you live. Continue to fight and die!"

Little Pete shouted in Chinese. Lai Choi San understood and pressed back. He had ordered his men into full attack. Drawing their hatchets, the Sum Yop *boo how doy* waved them high above their heads and launched a full-scale frontal assault. There could be no doubt as to the result.

By twos and threes, the hatchet men died.

Lai Choi San turned from the slaughter and watched Little Pete. The Sum Yop leader thrust a gun into the side of the Occidental and moved him along the warehouse wall until they reached the corner of the building. There Little Pete shoved the man around and they fled. While his own men were being massacred, Little Pete was getting away.

Lai Choi San pursued, drawing her own gun. Then she remembered it was empty and once more hid it among the folds of her clothing. A gleaming knife came into her hand. To dispatch Little Pete and get the information she needed from his prisoner, this was preferable.

Little Pete looked back and saw her running after him. He fired twice over his shoulder, then stubbed his foot and fell heavily. Lai Choi San vaulted over him and kept running. He shouted insults at her and struggled to stand, only to lose his footing again.

Then she was around another corner and running hard to catch Jason Stark. The man saw his pursuer and put his head down, sprinting to get away.

Lai Choi San knew she could overtake him—until he cut to the right. She saw that he veered to avoid a squad of marines marching along. The pirate found herself facing the lowered rifles of the marines.

She backed away, lowering the knife and holding it behind her out of their sight.

"Halt!" The sergeant in charge of the squad advanced. "No one's allowed this way."

"That man," she said, pointing. The sergeant never turned his head even when Lai Choi San began waving her arm about wildly. "What of him?"

"Get back or I'll have my men remove you. This whole area's under martial law."

She knew better than to argue. Every second counted in finding the running man. She retreated, found a side street and raced to circle the soldiers. By the time she got behind their position, she saw no trace of Stark. Lai Choi San cursed in four languages as she searched. No one had noticed a single man running amid the confusion caused by the marines and tong fighting.

She went to the end of a dock, looked out to where her junk was anchored, then slowly turned and hunted for any trace of the man who knew where the jade crown was hidden.

Nowhere. She saw him nowhere.

22

"No, this isn't right. I can't do it." Tess Lawrence pulled away from Slocum and started for the door of the curator's office. He stayed where he was, seated on the edge of the desk.

"You have to," Slocum said. "There's no other way."

"I can just . . . run away." Tess was close to tears.

The hike across town had been harrowing. Slocum had not realized there were so many policemen in the world, much less in San Francisco. Every mother's son of them had been on patrol, carrying shotguns and rifles and looking as if they were ready for a war. Slocum had heard gunfire near the docks but had discounted it. With all the police patrolling every street he could see, there were not enough of them to be involved. Whatever had riled them up, they intended to keep bottled up at dockside.

"Sure, you can run like a coward. You stole Sir William's exhibits. All the jade he risked his life to bring back. You can run off and let him think that not only the jade but you are lost."

"That's for the best." She sniffled now and wiped at her nose with the blanket she had around her. Tess still wore Slocum's shirt, but he had fetched his other one from his gear. "If he thinks I'm dead, how can he blame me?"

"Make it right," Slocum insisted. "Do it for your own reasons. You'll be miserable the rest of your life, knowing you double-crossed the man who trusted you." Slocum saw that was the right argument. Tess wilted before his eyes and finally broke down crying. She came to him and threw her arms around him. He felt her hot tears against his shoulder as he tried to ease her quaking.

He felt like a real bastard for pushing her like this. He cared less what she thought about stealing Sir William's jade than he did about getting the jade crown for his own purposes—for Ah Ming's. Slocum needed to use her and Sir William if he wanted to locate the crown to ransom the bones, and the best lever he had to move the man was Tess.

"I say, what's going on here? Tess!" Sir William rushed into the room and swung her around. He stared at her tear-stained face. "What have you done to her, Slocum?"

"No, no, Sir William, it's nothing like that," she sobbed out. "John saved me. I would have been flayed alive by pirates if he hadn't rescued me."

"Pirates? Lai Choi San?"

Slocum nodded.

"So she *was* responsible for stealing the jade. I knew it! The perfidious woman ought to be hanged from her own yardarm!"

"It's more complicated than that," Slocum said. "The jade was put on a cargo ship heading around the Cape. Someone named Jason Stark has the crown, though."

"The jade from the exhibit," Sir William said softly. "The pirate has it?"

"I'm afraid so, Sir William. I . . . we tried to keep her from taking it, but she just *took* it." Tess broke down crying again. This time Sir William awkwardly comforted her. Slocum saw that more explanation was not going to be necessary.

"We can track Stark and—" Slocum stopped when he saw Sir William look at him sharply.

"I know about Stark," Sir William said. "You think

I have done nothing while you were away? I called out the marines!"

"The gunfire down by the docks," Slocum said. "The marines caught him?"

"Blast it, no! He escaped. He had thrown in with a gang of Chinese—the Sum Yop tong."

"Did they get the crown?" Slocum saw everything falling apart around him. If Little Pete had gotten possession of the crown, any hope of ransoming Ah Ming's father was at an end.

"The tong men? No, I don't think so. Stark escaped. He still has it, I suppose," Sir William said, holding Tess a little closer to soothe her. She was only sniffling now but did not move from the circle of the man's arms. The longer she stayed, the more Sir William liked it.

"I'll get to tracking him down. A man like that can't hide in too many places." Slocum knew that Stark had cut himself off from most of the Chinese community by throwing in with the Sum Yop. Ah Ming might even know of the man's whereabouts through her far-flung web of spies and informants. If she didn't, Slocum knew he could ask some of the marines. Sergeant Lamont had been a forthcoming fellow. Any scuttlebutt passed among the marines would end up being whispered in his ear.

"No need, old chap," Sir William said. "I know where he got off to."

Tess pushed away and stared up at him.

"Where?" she asked before Slocum could.

Slocum saw what Sir William did not. The utter hatred burning in Tess's eyes told the story. She was a woman scorned and wanted revenge.

"No need to trouble yourself, my dear," he said patronizingly. "I am quite capable of handling this. You need to rest. Your ordeal has been unprecedented."

"She can stay here," Slocum said. Tess shot him a look he could not decipher. He was not sure if she was thankful or wanted him to plead her case to go along. What he could not dispute was her utter hatred of Jason Stark for betraying her feelings. He had used her, and she would not forget that.

"Jolly good," Sir William said. "Let me get more ammunition for my pistol, then we shall be off."

"Just tell me what you've learned, and I can find him." Slocum wanted to keep Sir William away from the crown to increase his own chances of recovering it. How he would turn it over to Ah Ming with Sir William nosing about was a problem he did not want to solve.

"This is good sport, old chap. We're in this together. Off to the hounds and all that." Sir William stuffed a box of ammunition into his coat pocket after reloading his pistol. He presented himself to Slocum. "Come along, now, Mr. Slocum. Time's a' wasting."

Slocum felt Tess's hot eyes on them as they left the museum. He chanced a quick look back to be certain she was not following them. As far as he could tell, she remained behind where it was safe.

Safe for him to steal the crown.

"Tell me what happened," Sir William said seriously. "Between you and Miss Lawrence while she was missing."

"It's exactly as we told you. Lai Choi San captured us separately. The pirate captain wanted the crown and tortured Tess. During a storm I freed her, we swam ashore and came straight back to San Francisco."

"So you missed the fight between the Chinese and the marines?"

"All of it," Slocum said. "I heard gunfire but thought nothing of it." He saw that the police still patrolled in squads of five or more. That told him the city was still uneasy over the tong war brewing. They cared less that the Chinese were killing one another than they did for it spilling over to threaten shipping or the upstanding citizens in other parts of the city.

"He's like a rat, you know."

"What? Stark?" Slocum jolted out of the reverie.

"Who else? He is not a smart man at all. It took me only a few minutes to find someone to, I think you Yanks call it, 'squeal.'"

Slocum doubted anyone Sir William bribed had told him the truth, but they were going to the docks. From all he had pieced together from Tess's story, Stark was a wharf rat and would not stray far from familiar territory. They walked along the Embarcadero, Sir William alert for details.

"There. I think that is the spot. The saloon with the curious feature of a trapdoor opening from its main room."

"Shanghaiers use it," Slocum said. "They drug their victims, then drop them through the trapdoor to a waiting dinghy. From there, the victim is rowed out to a ship and sold. By the time he comes to, he's out at sea."

"I know about all that, dear chap," Sir William said. "I pointed it out only because Stark comes and goes through that very same trapdoor. That means his lair is somewhere below the pier."

Slocum walked to the edge of the dock and peered over. The water lapped endlessly at the rotting pilings. A small rowboat bobbed on the waves, empty for the moment. When it got darker and the saloon at the end of the pier began drawing more customers, the shanghaiers would work overtime. Slocum strained and poked his head out even more, then caught his breath.

Slowly to avoid being seen, he drew back slowly.

"What is it?" demanded Sir William. "Did you catch sight of him?"

"Little Pete," he answered. "I saw the Sum Yop leader down there."

"Why—" Sir William cut off his question. A look of vexation caused him to look years older. "The tong found him. He escaped but the tong found him before we could."

"Little Pete might not have many of his hatchet men with him," Slocum said, thinking fast. "A lot of them were killed or wounded this afternoon by the marines."

"Oh, yes, a bloody lot of them were. The fight was a good one. Hardly any of the marines were injured."

"Little Pete knows Stark well enough to risk going after him by himself."

"Then we should go stick a pistol into this Little Pete's back and take Stark from him!"

"That might be easier said than done." Slocum went to the far side of the pier and studied it. He thought he saw faint rays of light sneaking out from between a boarded-up section of the pilings. That was the sort of place a man like Jason Stark would live. Hidden, affording him easy access up through the trapdoor or out by water, he could prey on the unsuspecting and have a hidey-hole to retreat to if things got too hot.

Slocum vaulted the railing and dropped ten feet to the rocky beach. He stayed in a crouch as he motioned Sir William to silence and to stay where he was. Duckwalking forward, he pressed his eye to the boards nailed up against the pilings. The coal oil lamp a few feet away on a low stool provided more than enough light for him to see everything in the room.

Stark cowered at the far corner of the tiny room. Little Pete had his back to Slocum but, from Stark's fright, pointed a gun at him. The waves breaking against the shore and the increasing din from the saloon above drowned out anything the men might be saying. It took little imagination to guess that Little Pete wanted the jade crown, and Stark was dickering frantically with him to stay alive.

If he rushed in, he might kill Little Pete. Slocum knew the complications arising from that act would outweigh anything else. Little Pete's successor as leader of the Sum Yops might not want to trade the crown for Ah Ming's father's bones. New leaders meant new deals. Better to let Little Pete wrest the jade crown from Stark.

Then Slocum could decide how to proceed. He might steal it away from the tong leader without him knowing who the thief was. That would be the best of all solutions.

Slocum could give Little Pete back the crown, get the body and satisfy everyone.

Everyone except Sir William.

Slocum jerked erect, hand going to his six-shooter when the far wall of the tiny room exploded inward.

"No," Slocum cried. He grabbed a loose plank and pulled with all his might. It came free. He thrust his six-gun through and fired. He missed Little Pete but hit the coal oil lamp. It exploded in a welter of glass and flames, adding to the confusion.

Slocum yanked free several more boards and forced his way into the room.

"Come on," he said to Sir William, who lay stunned on the plank floor. The explorer had been struck on the side of the head as Little Pete left by the most expedient route— over the fallen man. Slocum saw a muddy footprint in the middle of Sir William's back.

"Where's Stark?"

"I don't know. I heard them. I didn't know what you were waiting for, so I came in." Sir William looked confused from the blow to his head.

"Stark didn't go past you?"

"Only the Chinaman," Sir William said.

Slocum looked up. A knotted rope dangled from above. He shoved his six-shooter into its holster, jumped, grabbed the highest knot he could and quickly climbed until he banged his head against the trapdoor leading into the saloon. Doubled over, pressing his shoulders against it, he shoved with all his might. The splintery trapdoor flew open. Slocum tumbled down to the floor, got his feet under him and made his way down the narrow corridor into the main room of the saloon.

Dozens of sailors had already begun their binge. Slocum jumped to the bar and looked out over the room.

"Get yer dirty feet offa my bar!" The barkeep reached under the bar and pulled out a club. He swung it, but Slocum lithely jumped and avoided the bone-breakingly hard blow. Landing hard, he pushed his way through the bar patrons and out the door to stand on the pier. He looked hard but did not see Jason Stark. If Sir William had remained where Slocum had told him, the explorer could have nabbed the thief.

Slocum grunted in disgust and went to get Sir William. He had to find some other way of ferreting out Stark if he wanted to get the jade crown back.

23

Sir William Macadams lay on his face, unmoving. Slocum stepped carefully over the burned boards and knelt beside the explorer. He shook him gently and the man's eyes popped open.

"Good God, man, you frightened me," Sir William said.

"I thought you were dead." Slocum looked around Stark's hiding place and saw nothing but cinders and charred boards. Sir William had been in the middle, his clothing black with soot and burned in many places. "The fire didn't spread enough to burn the pier down, but . . ." Slocum looked around and saw the reason it had not spread. Sir William had sacrificed his coat to smother the flames.

Sir William coughed as he sat up. He motioned Slocum away.

"I'll be fine, not to worry, not to worry," he said. "Pray give a moment's silence for my dearly departed jacket, however."

"Why were you flopped out like that?"

Sir William grinned sheepishly. He let Slocum help him stand and took a few tentative steps before regaining some of his strength. Then he brushed himself off before he answered.

"The fumes overwhelmed me. It is not like me to forget

212

such things." He looked around. "This is an enclosed space. I hunted for the jade crown without noting how the timbers still smoldered. A foolish mistake."

"Yeah, foolish," Slocum said, disappointed. He doubted Sir William would have missed the crown if it had been here. Stark was a fool, but he was not so stupid that he would hide the Chinese Emperor's crown where he lived.

"Let's get back to the museum. I have to see if Miss Lawrence is feeling better. She did look a mite peaked, don't you think?"

Slocum saw concern in the man's expression and heard it in his words. He cared for Tess, even if he did not show it usually. Together, they slid through the hole in the wall and dropped onto the rocky beach. Slocum saw men hanging on the railing above and decided it was best if they walked a ways before returning to the street. Even after they worked their way into the crowds, Slocum walked with an eye peeled for trouble. To have gone back to the pier where Stark had lived would have invited trouble. Even here, surrounded by sailors and gangs of policemen, Slocum had the feeling of impending trouble.

He hailed a carriage and helped Sir William into it.

"What? You're not coming along, Mr. Slocum?" the explorer asked when Slocum gave the driver instructions to go to the museum but did not enter the carriage himself.

"Stark is still out there somewhere. This is the best time to find him, before he burrows down into a permanent hiding place."

"We burned that," Sir William said.

"A rat like Stark would have several hiding places. This was the most convenient." Slocum did not add that, since the jade crown had not been found, Stark had it somewhere else, somewhere he considered more secure. He had only gone to ground here because of Little Pete's hatchet men being hot on his trail.

"You know what you're doing, Mr. Slocum. I appreciate that. Be a good chap now, don't get yourself in a tight fix. I might not hear of it in time to come and get you out."

Slocum grinned crookedly and motioned for the driver to take Sir William back to the museum. As the carriage rattled off, Slocum felt the presence of someone behind him.

"I wanted to talk to you, Ah Ming," he said without looking. "Thanks for saving me the trouble of hunting for you."

"The whole town is aflame," she said. Slocum turned to face her. She looked small and helpless. He knew she was anything but that. If anything, she and Lai Choi San shared two traits above all others. They were deadly and determined.

"I kept Little Pete from getting the crown," he said. "That ought to keep things warm for a spell."

"You have only one day. Tomorrow. Sundown," Ah Ming said.

"I have to find Jason Stark. Little Pete almost beat me to him."

"If Little Pete gets the jade crown, there is no reason to return my father's bones to me."

"What have you heard?"

"His flesh has been consumed by rats."

Slocum shuddered involuntarily. That fate seemed peculiar to San Francisco.

"You will get his bones or you will die, John Slocum."

"I'm trying. What can you tell me about Stark?" He watched her expression closely for any hint that she might lie. When she answered, he saw nothing but her impassive face.

"I have never heard of this man."

"Ask around. He hangs out at dockside. That means he works for someone, maybe as a shanghaier." Slocum remembered the room under the saloon. It was the perfect setup for someone engaged in shanghaiing drunk or doped patrons of the bar and getting them into a skiff so that they could be sold to ships' captains hungry for crewmen.

"He has the crown?"

"He knows where it is," Slocum said.

"I will see what others have to say, though they might not be willing to talk freely."

"The tong war," Slocum said. He frowned as an unpleasant thought came to him. "If the Sum Yops and On Leongs are fighting so openly, what good's getting the jade crown? Little Pete would only kill whoever tried to make the exchange."

"That is why you must do it," Ah Ming said. "You are not On Leong. And Little Pete is greedy. He has some use for the crown."

Slocum looked past Ah Ming toward the harbor. The only one who wanted the jade crown so badly she would kill for it was Lai Choi San. What sort of a deal had Lai Choi San and Little Pete come up with?

"Do you know what cargo ships are due to port here in the next week or so?"

Ah Ming shook her head.

"That might give some clue as to why Little Pete wants the crown and would give up a hated enemy's bones for it."

"You have until tomorrow at sundown," Ah Ming said.

"Find out what I need to know!" Slocum called after the slowly retreating woman. Ah Ming did not show that she heard.

Slocum slumped, then regained some of his composure. Ah Ming might take days to find what Slocum needed to know right now. All he knew of Stark came from Tess's biased view of the man. He had been a charmer, she said. He had swept her off her feet and convinced her to steal the jade from her employer. Hearing how valuable the crown was, Stark had added a little something to the larceny he had already connived to involve Tess in.

Slocum had met men like Stark before. They could charm an angry rattlesnake and make the flowers bloom with their bright smiles. Appearance mattered less than manner, and their manners were always perfectly on target. They read people like a newspaper and ingratiated themselves with whatever their marks wanted to hear. In Tess's case, it had been more than ingratiation. She was a lonely woman whose love for her employer went unrequited. That made her doubly easy for Stark to take advantage of.

"Maybe a shanghaier and certainly a snake oil salesman," Slocum said. "He won't be far from his usual haunts."

Hitching up his gun belt, he went back down to the docks. He steered clear of the crowds of sailors pouring into the watering holes and tried to keep a sharp eye out for Stark. The depth of the shadows and lack of lighting made it difficult, but Slocum kept moving. Twice he had to avoid being attacked by roving gangs of thugs, the last one obviously shanghaiers intent on filling a quota.

As Slocum watched them surge past where he had taken refuge in the mouth of an alley, an idea came to him. Stark was likely in cahoots with shanghaiers. If not these, then another gang. Slocum hurried from the alley and trailed the gang as they made their way along the docks, waiting outside saloons and occasionally going in. When this happened, they never came out. Slocum chanced a look over the side of a pier and saw that many of the saloons had trapdoors for the shanghaiers to get their victims out without being seen.

When the gang was down to a handful, Slocum singled out one, came up behind him and quickly muffled any outcry with a hand over the mouth. Bending him backward, Slocum dragged the man into an alley and swung him around so hard he crashed into a brick wall.

"Don't turn around," Slocum said coldly. "If you do, I'll blow your spine into powder." He shoved the muzzle of his Colt Navy into the man's back to prove he had the means to carry out his threat.

"Take what I got, mate, jist leave ma a nickel for a beer."

"Jason Stark. Where is he?"

"Who?"

Slocum slugged the man and drove him to his knees. This time he pressed the cold metal muzzle against the man's temple.

"You're within five seconds of having your brains blown out."

"I . . . I seen him earlier. He was at the Pole Star. It's a dive down a ways along the Embark!"

"How much earlier?"

"Twenty minutes, maybe more."

Slocum slugged him. When the man stirred he hit him again. Considering his occupation, Slocum considered shooting him but decided he might need the ammo later. Cramming his six-gun into his holster, he set out for the saloon where the shanghaier claimed to have seen Stark.

Barely had he stepped into the smoky, crowded saloon when he spotted Stark. The man hunkered down in the corner of the room, trying not to be seen. The act of trying to be invisible set him apart from everyone else in the room. Slocum dodged two sailors as he started across the room for Stark when another crashed full tilt into him, sending him staggering back.

"Where ya goin' in such a hurry, little man?"

Slocum looked up into the giant sailor's eyes and saw only bubbling hatred there. The man was ashore and looking for someone to fight—or kill.

Without hesitating, Slocum drew his six-shooter and swung with all his might. He grazed the sailor and opened a gash just above his eye. The sudden spurt of blood blinded the sailor, but this was obviously nothing new for the man. He let out a bull roar and charged, arms wide to scoop Slocum up and crush him in a powerful embrace. Slocum ducked, swung for the man's belly with both hands on his Colt and then stepped away.

By now half a dozen fights had started. Slocum wanted no part of them. The sailors fought for the sheer joy of it. He wanted Stark.

Jason Stark had vanished.

Slocum glanced over his shoulder. Wherever Stark had gone, he had not gotten past and back out onto the dock. Kicking and punching, Slocum made his way to the table where Stark had been. The sawdust on the floor was liberally speckled with fresh blood leading toward a back room. Slocum started for the room, only to have the barkeep step in front of him.

"Sorry, mister. You can't go back there."

Slocum never broke stride as he buffaloed the bartender
and knocked him to the floor. Kicking in the door to the
back room revealed to Slocum what he feared most. A
trapdoor in the floor stood open. He went to it and saw two
men grabbing oars. Jason Stark lay unconscious in the boat
behind them.

Slocum aimed and fired. One bullet drove through the
bottom of the rowboat but did not put a big enough hole in
the wood to cause any real damage. The way the boat
leaked, another hole would hardly be noticed.

He fired a second time, but the bullet *plinked!* harm-
lessly into the water. Slocum dropped down the ladder, not
bothering to use the rungs. He hit the small landing hard,
ready to fire again. The two men rowed with a vengeance
and were only dark lumps amid the choppy waves. In frus-
tration Slocum fired until his six-shooter came up empty.
He took the time to reload, then looked around.

Another rowboat banged restlessly against the small
dock, tossed on the waves. He jumped in and cast off.
Grabbing both oars, he started rowing. All the aches from
his earlier trip into the bay returned, but Slocum felt victory was close at hand. Stark was being shanghaied. If he
could rescue the sneak thief, he would be grateful enough
to turn over the jade crown. And if he wasn't grateful,
Slocum considered all the ways Ah Ming might have of
making him tell her where the crown was. Little Pete's tor-
tures might be cruel but Slocum had no doubt Ah Ming
could surpass the Sum Yop leader's worst.

After a few minutes' rowing took him away from the
docks and out into the bay, he looked around for a likely
ship. The dark hull of a clipper ship a quarter mile off
looked like his best chance. He rested a few seconds,
chanced standing and sighted what he thought was the
boat with Stark making for the cargo ship. Slocum put his
back into rowing again, the effort paying off. Although
two rowed the other boat, he narrowed the distance between
them.

Then he noticed he was shipping water. Rowing became

harder and harder as the bottom of the boat filled. Cursing, he grabbed a small bucket and began bailing. By the time he had enough water removed, the other boat had disappeared. Determined, Slocum rowed for the three-master ship and bumped gently against the towering schooner's hull. He saw lines dangling down, and, using one to fasten his boat, he clambered up another, ready for anything when he got to the deck.

The captain and two seamen looked up in surprise when he dropped onto the deck, his six-shooter drawn and pointed at them.

"You got a friend of mine there," Slocum said. "I want him back." Stark moaned and thrashed about weakly on the deck. "Those two shanghaied him back at the saloon—the Pole Star, it was."

"Who the hell are you?" demanded the captain, strutting over. He wore enough gold braid, all faded from sun and saltwater, to anchor his ship. On his chest he wore several medals. Slocum recognized them as Union commendations. Whether the master of this ship had ever fought for the Yankee navy or simply wore the medals out of arrogance did not matter to Slocum.

"The man who's going to take your new recruit back to shore," Slocum said.

"Like bloody hell, ya will!" the captain roared. "I paid good coin for him. He's shippin' to China."

"You can have him back when I'm done with him," Slocum said. "I got a bone to pick."

He heard movement behind him. Slocum ducked and slipped to the side, but the sounds he heard came not from the deck but the rigging. A sailor aloft swung a heavy pulley that collided with the middle of Slocum's back, sending him sprawling. As he fell, he fired. He hit one of the shanghaiers but did nothing to slow both the captain and his crewman above from falling on him like a ton of bricks.

Slocum gasped as the air rushed from his lungs.

"Looks like we got two fer the price o' one, Cap'n," Slocum heard. A giant surf roared in his ears. Every breath came like a dagger driven into his chest. He pulled his arms in and realized he still clutched his six-shooter.

"Git 'im to his feet and put 'im to work alongside his matey over there," Slocum heard. His eyes refused to focus. That didn't stop him from turning in the direction of the voice and firing. A loud cry of pain rewarded him. He fired again, swung around and kept firing. By the time his six-gun came up empty, he was able to make out the clipper ship's crew in disarray.

He stumbled toward where Stark still sprawled on the deck and realized he would never get to him. The shock of seeing two of their mates gunned down was wearing off. Slocum caught a quick glimpse of the captain. The man clutched his sleeve, now turned red with spurting blood. He had been winged, too.

Realizing he had overstayed his welcome and had no chance of fetching Stark back to San Francisco, Slocum turned and fell rather than dived over the railing. He crashed into the cold water of the bay and came to the surface, sputtering for breath.

The bullets sending up tiny water spouts all around him lent urgency to his flopping into the rowboat and putting his back into the oars. In a few minutes he was beyond the range of the piss-poor marksmen aboard the schooner. By the time he had fully regained his senses, he realized he was rowing out to sea. The huge dark mountains on either side of the Golden Gate loomed.

Slocum began rowing for his life—and losing.

24

Slocum slewed the boat around and tried rowing for land but the current flowing out of the bay was too strong. For what seemed an hour he rowed until he was no longer able to continue. Slumped down over the oars, he fought to get his strength back. To be carried out to the ocean in such a small boat was death.

"I swear, I'll never so much as take a bath again," he muttered, sick of the sight of so much water. The sound of the waves sloshing over the sides of his rowboat drowned out his words. He straightened, gripped the oars and pulled hard, only to crash into something hard enough to throw him forward. He pulled in the oars and turned to see what had happened. If he had hit a rock, he might be saved. That meant he was close enough to land to hail someone on the shore.

He looked out and saw only blackness. Then he looked up and saw the masts of Lai Choi San's junk outlined against the night sky. He stared at the white-clad figure on the stern deck and knew she had spotted him. Slocum shipped the oars, turned around in the boat and tried to lift his hands high over his head. They hardly budged.

"I surrender," Slocum called. His voice was hoarse, and

he knew that Lai Choi San could have her marksmen shoot
him where he bobbed on the waves—if she wanted to be
merciful. Otherwise, she would let the current carry him
out into the Pacific Ocean to die a lingering death from
lack of water.

Two of the Chinese pirate's crew jumped into the water
and swam like fishes to row him alongside the junk. They
helped him up and when he got to the deck, he almost
collapsed.

"You seek death?" Lai Choi San asked.

"Just out for an evening's sightseeing," Slocum said.

"The crown," she flared. "The jade crown! I want it!"

"Don't seem to have it on me," he said. The two Celestials who had pulled him up into the junk moved behind.
Slocum winced as both thrust knives into his back enough
to hurt.

"I will flay the skin from your body. I will make what I
did to the woman look tame. Tell me where you have hidden the crown!"

"I'm still hunting for it, too," Slocum said. He jumped
when both men behind him drove the tips of their knives a
little deeper into his flesh. "I tried to find out from the man
who has the crown what he did with it, but he got shanghaied. That clipper ship back in the harbor. He's a new—
and unwilling—crew member now." He jerked his thumb
in the general direction of the ship he had just escaped so
narrowly.

Lai Choi San looked from Slocum into the bay.

"That one?"

"Can't tell in the dark. It was a clipper ship with three
masts. The man who stole the crown got himself shanghaied. Getting him back proved a mite more troublesome
than I expected."

"I heard shots."

"Reckon that was me," Slocum said. "A couple of the
crew got winged. So did the captain. Last I saw, though, the
man who knows where the jade crown is was still alive and
kicking."

"If you are lying, I will cut out your tongue. *Then* I will begin the torture."

"Don't doubt it," Slocum said. "I'm not lying." The edge in his voice convinced Lai Choi San. She gestured. The junk shuddered under his feet as sails were lowered and the rudder turned enough to direct the ship toward the clipper.

Slocum propped himself against the railing, marshaling his strength. In spite of himself, he stared in wonder as the junk cut silently through the water and approached the clipper ship. The schooner lay at anchor, and the junk could easily slide right on past. Lai Choi San maneuvered carefully until the junk bumped against the other ship's hull.

Slocum expected Lai Choi San's crew to let out earsplitting screams as they swung over on ropes. They were as silent as their ship in the night. He watched as two of the schooner's crew died. But there was no chance the Chinese could go undetected forever. The lookout high in the crow's nest finally sounded the alarm.

"Where is he? The one who knows?" Lai Choi San hissed like a snake.

"Doubt he's above decks since he was brought aboard against his will. Likely they have him in the cargo hold or chained up somewhere."

Lai Choi San shouted in Chinese. Four of her pirates pulled back a hatch and dropped down. Slocum stood a little straighter. He heard the commotion from belowdecks on the schooner and wondered who was getting killed. The answer came seconds later when three of the four Celestials popped back up. They stood at the corners of the hatch while the fourth climbed up, a man slung over his shoulder.

"I should identify him," Slocum said.

"Stay here."

"I want him alive, too." Slocum's mind raced on how he could get Stark away from the pirates and back to San Francisco. Without the jade crown as ransom, Ah Ming had no chance of recovering her pa's body—his bones.

"You want the crown for your own purposes. I want it for ransom."

This shocked Slocum. He stared at the pirate and frowned.

"You look surprised," Lai Choi San said. "The emperor has my husband in a dungeon in the Forbidden City. If I do not return with the crown before the summer festival . . ." Her words trailed off.

"Your husband's life is on the line," Slocum said.

"Look out!" Lai Choi San shouted in English, then switched to Chinese.

From the captain's cabin aboard the clipper ship came three men, all armed and firing. The lead sprayed wildly. One died almost instantly from a thrown knife, the other two dived for cover but kept shooting.

The pirate carrying Jason Stark sprinted for the railing, jumped lightly to it and judged distance. With a powerful spring, he landed on the junk's deck.

"All hands on deck, all hands!" screamed the schooner's captain. "Repel boarders! We got pirates!"

Only one other of Lai Choi San's pirates aboard the schooner made the leap to safety. The junk banged hard against the other ship's hull before veering away. The sporadic gunfire from the clipper ship amounted to nothing as the distance increased.

"Will he come after us?" Slocum asked, watching the other ship recede.

"He cannot raise anchor quickly enough. And what would he do for one new crew member?" Lai Choi San laughed and waved her hand airily, dismissing such a notion. "Let us see what your jade stealer has to say for himself."

Slocum stepped to one side as Lai Choi San went to where Jason Stark had been dumped on the deck. In the darkness he saw a darker pool spreading under the body. His heart jumped into his throat. Even before Lai Choi San rolled Stark over, Slocum knew the man was dead.

He knelt and looked at Stark's body. The man had been plugged square in the back of the head by one of the wayward bullets.

"He is not going to tell us anything," Lai Choi San observed. She whipped out her knife. Slocum sucked in his breath, sure she intended to use it on him. Then the pirate captain proceeded to cut the clothes off Stark's body until there was no question he did not carry the jade crown hidden on him.

The knife vanished as quickly as it appeared.

"What are you going to do?" Slocum asked. He feared the worst. If the woman's husband was locked up in their emperor's dungeon, he was likely to die there. Stark knew where he had hidden the jade crown. No one else knew. No one.

Lai Choi San studied him for a moment, then bowed slightly.

"Put this one ashore. Dump the other over the side for the sharks."

Slocum worried that the woman meant for him to become chum for the sharks, but either the crew got her orders wrong or Slocum worried for nothing. Two crewmen grabbed Stark by arms and legs and heaved him over the side. The resounding splash told of the man's watery fate.

"Why are you letting me go?"

Lai Choi San stared at him with unfathomable eyes, then said, "There is no reason to kill you. If only he knew where the crown is, the secret died with him." She spun and walked off, making no sound as she moved. Slocum stared at her back and then was urged to go over the side himself, to his rowboat.

When the junk passed within a few hundred yards of the docks, Slocum cast off and managed to row ashore. He beached the boat near a dock and scrambled from the rowboat vowing to never again so much as touch a drink of water. On shaky legs, he climbed a ladder and got to the pier. He sat heavily, legs swinging over the edge as he locked his arms over the lowest rail and leaned forward. The junk had disappeared, sweeping past the Embarcadero under partial sail. Out in the harbor he saw the schooner, riding the waves and looking so damned peaceful it made him want to take out his six-shooter and try shooting holes in it. The range was too great, and he was out of ammo.

Slocum rested and thought hard. Stark had hidden the jade crown but he was not a clever man or one taken to doing things right. His expertise had been in duping the gullible, spinning tall tales and making a few dollars off his lies. The more Slocum thought about it, the more he wondered why Stark had been in the Pole Star drinking when he knew Little Pete, Ah Ming, Sir William and Slocum all hunted for him. If he had a hiding place, he should have holed up there after his other den had been destroyed.

"He would hide the crown where he thought it was safe, but he didn't have much time to find a place." Slocum stood, used the railing for support and slowly felt strength coming back into his arms and back fueled by a potent thought.

He was not quite sure where he had landed, but it took only a few minutes for him to find the Pole Star Saloon perched on the end of the dock. Rather than going inside, Slocum studied the place. It was built out of what might have been driftwood and flotsam from the harbor. A good, strong wind would blow the place into kindling. The crowd of sailors going and coming made this far too public a spot for Stark to have hidden the crown.

"He'd want to keep an eye on it," Slocum said slowly. He pictured the interior of the saloon again. There were a couple windows but looking out across the harbor would not have availed Stark of anything. Then Slocum remembered how Stark had been slumped in the chair, eyes downcast. He had thought the sneak thief was trying not to be seen.

He was trying to keep something in sight.

Stride long and sure now, Slocum went to the side of the Pole Star and saw a walkway hardly wide enough to balance on. He dropped to hands and knees and looked hard at the wood. A few splinters had been broken off the wood recently. The saltwater and weather had not darkened the wood yet. Crawling, Slocum went along the walkway until he reached a spot where he estimated Stark had been sitting on the other side of the wall.

Flopping on his belly, he looked over the edge. Nothing. He reached around and began searching blindly for the crown. He came away with a filthy hand covered with slime and rot.

Not about to give up, he fumbled out his tin of lucifers and struck one. Moving quickly, he thrust it under the planking and looked around. He saw a large hole about where Stark's feet would have been. Before the match burned his fingers, Slocum followed the line of sight down along the pilings.

His heart almost exploded when he saw a small package secured to the support. Unable to reach it, he dropped over the side, held the edge of the walkway, then wrapped his legs around the piling. Risking splinters, he released his grip and dropped a few inches. He shifted his hands and found a knotted rope dangling down. He tugged on it and decided it was strong enough to support him.

Using this, he twisted around and got his fingers around a slick package tied to the piling. Fumbling, cursing, he worked the knots free and came away with an oilskin pouch. Still dangling from the knotted rope and with his legs gripping the piling, he peeled back the oilskin to reveal the contents.

He had found the jade crown.

25

He had to move fast because someone was following him. Slocum tried to guess who it might be and failed since the list of possible trackers was so long. He was out of breath by the time he reached the small museum and ducked into the front door. He pressed himself flat against the wall and peered through the inch-wide opening he left. There might have been movement in the shadows outside or it could have been his imagination.

"John? What are you doing?" Tess Lawrence stood in the foyer, staring at him.

"I found the crown, but somebody followed me here. I want to get a glimpse of him."

"Does it matter who it is?"

Slocum started to answer, then laughed. It did not matter one whit.

"Smart girl," he said, closing the door and bolting it. "I've been so caught up in everything, I stopped thinking."

"Oh, never that, John," she said, smiling.

"Where's Sir William?"

"He's out talking to Captain Johnson. He's raising Cain about the way the marines have been used, and the captain is getting a bit tired of hearing about it."

"I can imagine," Slocum said. He looked past her into the gloomy museum. "Are you alone?"

"As alone as I can be with you here," she said, coming forward. She pressed her hand against his chest. "You have such a strong heartbeat."

"Beating faster now that you're in front of me."

"Sir William won't be back for a while. He's down at the dock—" she started.

"Talking to Captain Johnson," Slocum finished for her, then cut off any further words with a kiss. Tess flowed into his arms and pressed close to him. Slocum felt the beating of her heart as he reached down to press his hand onto her breast. She moaned softly and tilted her head back, eyes half closed.

"Yes, John. We should celebrate. The crown."

"The crown," he said, hardly thinking about it any longer. He bent slightly and scooped her up into his arms. Her skirts flared as she threw her arms around his neck so she could bring his head down to kiss him again. Their passions mounted as he carried her through the darkened museum toward the curator's office.

"Not there, not again," she said. "There's a fancy bed at the back of the next exhibit room. A Russian empress's bed."

"Sounds just like what's needed," Slocum said. He turned this way and that so Tess avoided banging into any of the glass cases that had been moved back into place in the large room. He found the corridor leading off. He had prowled the museum earlier, looking for ways in and escape routes should it be necessary, but he had never taken a serious look at what was in the room. He did now.

There was an elaborate four-poster bed on display amid minor items from Russia.

"Catherine the Great slept in this bed," Tess said breathlessly.

"And we're going to make love in it," Slocum said gently, placing Tess on the bed. He sat beside her, his hand reaching up under her skirt. He felt her warm calf. He slipped his hand higher. She shivered now, and it was not from the cold. Moving slowly, he worked upward to her warm inner thigh. She sighed deeply and lay back on the bed.

"That's so nice, John. I love the—oh!" She let out a gasp when he reached the tangled nest hidden between her legs. His fingers stroked over the now-slippery nether lips and then parted them slightly. He turned on the bed and ran his other hand up to join its partner. Working slowly, carefully, he stoked over her most intimate regions and then slid a finger into her. She began thrashing about on the bed, her legs spreading wider in wanton invitation to him.

He pushed her skirt out of the way. He had intended to make this a long, slow lovemaking, but she was so aroused that he got hotter by the second and knew he could hardly wait. Getting her skirt bunched around her waist forced her to lift her rump off the bed. As she did so, he pressed his face down into the fragrant jungle and began licking.

Tess cried out. Her knees rose and then she thrust her legs out on either side of Slocum's head. He continued to lick and stroke with his tongue like a cat lapping up cream until she was moaning incoherently with pleasure.

When she climaxed, she clamped strong thighs onto his head. For a moment Slocum was deliciously blind and deaf. He never stopped his oral assault. His fingers found the little pink nub at the top of her sex lips and pressed down. Another loud cry of release escaped her lips. She tensed all over and then relaxed, her legs draped over his shoulders.

"My turn," he said. Slocum moved deliberately, letting her legs slide along his shoulders until her ankles rested atop them. He rose above her. Together they managed to get his gun belt off and his jeans popped free. With a sigh of relief, his erection was released from its cloth prison. She reached around and steered him inward, but her legs prevented her from doing too much. That didn't matter. Slocum knew where he wanted to go. And he did.

With a smooth, slow thrust, he sank balls-deep within her. Bent double, ankles on his shoulders, Tess experienced a new sensation. For Slocum it was even more intense. It felt as if she crushed him flat.

He hesitated once he was fully within her, then drew back. His ache grew and his desires threatened to consume him. He began thrusting with more and more speed until there was no turning back. With a surge he shared the release Tess had experienced. He sank down and shrugged his shoulders. Her legs dropped to the bed. She stared up at him and smiled.

"I wish Sir William wasn't coming back anytime now."

"Oh? What if he wasn't?"

"There's another bed in the back room," she said suggestively.

Slocum turned slightly and listened. He heard movement out in the museum's main room. Tess heard it, too.

"Sir William!"

"Get decent," Slocum said, jumping off the bed. He hitched up his pants and grabbed for his six-shooter. The sounds out in the museum might not be caused by Sir William. Slocum had never caught sight of whoever had trailed him from the docks.

He slung his gun belt and moved silently. He relaxed when he saw that Tess had been right. Sir William stood in the room, looking around.

"I say, there you are, my good man."

"Did you see anyone lurking around outside?" Slocum asked.

"Why, yes, I believe so. There was a Chinese chap." Sir William sobered. "They are after you?" Then the explorer brightened. "You found it! They're after you because you found the crown!"

"Reckon you're right on both counts," Slocum said. His mind raced. He had a plan but it required so much to be done—right now.

"I came to be sure Miss Lawrence was all right," Sir William said.

"I am," Tess said, coming from the back room. Her hair was mussed and her dress was slightly askew. Sir William frowned when he saw her. His eyes darted to Slocum and then back.

With some disapproval he said, "I wanted to tell you that Captain Johnson has launched a raid on the Sum Yop headquarters in an attempt to end the tong war." Sir William chewed a moment on his lower lip and finally spat out, "What have you been doing, Miss Lawrence?"

Tess's eyes widened in surprise. "You remember my name."

"Of course I do, dear—Miss Lawrence."

"I told her to hide while I looked for the hatchet man trailing me," Slocum said.

"That's right," she hastily confirmed. "Mr. Slocum feared an attack since he has the jade crown."

"The crown," Sir William said, distracted once more. "I must see it!"

"Show him," Slocum said to Tess. "I'll see if there are more than the tong killers after me."

Neither Sir William nor Tess asked who else might be tracking him. Slocum knew that the chance was good one of Little Pete's *boo how doy* was on his trail, but it could also be one of Lai Choi San's crew. She had let him go too easily and had not believed him.

He went to the front door and dropped to his belly before looking out. He waited several minutes before seeing movement in the bushes at the edge of the museum property near the road. Try as he might, though, Slocum could do nothing more than find where the man hid. Who had sent this spy, Slocum could not tell.

Closing the door, he got to his feet and went back into the museum where Sir William and Tess stared at the crown.

The explorer looked up, his face lit with enthusiasm once more.

"You are a man among men, dear chap. You found it! Tell me all about the hunt and—"

"There's no time," Slocum said. "If the marines are attacking the tong strongholds, you've got to get out of town right away. There's a train leaving in less than a half hour. We just have time to get you on it."

"We can take the crown. It's not as good as showing the entire collection in Boston, but the jade crown will still be quite a draw."

"You got your belongings packed?" Slocum looked straight at Tess. A moment passed, then she nodded slowly. They both realized what he was asking—and what they both were agreeing to.

"I'll never let this out of my sight," Sir William said, hands on the crown.

"Get it packed up," Slocum said, watching Sir William go about the chore. He tried to take it, but the explorer refused to let it go.

"Check the back of the museum while Tess gets her valise," Slocum said. "I won't let anything happen to it. I promise."

Sir William looked around, then reluctantly hurried off. Tess disappeared into the curator's office to get what she needed for a long trip across the country. And Slocum set about doing what was needed.

He spun, his six-shooter coming out of his holster in time to get off a shot at the Celestial coming through the front door. The Chinaman ducked back.

"What happened?" Sir William rushed up.

"We need to get out of here right now. I didn't even wing him."

"Wing him," said Sir William, chuckling. "That's one of their surnames, you know. Did you wing Wing?" Sir William laughed aloud.

"I'm glad you appreciate your own joke. Is the back way clear?"

"Oh, quite." Sir William reached out with both hands and pulled hard. "Let me have the crown."

Slocum released the package. Sir William clutched it to his body like a mother with a newborn.

Tess, Sir William and Slocum went out the back door.

Two streets away Slocum hailed a passing cab and bundled them into it.

"John, you're not coming with us?" Tess looked upset but the moment of decision had passed back in the museum. Both knew the answer.

"You and Sir William go to Boston. I have business here."

"With the Sum Yop?" asked Sir William. "It cannot be a secret the way you look whenever they are mentioned."

"If I hurry, I can get something Little Pete has stolen," Slocum said.

"Captain Johnson will be on the attack by now. Good luck, old chap." Sir William transferred the crown to his left arm and shook Slocum's hand briskly. Tess reached out and lightly touched his hand.

"Train station," Slocum called to the driver.

"Be quick about it, my good man," Sir William added. He was pushed back into the carriage by the sudden start. Sir William did not look back. Tess did.

Slocum heaved a sigh and knew her departure was for the best. He returned to the museum. He had to get to Little Pete before the marines raided his headquarters and destroyed everything in it.

26

"There's no need to cry, my dear," Sir William said. He clutched the box holding the precious jade crown tightly but managed to reach over and pat Tess's arm. "He will be just fine. Mr. Slocum is a very resourceful man."

"I know. It's just that so . . . so much has happened," Tess said, dabbing at her eyes. She looked at Sir William, who favored her with a bright smile. He had no idea what she really meant.

"Things will work out swimmingly from here on. It's best to leave this terrible frontier city for a more refined metropolis."

"Boston," Tess said, dabbing ineffectually at her tears with her handkerchief.

"You will find that you have left nothing of any real importance behind, my dear," Sir William said. "Everything bright and wonderful lies in front of you. Such a stellar future! All of high society will flock to see the crown—and us!"

"What do you mean?" She finished mopping the tears and turned slightly on the hard bench seat to look at him.

"The exhibition will be talked about for years." He stroked the box as if it were a pet. "We will be the toast of the town. We can go to Europe. Dazzle the crowned heads of all the better countries. England, of course, but also Austria and Italy. You will love Italy. The opera!"

"You'd take me along?"

"I'll need an . . . assistant," he said lamely. Sir William swallowed hard, trying to find the right words. He hinted broadly that he wanted more from Miss Lawrence than services as an assistant, but she seemed obtuse to what he was suggesting. Damn her!

"Oh," she said. Tess leaned back and stared straight ahead. What she had wanted before no longer seemed important. Sir William had been so bold and daring—until she compared him with John Slocum.

The train rattled and clanked as the engine began to grind away, moving the imponderable tons of steel along the rails. An unexpectedly loud steam whistle made Sir William cringe for a moment. He recovered immediately. It would not do to show any kind of consternation at this moment. Not when he was trying to woo a lovely young lady.

"The entire of Europe will be ours—yours," he said, sidling into a more definitive question. She had been loyal and had shown nothing but attention to detail. She was not uncomely, and it was high time he find a wife. That would be expected of him as he dazzled the crowned heads of Europe. A wife was a definite asset at dinner parties and the like.

And settling down. Sir William swallowed hard again. That would be difficult. Of course, there was always the chance of a *short* adventure in Africa or somewhere near England. What wife could possibly deny him that? Until she was with child, she might even come along on his grand quests. Miss Lawrence took meticulous notes that would be perfect for his memoirs, after all.

"I'm not sure what to say, Sir William," she began.

His eyes left her face and darted to the rear of the passenger car.

"Stop that man!" Sir William leaped to his feet and pointed at the Chinaman. "He's a killer!"

The *boo hoy doy* drew a hatchet and brandished it, then

opened the door connecting the two passenger cars and ran off. The door slammed behind him.

"Here, don't let this out of your sight," Sir William said, thrusting the box with the crown into Tess's hands. She looked up in surprise.

"What's going on?"

"They've come aboard to steal the crown, I fear. I must stop them now or we'll be plagued with the yellow vermin all the way across the country."

"Sir William!" She reached out and put her hand on his arm. He had drawn his small pistol.

"I'll be careful, my dear," he said, then pushed past her into the aisle and made his way to the rear of the car. The other passengers looked at him curiously. More than one of the men moved coattails back to expose their own six-shooters. Sir William ignored them and ran to the rear of the car. He peered out onto the small platform between cars and then threw open the door. As he took a step out, he froze. Something was not right.

He spun about in time to see two more Chinese beside Tess. One threatened her with a knife and the other wres-tled with her for the box she held tightly.

"Stop, I say! Blighters!" Sir William fired. The first shot missed. The second frightened Tess into releasing the box holding the jade crown. One Celestial shoved her back into the seat and drew a pistol of his own, returning fire. Sir William ran forward, shooting as he went. The train lurched and sent him sprawling. By the time he got to his feet, both Celestials were gone.

"Tess, are you all right?"

"Yes, Sir William. I'm shaken up. They stole the crown!"

Sir William looked at her for an instant, impulsively bent, kissed her cheek and then ran after the two thieves. He flung open the door between cars in time to see the sec-ond Chinaman jump to the ground. Sir William never hesi-tated. He jumped, too, hitting the ground hard enough to rattle his teeth. His legs buckled and he rolled until he came to a halt some yards away from the train.

He sat up and saw the conductor on the back platform with a lantern, as if hunting for his lost passengers. Then the train rounded a curve and disappeared from sight.

Sir William got to his feet and went hunting for the two thieves. They had decoyed him away with the first hit, then had attacked and stolen the crown with the other two who had been lying in wait.

"Bloody sneaky thieves!" Sir William began hiking back to the spot where the Chinamen would have landed.

He found the second one on the ground, his head canted at an unnatural angle. The man had not made his exit from the train too well, and had slipped and fallen, breaking his neck. Sir William knelt and examined the man, then stood.

"By damn, that chop tattooed on his arm makes him a Sum Yop!" He had thought they were tong members because they had brandished hatchets. But the distinctive mark identified the exact tong responsible for the theft.

"Little Pete!" The name escaped his lips like a curse.

He began hiking along the tracks, heading back into San Francisco. He had a tong leader to find.

It was nearing sundown when he trooped back to the railroad depot. Sir William had not walked this far since his guide and most of his expedition had been killed in a freak lightning storm in Borneo. The exercise invigorated him and made him feel more alive than he had in months. Chasing after the society doyennes for money to finance future expeditions wore down on him. He was a physical man who enjoyed adventure, although some of the society matrons had provided some things more adventurous for him than being hounded by cannibals.

He hopped into a carriage and ordered, "To Chinatown. Right away, my good man!"

The driver turned and squinted at him.

"Ain't ya heard? You jist git in?"

"Heard what?"

"The marines're cleanin' out the dens of them filthy yellow bastards. 'Bout time, I say. It ain't safe to go nowhere near Chinatown or the docks 'til they're done with the exterminatin'."

"As close as you think safe, then," Sir William said. He knew better than to argue with a man looking out only for his own safety. Even money would not win over this recalcitrant individual.

"Yer money, yer scalp," the driver said. Sir William sat back and fumed as the swaybacked horse clopped along at a pace hardly better than walking.

"Here we go," the driver called when they halted more than half a dozen blocks away from the main street running through Chinatown. Sir William heard gunfire and smelled the sharp tang of gunpowder in the air wafting from the east. He stood and saw orange flashes—muzzle flashes. "That'll be six bits."

Sir William handed him a dollar bill.

"Thank ye kindly, mister. Don't go gettin' too near the fightin' till they's done. Then you kin go see what a mountain of dead chinks looks like."

Sir William almost grabbed the money back and gave the man a thrashing. He instead ignored the driver and directed his attention toward the furious bursts of gunfire. He barely had gone a block when a marine stepped into the street and barred his way with a lowered rifle, bayonet affixed.

"Can't go down there," the marine said. "Not till the fightin's done, sir."

"They are fighting the tongs?"

"Reckon that's right."

"There doesn't seem to be any fighting here at the moment. What of Chinatown?"

"When we clean out the vermin along the docks, then we'll move there. My orders are to keep citizens away, so don't think of goin' there 'less you want to get yourself kilt dead."

"Far from it, my good chap, far from it. Thank you for the warning." Sir William backed away from the marine, went a few blocks west, changed back northward and cut across to Dupont Gai as fast as he could. Up the hills behind the marine guard and into the heart of Chinatown he went until he sweat in spite of the cold wind blowing off the bay. The deeper into the heart of the Chinese quarter he went, the fewer people he saw. Ghosts flitting through would have been easier to find. Usually Sir William noted furtive glances from half-shuttered windows or saw store proprietors watching resentfully. Not this evening. The dearth of population meant the tong war had become a serious concern for all.

"Where are you, you thieving, conniving bastard?" Sir William muttered to himself as he made his way through the maze of streets to find the Sum Yop headquarters. He was certain Little Pete's henchmen had stolen the jade crown. If he wanted it back, he had to be cagey and go against great odds, but then he usually did. That was how he had gotten the jade crown away from the imperial guard so many months ago. They had been arrogantly neglectful, thinking no one would dare spirit away the emperor's crown. He had been too clever for them and had won the most important possession of the emperor's court.

His heart leaped into his throat when he saw the tiny tendrils of oily black smoke leaking from cracks in the brick walls of the old building housing the Sum Yop tong. No obvious fire worked to consume the decrepit structure, but something inside was seriously amiss.

He kicked in the side door and choked at the blast of smoke billowing outward. Sir William turned his face and waited for the smoke to clear enough for him to go into the building.

"Little Pete!" His shout was swallowed by the vast, empty building. Sir William went deeper into the building, following the path of destruction that marked the solution to the maze and finally found a small room. He stepped forward, hoping against hope he would find what was not likely here.

A vault door lay on the floor, torn from its hinges by brute force. A quick glance inside showed that all the contents had been removed. With the smoke making his eyes water, Sir William started to leave, then noticed a leg poking out from under a table. He pushed the overturned table away and saw a dead Chinaman.

A dead Chinese sailor. It took him a few seconds to understand what this meant.

"Lai Choi San, you are my last chance to get the jade crown back."

With hope burning bright again, Sir William headed for the docks.

27

"I do not want the crown," Ah Ming said. The fury in her dark eyes burned Slocum as if she had thrust a branding iron into his guts.

"You can swap it for your pa's bones," Slocum said, holding the crown out to her. He had felt a twinge of guilt for a few minutes after watching Sir William and Tess drive off. He had switched the real crown for a box of artifacts from the museum that were about the same weight. Sir William would be disappointed, but Tess might not care if she convinced the explorer that he loved her and they married eventually. For her that would be a prize beyond any Chinese emperor's crown.

"The Sum Yop are scattered throughout the city," Ah Ming said.

"You'll stand a better chance of finding Little Pete and giving him the crown in return for—"

"You fool!" Ah Ming's towering rage caused Slocum to take a step back. "The Sum Yop headquarters has been destroyed."

"The bones will be left," Slocum said. He had seen men struck by lightning and their skeletons remained. No fire in a city could match that for pure destructive power.

"They are gone," Ah Ming said, her anger becoming a colder rage that worried Slocum more than her hot fury. "I saw with my own eyes that the Sum Yop vault was looted and completely empty. My father's bones were not there."

"Little Pete," Slocum began. He paused to think on the matter. If the Sum Yop leader had looted his own vault, he would have taken whatever gold and other valuables were there. Even if his hatred for the On Leong leader was the sole driving force in his life, keeping the gold would take precedence so he could maintain power over his hatchet men. Without control of the killers following him, he was nothing.

"If he took them, it's all the more important that you trade the crown," Slocum said. He held it out. Ah Ming's eyes did not even flicker in the direction of the box.

"He did not. He is hiding. Little Pete was ambushed before he returned to his fortress. There were dead sailors."

"Lai Choi San?"

Ah Ming said nothing, but Slocum read the answer on her face. He tucked the jade crown under his arm as he considered all the possibilities. This might be working out better than he had thought.

"I'll be back soon with your father's bones," Slocum said.

"If you are not, you will die. I will personally drive a knife through your eyes and feed your worthless, blind carcass to the rats."

Slocum did not doubt Ah Ming meant every word.

"Is the dock area clear now? The marines were shooting anything that moved there."

"The soldiers are everywhere, killing anyone Chinese they see."

"Then they won't think twice about taking a shot at me," Slocum said grimly. If Captain Johnson had barricaded the docks, there might be no way to get out to the junk anchored once more in the harbor. Slocum knew he could not swim such a distance in the cold water, especially not carrying the crown. If he had no other choice, he would hijack one of the navy boats and force the crew to take him out there. If Lai Choi San did have the bones, she might not keep them long since they meant nothing to her.

Slocum made his way through the darkened streets and avoided two military patrols before reaching the Embarcadero. There he found several buildings on fire and workers milling about as firemen worked to put out the blazes. He ignored the obvious places where he might find a boat and went down to the shoreline, hunting for shanghaiers. It took him less than ten minutes to find two of them struggling to get a burly sailor into their boat. The sailor had been drugged but fought strongly enough to make one shanghaier wonder aloud if they ought to cut his throat and go find another victim.

"Dump him," Slocum said, six-shooter pointed at them.

"You ain't cuttin' in on our trade," one said. Slocum shot him in the leg. The man screeched like a barn owl and then began cursing. Slocum shifted his six-gun to center on the other shanghaier's chest.

"You got any complaints?"

"Naw, this one was more trouble 'n he was worth."

"Into the boat," Slocum said.

"What? No, no way! You ain't sellin *me* to—"

The man paled under his tanned leather skin when he saw that Slocum would kill him on the spot if he disobeyed.

"Look, we kin make a deal. Him and me, we got a sweet plan for collectin' them 'recruits.' We kin cut you in. Make you a partner."

"Recruits," Slocum said, shaking his head sadly. A recruit volunteered. These men were slavers peddling human flesh they did not even pay for. "Into the boat." Slocum stepped into the stern and sat, his pistol never wavering. "Push off and start rowing."

"Lars, help me," begged the man at the oars.

"You'll be back inside an hour," Slocum said. "I'm not doing to you what you've done to dozens of others."

"Hunnerds," Lars grumbled. He whimpered a little

more as he tried to stand. Slocum reckoned he had broken the man's thighbone.

"Row me out to the junk, and you can come right back," Slocum said. "Your partner's going to need a doctor to fix him up or he'll lose the leg."

"Ain't no big thing, that," the man in the boat said. "Might actually be useful havin' a peg leg. The salts see it and want to hear the tale. Then they gets themselves Mickey Finned and—"

"Stop planning, start rowing," Slocum said harshly. He cast a final look at Lars. The man had collapsed onto the shore. Whether he had passed out or not, he was no longer a problem.

"The junk? The one what's captained by the Chinese bitch?"

"That's the one," Slocum said. He tucked the box holding the jade crown under his left arm.

"What business you got with her? We ast and she don't want no more crew. Word is she's lost quite a few but won't take on more, not even chinks."

"She's certainly lost her first mate," Slocum said, remembering how he had shot Sung. The man could not have survived. "Maybe you'd be interested in signing on? I can put in a good word for you." Slocum laughed as the man rowed faster.

"You tellin' the truth when you said I could leave right away? I don't want nuthin' to do with them dragons."

Slocum grew increasingly anxious as they approached Lai Choi San's ship.

He lowered his six-shooter so it was at his side and out of sight of the lookout high in the rigging. Shouts in Chinese were passed from the lookout to Lai Choi San on the main deck. She leaned against the rail, watching Slocum's approach.

"Why should I not shoot you out of the water?"

"I have the crown," Slocum called back. Even in the dark and at a distance he saw her reaction. Lai Choi San stood upright and began barking orders to her crew.

"You weren't joshin' 'bout knowin' her, were you?" The shanghaier looked as if he would be sick to his stomach at any instant. "Look, you tell her we didn't mean nuthin' by grabbin' those two from her crew. They was struttin' 'round, actin' all high and mighty. It was a challenge, it was."

"Shut up," Slocum said.

The rowboat banged against the side of the junk. Ropes came snaking down. Slocum secured the rowboat with a rope and turned to the shanghaier.

"Come aboard or swim for it."

"My boat! I need it!"

"Your choice."

The man never hesitated. He dived overboard and began swimming amid thrashing arms and legs that produced more froth than speed. Slocum never gave the shanghaier a second look. He made his way up a rope, hanging on to the box as he went.

"Is that it?" Lai Choi San pointed the instant his feet hit the deck. Slocum held out the box with the jade crown.

"A trade. I think you have something I want in return."

"I have the contents of Little Pete's vault. He thought to trade me the crown for a shipment of arms." Lai Choi San snorted in contempt. "I never planned to steal the weapons, only the crown. Give it to me."

"The bones," Slocum said, squaring his stance and letting his right hand rest on his belt buckle. In this position he could whip his Colt Navy from the cross-draw holster and get off one shot—at Lai Choi San. The rest of her crew would kill him, but she would pay if she tried to take the box without swapping. Or she could play it square.

"Such a bag was found in Little Pete's vault. Those belong to the On Leong leader?"

"They do. Ah Ming wants the bones for a proper burial."

"In China?"

"I reckon so."

Lai Choi San called out to a pirate sitting with his feet dangling down into an open hatchway. The man straightened his body and vanished from sight. Slocum heard his feet hit the lower deck and then scamper off. In less than a minute, the sailor returned with a rattling burlap bag filled to overflowing with bones.

Slocum started to hand over the crown when he heard the distinctive sound of a six-shooter cocking behind him. He froze.

"You blighter," Sir William cried. "You would give the most valuable artifact ever taken from China to a pirate? To a *pirate*?"

Slocum saw that Lai Choi San was as startled by Sir William's sudden appearance as he was.

"I had to do it, Sir William. It's a matter of a promise I made. My reputation's at stake."

"You're a thief. You switched boxes at the museum."

"How long did it take for you to find out?"

"Three of Little Pete's hatchet men stole the box. I tracked Little Pete down and all he had was a box of worthless trinkets. If he didn't have the crown, I knew it would end up on this pirate ship eventually. I was right."

"She'll kill you," Slocum said. "She doesn't care a whit if you kill me, but you shoot and her crew will slaughter you."

"I'll take my chances," Sir William said.

Slocum handed the box to Lai Choi San.

The pirate captain took the box but did not rip it open to examine the contents as he had expected.

"You are a brave, foolish man," she said. Slocum didn't know if she meant him or Sir William. It hardly mattered. From the corners of his eyes he saw her crew slowly forming a ring around them. Even if both he and Sir William started shooting, there was no chance they could escape with whole skins—or at all.

"Finding the crown was the pinnacle of my career. I will not give it up."

"Perhaps you will not have to," Lai Choi San said.

"You're giving me the bloody crown, just like that?" Sir William sounded skeptical. Slocum didn't blame him since he knew what the crown meant to Lai Choi San. She would do anything to free her husband from the emperor's dungeons.

"I cannot," the pirate said. "I need the crown to ransom my husband. The emperor is holding him prisoner and will execute him if I do not return with the crown."

"But how—?"

"I have no love for my emperor. Once, you stole the crown. Together we can do it again."

"Together?" Sir William said in a hushed tone.

"Together with my husband and me," Lai Choi San said. "There are vast treasure ships sailing the South China Seas. Much of the cargo is worthless to us. For you, it might be valuable."

"Why, yes, it would. You would not try to stop me from stealing the jade crown back?"

Lai Choi San said nothing.

"I could sail with you?"

"You are an adventurer, a brave man, intrepid," Lai Choi San said. "See what life on the sea is like for a pirate. It would make a fine chapter in your memoirs."

"Bloody hell, that's a capital idea!"

Sir William pushed Slocum aside as he came around and thrust out his hand. Lai Choi San shook it, then bowed slightly.

"Welcome aboard, Sir William."

"When do we sail? The sooner you hand over the crown and get your husband returned, the sooner I can steal it back."

"With the morning tide," she said.

"Then there's no reason you'd want to keep these?" Slocum held up the bag of bones.

"I wish only to return to the Flowery Kingdom for my husband," Lai Choi San said. She bowed a little deeper in Slocum's direction.

"Damn me, Slocum, this has worked out quite well."

"What happened to Tess?"

"Miss Lawrence?" For a moment it seemed that Sir William could not place her name. Then he brightened.

"Why, she is still on the train bound for Boston. She will find it a far better place than San Francisco, I am sure."

The explorer was probably right. Tess was a lovely woman with just enough touch of larceny in her soul to do well wherever she was. Boston would be her oyster to open and devour. And, Slocum had to admit, she was better off not pining after Sir William. He already had a mistress with whom no mortal woman could compete. The lure of adventure was more powerful than sex or opium.

Hefting the bag of bones, Slocum silently bid good-bye to Lai Choi San. The pirate captain bowed again in his direction and a sly smile curled her lips before she turned her attention back to Sir William. The two deserved each other.

Slocum got his leg over the railing and then jumped, falling into the rowboat. The bones of Ah Ming's father rattled as he tossed them to the bottom of the boat and then set about rowing back to shore. Ah Ming would have the bones by dawn, and Slocum could be on the trail away from San Francisco soon after.

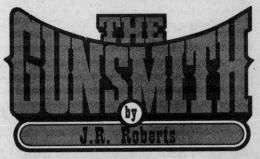

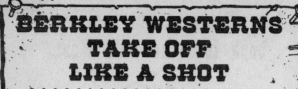